Abhainn's Kiss
By Carolan Ivey

Avalon reborn...

Hidden away on a misty island off the Irish coast all her life, Abhainn has no idea she is the last of her Faery race—until a troll tries to kill her.

Her peaceful world shattered, she has only days to fulfill her destiny. She must defy a curse that dooms her to hide from the sun, and take her rightful place in the Great Circle on the Isle of Avalon. Only Abhainn can restore the balance of Dark and Light, and heal the rift between humans and Fae. That's a tall order for one fragile Faery.

Michael Craig is on a quest of his own, one grounded in cold, hard reality. Fairy tales? They're for children and dreamers. But when he rescues Abhainn from certain death with an accidental kiss, he finds himself thrown into a very different reality. One he's reluctant to accept, even as it unfolds before his eyes. Only one thing holds him there—Abhainn will die without him.

Abhainn's life depends on Michael's kiss, his sword arm...and his ability to believe.

Warning: This book contains violence, unruly Faeries, scary sea creatures, evil queens, graphic sexual content and language.

The Heron's Call
By Isabo Kelly

Only the brave will answer the Call...

Kael Zyhn is a Heron sword mage and the first of his kind to forge a mage sword in more than a generation. But the trance that took him just before forging the sword disrupted Kael's first meeting with his *raynia*, his soul twin. Twelve years later, he's recovered from his ordeal and ready to claim his mate. Only to discover she wants nothing to do with him.

Rowena, an Aleanian sword sworn, can't forgive her long absent *raynei* for deserting her all those years ago. But she admits that she needs him to survive her latest mission. Unfortunately, the longer she's in Kael's presence, the more she wants him, despite the protests of her damaged heart.

To succeed in her quest, Rowena must learn to trust Kael. But can she dare trust him with her heart again? And will she risk his life by giving in to her desires?

Warning, this title contains the following: explicit sex, graphic language, mild violence, a little light "tie me up, tie me down", and a lot of sword fighting.

Thief of Hearts
By J.C. Wilder

Honor among thieves...

Harper Wilde was a woman on a mission. When she'd retired from the life of a professional thief, she never dreamed it would be a family member who forced her back into it. With her stepbrother's reputation on the line, she accepts the task to steal blackmail material a local mobster was using against him. In the midst of one of the most important jobs of her career, she runs into a shadowy figure from her past, Chase, the man who'd broken her heart.

Can two thieves trust each other long enough to escape with their lives?

Warning: Explicit, hanging from the chandeliers style sex.

In The Gloaming

A Samhain Publishing, Ltd. publication.

Samhain Publishing, Ltd.
512 Forest Lake Drive
Warner Robins, GA 31093
www.samhainpublishing.com

The Gloaming
Print ISBN: 1-59998-639-6
Abhainn's Kiss Copyright © 2007 by Carolan Ivey
The Heron's Call Copyright © 2007 by Isabo Kelly
Thief of Hearts Copyright © 2007 by J.C. Wilder

Editing by Jessica Bimberg
Cover by Anne Cain

Abhainn's Kiss electronic publication: February 2007
The Heron's Call electronic publication: February 2007
Thief of Hearts electronic publication: February 2007
First Samhain Publishing, Ltd. print publication: February 2008

Contents

Abhainn's Kiss

Carolan Ivey

Acknowledgements

Inspired by the works of Brian Froud, Pierre DuBuis, Nancy Arrowsmith and George Moorse.

Dedication

For Rick—with all my Celtic heart.

Pronunciation Guide

Abhainn: Ā-vawn

Nuala: NOO-lah

Màthair: MAH-hair

Mícheál: MIH-hahl

Inisghriann: IN-ish-reen

Dun Laoghaire: dun L'HEER-y

Chapter One

"Awake, Cadwyn. It is time."

Cadwyn stirred and stretched, blinking in the rising light of dawn. *Ah, it must be spring,* she thought, drinking in the green smells of earth, new grass and water only recently freed from its winter prison of ice.

"Hurry. You must begin." The voice, though kind, held an undertone of urgency.

Cadwyn shook off the last of the cobwebs of her stone-sleep and rose from her mossy bed by the stream bank. She had long ago mastered the art of transforming herself from her sleeping form of a small stone to her waking form of a Spinner.

"How long have I been sleeping?" She yawned, flexing her fingers and toes, feeling the delicious stretch of muscles that had too long lain in sleep.

"That is unimportant," said the woman, backlit and indistinct against the pale sky. "What matters is that you must begin."

Cadwyn blinked up at the woman who addressed her, and brightened.

"What life am I to spin for this time?" she asked eagerly. Then the elder voice laughed softly, and hope dimmed. *Oh, please, Goddess. Not another grasshopper. Not another Pillywiggin. I'm ready to spin the lifethreads of bigger things!*

"Bigger things?" The elder woman's voice held amusement and a trace of chiding. "Each thread in the web of life has importance, Cadwyn. This much you should have already learned."

Cadwyn flushed that the woman could read her so easily. She dropped her gaze in embarrassment. "Forgive me, Mistress," she murmured. She felt a gentle finger hook under her chin, and reluctantly she raised her head.

Cadwyn gasped and instantly averted her gaze. This was no ordinary Mistress sent to set her on her next spinning task. *The Old Mother. The Lady herself has come to me.*

"Look into my eyes, child."

Cadwyn paled and gave her head a small shake. "I...I cannot. The other Mistresses told me..."

"That a mere Spinner must never look into the Old Mother's eyes?" The voice hinted laughter. "Have no fear, little one. I have been watching you since you were a tiny pebble in this very stream. You are the one I seek for this task."

Cadwyn stubbornly kept her gaze on her shoes, which she realized in dismay were not terribly clean. "Perhaps one of the larger stones..."

"Do not waste time trying to avoid your duty, Cadwyn."

Cadwyn instantly jerked her head up. "I would never do that, Lady." She found herself eye to eye with the Old Mother and held her gaze despite her fear.

The brightening dawn light revealed the Lady's long flowing hair. Not grey, exactly. More like black, but frosted by millions of tiny diamonds shimmering in moonlight. Ageless beauty, hard-won wisdom, and many lifetimes of cares traced the fine-boned face.

The Old Mother smiled, the resulting creases taking nothing away from her riveting face. She lifted a graceful arm, draped in green cloth of unimagined texture and hue, and again took Cadwyn's chin so she had no choice but to look into her Lady's eyes.

They swirled with all the colors of the earth—blue, then green, grey, brown, orange, gold, silver. Cadwyn could have watched them forever, but for the worry and urgency that radiated out of them, along with the glint of ancient wisdom.

Self-conscious, Cadwyn looked away and hastily smoothed her sleep-rumpled hair and brushed at the moss that clung to her apron. And her skirt. And her sleeves... She stared at the variety of little plants that had grown upon her while she slept, brushed at pale green lichen that clung in bits to her skin, touched her hair and found it full of twigs—or possibly tree roots. She looked up at the Old Mother, alarmed.

"Exactly how long have I been sleeping?"

For the first time, she saw the Old Mother hesitate.

"Walk with me and I will explain along the way," the Lady invited with a sweep of her arm. "There is not much time. Come."

At the touch of the Lady's hand on her own, Cadwyn found herself transported from the quiet glade of her sleep to a star-filled chamber. A multi-hued, incredibly complex web of light was flung across the room, from end to end, side to side, top to bottom, stretching into invisibility in all directions. And all over this web, her sister Spinners worked.

Cadwyn had been here many times in the past, adding her own little weavings that represented the lives of the smallest and least complicated of the Fae. But something felt different now. A sense of the frantic permeated the web room, and its Spinners bent to their tasks with frightening ferocity, fingers flying, spindles clattering at a terrible speed.

Cadwyn reached out a hand and lay her palm on the nearest matrix of life-threads, which looked alarmingly fragile. She swayed and nearly fell to her knees. In her buzzing ears, she heard flatly spoken words.

"Ah, now you begin to understand, Cadwyn, Lady of Stone."

"What is wrong with the earth?" Cadwyn cried, both hands now racing over the strands. "The water... I can taste it. Something fouls it. The air... Oh, sweet Goddess, the trees. What has happened to the trees? And my dear birds...oh...my flowers..."

The Old Mother gently but firmly grasped Cadwyn's frantic fingers and pulled her around. "Do you see all these Spinners, child? They are not only adding to the web of life, they are trying to repair it. Every Spinner in the kingdom is at work. Everyone—" the Lady sighed "—but you. You, we have allowed to sleep as long as possible. A thousand years."

Cadwyn felt her insides go hollow. The scope of her vision widened, and she spun slowly in a circle, seeing now that what the Lady said was true. Hundreds, thousands, many millions of Spinners worked the web, barely sparing a glance for her or the Lady. She had wished for bigger things, but this was too big. The web had grown immeasurably in her absence, but also stretched thinner.

Hands shaking, she reached into a deep pocket in her dress and brought out her spindle.

"I am ready."

The Old Mother took her hand and led her through twisting passageways within the web, then to a long, wide corridor where the web looked to be split nearly in two. She followed the

Old Mother to the end of the corridor, out to the very edge of the matrix, where a ragged piece of web floated almost separate from the main structure, linked to the two halves by one fragile strand.

"Begin here," said the Lady, her manner brisk, but not unkind. "Careful," she warned when Cadwyn reached out to touch the drifting piece. "This race of Fae are very fragile, like the waters to which they are bonded."

"A water Faery," Cadwyn whispered in wonder.

The Lady suddenly stiffened and drew in a sharp breath, briefly closing her eyes. "Quickly," she said with sudden urgency. "A child of this race is about to be born. You must begin spinning for it now!" She waved her hand and a pool of dark, moonlit water appeared at their feet. "Use this."

Cadwyn trembled. *Moonwater*. What creature merited this most precious of substances? Most lives were merely touched by it; no Spinner had ever woven an entire life out of it. Self-doubt pressed down on her spirit. She turned to the Lady in appeal. "Is there no one else?"

For the first time, the Old Mother's expression turned thunderous.

"There is no one else. You must begin now. Look..." The Lady opened a portal, and Cadwyn look through it, down into the interior of a tiny cottage. A woman lay in childbirth, and another lone woman attended her. "The child comes. If you do not begin to spin her lifethread now..." She paused, and Cadwyn had the distinct impression she was trying to think of anything but what she was about to say. "...this race will be lost."

Cadwyn seated herself and swallowed hard. Picking the laboring mother's lifethread from the ragged edge of the drifting piece of web, she resolutely plunged her hand into the

17

Moonwater pool, pulled out a healthy handful and began to spin, working the new thread into the mother's.

The Moonwater wasn't nearly as fragile as she had feared. It flowed rapidly through her fingers as she watched the birthing process through the portal, voices of the two women in the cottage drifting across the barrier.

"*Please*, Ardaith," the midwife implored as she squeezed copious amounts of water over the mother's skin. "The dawn is almost upon us. You must allow me to move you to a safe place!"

The laboring woman, Ardaith, tossed her head from side to side on the pillow. "No, Nuala! The bairn comes now." A contraction gripped her bulging belly, and she raised herself up onto her elbows, curled her back, and groaned in such animal tones that Cadwyn nearly dropped her spindle.

"Quickly now," urged Nuala, moving into a position between Ardaith's upraised knees, a large cloth at the ready. Between anxious glances at the cottage's east-facing window, she exhorted the mother to push, push hard, *hurry*!

Ardaith fell back on the pillow, sobbing her exhaustion. "If I cannot do this, Nuala..."

Nuala began to wildly shake her head.

"Nuala, listen to me! You must take the child and wrap it in your black shawl. Wet it down first. Take the child to my...uuuunh...take her underground. You know the place. You must run! You have only a few breaths to do this, or she dies."

Nuala nodded, sobbing, as she hurried around the bed to adjust the tight-woven, dark blankets that kept out the sun. "Maybe if we keep the windows covered—"

"We must not take the chance. The sun is above the horizon; I can feel it weakening me. Leave me and take her to my safe place. Aaaahhhh! Now! She's coming now!"

18

The next moments passed so quickly, Cadwyn blinked and missed most of what happened. Events unfolded in a blur.

Ardaith bore down one last time. Nuala cried out in triumph as the wet, slippery baby tumbled into her outstretched hands. She held the child up for Ardaith to see. Ardaith, smiling through tears, reached for her child.

With a slight *snick*, something sliced neatly through the window cloth, something that left the narrowest of slits behind and embedded itself, twanging, in the opposite wall. A bright streak of sunlight streamed through the slit, falling on the dull, quivering shaft of black, barbed arrow. Cadwyn blinked at it for a moment, then turned her gaze back to the childbed.

Ardaith was gone. The rumpled blankets where she had lain dripped with glowing blue water, its brightness rapidly fading in the rising dawn.

To her horror, Cadwyn realized the thread had gone slack in her hands. Her gaze flew to the web. Ardaith's lifethread dangled free, apparently having frayed and snapped while Cadwyn's attention had been anywhere but where it belonged— on her spindle. The child's thread lay limp in her frozen fingers, barely begun but already fading before her eyes.

I must somehow reattach this thread into the web. But it is so weak now, I know it will snap.

The pool of Moonwater at her side wavered and threatened to vanish. Casting about wildly, her eyes pounced on a thread that strayed from the edge of her own mistreated apron. Without thought, she snatched the thread, pulled it free, plunged it into the Moonwater, and bent her head to her task, holding her breath as she worked the moon-spun thread around the sturdier Stone Maiden strand.

I will not fail this child as I failed her mother. She will live!

She looked neither right nor left, hearing but never seeing when Nuala raced from the cottage with a tiny, weakly crying bundle in her arms.

Cadwyn worked the child's thread into the floating piece of web, willing with all her might that the child would live. She dared let out a breath as the thread grew stronger in her flying fingers. To her amazement, it began to glow.

She allowed one word to penetrate her fiercely focused thoughts.

Asrai.

She sensed a presence behind her, but did not look up, knowing whom it was without looking. She worked on, desperately hoping the Old Mother hadn't seen her mistake, hadn't seen the furtive addition of her own apron thread to correct it.

"Yes," said the Old Mother, her voice heavy and for the first time, sounding old. "The child is of the Asrai."

"The Asrai are cursed," said Cadwyn and then bit her tongue, scolding herself for telling the Lady what she already knew.

"Does this make a difference to you?"

Cadwyn spared a few moments' attention to consider. Mentally she replayed what she had seen below, remembering the thin, black arrow embedded in the wall. "No," she said finally, "it doesn't."

"Good." The Lady sighed. "Aye, the Asrai have been cursed these past thousand years for breaking the Great Circle. You have seen the result." She lifted a hand to touch the damaged, dirty web. "Because of one Asrai's love for a human, Camelot fell and set the Earth on the path of destruction, and our own world with it. I suspect Queen Berchta had a hand in the Asrai's downfall," she went on, "but I have no proof. For the

Asrai queen's failure to take her place in the Great Circle, all her kind have been forbidden to show themselves in the light of day. If they dare, their punishment is to dissolve into the very waters to which they are bonded."

Cadwyn felt the Lady's strong hand on her shoulder.

"This Asrai child is the last hope that the Circle can be healed, and save us all."

"Someone is trying to kill the child, Mistress. Who?" She felt the Lady's hesitation.

"I do not know at this time," the Lady said finally. "There are dark forces in our world, as dark as those of the world of Men. You have not been exposed to this darkness before now."

The Lady fell silent, and Cadwyn felt her eyes on her, as if waiting for any sign of faltering. She set her jaw and quelled her panic.

"Can you do this, child?" came the Lady's voice.

Without looking up, Cadwyn nodded.

The Lady turned to the larger web of Life, selected a strong-looking portion, and touched it.

"Attach the child's lifethread here. No one will think to look for her here."

The Lady stepped quietly away from young Cadwyn, out of hearing range, then released a long sigh.

She had seen Cadwyn falter, seen the young Spinner snatch a thread from her own garment to keep the baby's lifethread alive. The Lady had stilled her instant urge to intervene, cooler thoughts prevailing.

Cadwyn has bonded this Fae child with both water and stone. What does it mean? Will the tiny thread of stone

21

strengthen the child? Perhaps...temporarily. We will have to wait and see if the law of water on stone holds true.

When water drips upon a stone, eventually the stone weakens and breaks.

A movement in the portal caught the corner of her eye. Careful not to disturb Cadwyn, the Lady took a silent step closer to it and peered through. Time ran differently here, and she knew that Cadwyn's flying fingers had already taken the child well past babyhood.

She caught her breath. Cadwyn—young, earnest, clueless Cadwyn—had not noticed that the far end of the Moonwater thread had brushed against another part of the web. One containing the lifethreads of humans.

Cadwyn had unwittingly brought a human into the picture.

With silent movement, the Lady touched the human lifethread, sensing, assessing.

Here beats a strong heart. The heart of a knight. But the time of the knights was over, long ago. Will this heart be allowed to beat free?

Was Cadwyn's mistake unwitting, after all?

"There are no accidents," she mused as she watched the scene in the portal unfold before her.

"Lady?"

The Lady didn't take her eyes off the portal, but patted Cadwyn on her rhythmically swaying shoulder. "Never mind, child. Keep to your work."

This human may have some part to play. If not, his thread will loose and drift harmlessly away. We will simply wait and see.

The Lady's gaze lingered long on the human's lifethread. Considering.

No. I cannot interfere with this human's free will.

But...it won't hurt to light his path—should he so choose to take it...

೮೩ಬಿ೭೮೦

"It's *my* turn to be Lancelot!" The Faery child plunked herself down on a pile of stone, white-gold hair floating in a wild cloud about her face. She poked her bottom lip out at the wiry boy who circled her on a sturdy island pony.

"You can't be Lancelot, you're a girl." His voice jounced in time to the pony's trotting feet. "And you're too short, besides. My daddy calls *me* puny, and you don't even come up to my elbow."

She puffed out a breath. "But I'm tired of standing about like a ninny while you get to joust and wield swords..."

"Gwenhwyfar was *not* a ninny, you ninny. She was a queen. *Arthur's* queen."

"Well, all right, but this time I get a sword. I mean, what if all the knights are busy and Mordred sneaks into the castle?"

"That makes sense, I guess. She didn't get to be queen by lying around and letting everyone do everything for her. Arthur wouldn't have thought much of someone like that."

The Fae child smiled in satisfaction. Springing up from her rock, she grabbed the pony's forelock, bringing it to a jolting halt with barely a touch, and whispered something in its ear. Instantly the animal stood on its hind legs, dumped the protesting boy onto a pile of soft moss and showed its heels as it cantered away.

"Not fair!"

The girl danced around him in a circle, mocking his indignant tone and sticking her tongue out at him.

The boy leaned back on one arm and wiped his brow with the other. "It's hot. Do y'all have a swimming hole around here?"

The girl went still. "A what?"

"A swimming hole. A place to, you know, cool off in the water when it's hot out."

The girl's face folded into a frown. "No."

"Okay, then, let's go down to the beach and... What's wrong? Are you hiccupping?"

"I never go, *hic*, near the water," she whispered, her voice shaking, low.

The boy stared at her for a long moment, then shrugged. "All right. You wait here. I'll go down to the beach and take a quick—"

"*Hic, hic...* No!" The girl closed the distance between them in an eye blink, so fast that the boy yelped in surprise when he found her clinging to his arm, tugging for all her tiny body was worth. Though he could have flicked her away as easily as a fly, something deep in her sun-on-green-water eyes caught and held him fast. A tear, glittering with strange sparkles in the sunlight, appeared at the corner of her eye, brimming and threatening to spill over.

As if in answer to her fearful plea, a cool breeze sprang up, drying the sweat on his forehead and sending a shiver across his skin. A dip in the chilly ocean didn't appeal so much now. Presently he gave an exasperated sigh, reached up and playfully dashed her tear away, absently noting how it shone like quicksilver on his knuckle before it sank and disappeared into his skin. "You win," he grouched, flexing his finger once, then forgetting about it. "We'll do something else. But we'd better do it quick before your mama calls us for dinner."

In the flicker of an instant, the girl seemed to forget all about her distress. And her hiccups vanished. "Let's play dragonslayer," she said happily. "This time, I want to slay the dragon and for a change, I'm going to rescue *you*."

The boy rolled his eyes as he levered himself up from the ground. "Whatever pleases you, Your Highness."

CʒƧƆ୨ৼƆ

Hidden behind the tallest of the ring of Faery stones, Nuala spied on the two children and listened intently to their play-acting. She stiffened at the boy's off-handed declaration to do whatever the Fae child wished. *Stupid boy! His kind know not the binding power of innocent words!*

The quicker she got rid of this human boy, the better. From the moment they had found the lad washed up on the rocky beach of Inisghriann, along with the pieces of his broken *curragh*, little Abhainn had taken to him. Too quickly, and too completely. Why, thought Nuala sourly, when she had always been warned of the dangers of humans, a race of creatures notoriously blind to aught but their own narrow view of the world?

And what tales would he carry home with him? With what careless words could he expose Abhainn to the very evils Nuala had worked all these years to protect her from?

For a moment longer, she watched Abhainn play with her newfound friend, this boy called Michael in the hard tones of his own language. Her heart ached for Abhainn at what she was about to do—what she *must* do.

She took a breath and stepped from behind the stone, hesitating almost a second too long.

Abhainn, delighted with getting her way, leaned forward and pooched out her bow-shaped lips. "Seal your promise with a kiss!"

The boy's jaw dropped, but then a devil danced in his eyes and he leaned toward the girl.

Nuala gasped. *No! That boy is young, but he's just old enough to oblige her, even if it is only in fun! One kiss could bring disaster down on us all!*

"*Mícheál,*" she called out, making her tone sharp enough to stop both children in their tracks. Mícheál's ears reddened as he straightened away from the girl.

Thank the Goddess... I stopped them just in time! I was such a fool... I should have sent the boy off with the Selchies straight away.

"Word has come. Your family searches for you and they are near, just beyond the mists. It is time for you to go."

Both children's shoulders slumped, and Nuala could almost hear their imaginary swords clatter to the ground. Mícheál, gangly with the human's awkwardness of youth, pushed the mop of black hair out of his eyes. He slowly squared his shoulders as if trying, like most of his kind, to grow up too fast.

"But *Màthair...*" Abhainn's voice trembled, and her eyes filled with the tears Nuala knew would form a small creek if the child let them fly. This was a sight this human boy must not be allowed to see. So far, he had seemed to think nothing of the girl's delicately pointed ears that peeked out from the cloud of bright hair. Such was the ease with which all human children accepted the Fae world. But Abhainn's prodigious tears would be a tale that must never leave these shores, lest the wrong creature overhear it.

Nuala hardened her heart in the face of Abhainn's distress as she took each child by the hand, inserting herself firmly between them. Mentally, she rehearsed the spell that would erase the memory of this place, of Abhainn, from Mícheál's mind.

On Mícheál's hand, she detected the traces of Abhainn's tear on his skin. She frowned mentally and redoubled her efforts to find words that would make the spell twice as strong, twice as binding.

She held out little hope that the spell would affect Abhainn, as well. It took an especially powerful spell to affect a Fae such as Abhainn, and Nuala knew her spellwork was woefully inadequate to such a task. She would simply have to try to explain to the child why Mícheál must leave here without a shred of memory of having set foot in this realm.

"Come, children," she said, trying to gentle her tone. "It is time to say goodbye."

Chapter Two

Isle of Inisghriann, 20 years later

Had I kissed him but once, he would have stayed.

Abhainn stepped to the door of the cottage she shared with Nuala, braced her hands on either side of the door frame and leaned out into the cool morning air. She closed her eyes and breathed deeply, pondering the words that drifted softly through her mind.

The errant thought brought with it a subtle, taut sense of expectation that made the flavor of this day somehow different from other days.

Behind her, she heard Nuala stirring about, rolling freshly spun wool into bundles and retrieving the kelp basket from its hook on the ceiling. Normally Abhainn helped her mother take the wool down to the beach, where she would hang far back from the water's edge while Nuala met with the Selchies who would take the skeins beyond the mists. But today...perhaps today Nuala would release her from this chore. Abhainn turned her head and glanced hopefully at her mother.

Nuala laughed gently and waved her hand. "I see that look in your eye. You'll be of no use to me today."

Abhainn smiled and wasted not one more second of this precious morning of sun. She ran lightly toward the Faery circle, taking care to avoid treading on the delicate spring flowers and the tiny Faeries who tended them. Their airy wings brushed her ankles as she made her way up the hill.

As she stepped between the two head stones, greeting them as the old friends that they were, the sense of expectation tickled her consciousness again, along with a vague sense of wistfulness. She let out a long sigh. Odd that on such a beautiful morning, melancholy should intrude into her thoughts.

Spring water bubbled out from the base of the tallest stone, forming a small pool the size of one of Nuala's round bread loaves. Abhainn scooped a swallow of water into her mouth, letting the cool wetness trickle down her throat. This spring quenched her thirst like no other.

And it was the only body of water anywhere that didn't strike terror into Abhainn's heart.

Her friends didn't let her linger alone for long. Equillian Faeries, keepers of the wild pony herds, kept her busy for the better part of the morning, laughing, giggling and braiding manes and tails with summer flowers. Abhainn finished the last braid, tied it off with a strand of green grass, and then sent the pony on its way to join its waiting companions down the rocky hillside.

Content to be alone at last, she folded her bare legs into a shallow stone depression in the center of the circle. Nuala had told her once that many a Druid seer had sat in this spot to receive visions, but that was long ago. She closed her eyes and turned her face up to the sun she loved so well. It shone so rarely here for any length of time. A morning of unbroken sunshine was a rare gift.

The strange sense of expectation pulled at her core yet again. Unbidden, the face of a dark-haired boy reared up in her mind's eye, a boy with eyes the deep grey of sea-drenched stone cliffs. The picture in her mind stared back at her, as if he saw her as well. She gasped softly, wondering if this hollow Druid stone still held some vestige of power.

Had I kissed him but once...

Mícheál.

This was the second time that day she had thought of him. Strange, after so many turns of the seasons. The boy, whose borrowed boat had been swept here on an errant current, had stayed only a fortnight until his family had found him and taken him away. Many seasons had spiraled by before Abhainn had stopped keeping vigil for him on a rock outcropping well away from the water line. Before she had finally accepted Nuala's insistence that he was better off in his own world, where time ran differently. Better off with no memory of this place, so that he could not spread tales to the wrong ears. It was for his own safety, as well as hers, Nuala had explained. So long ago...

Ancient Ones, who sat upon this very stone and dreamed, what do my thoughts of him mean? Are they a sign? Is he well? The runes told me nothing, as if he never existed. Does that mean he does not remember me at all?

The stones around her groaned a warning.

Abhainn opened her eyes and studied the stones, knowing that as long as the sun was up, they would stay frozen in their places in the circle. Usually, if she listened hard, she could hear them whispering among themselves. But this time she didn't have to strain to hear—they called out with a screech like two stone slabs sliding past each other.

"What is it?" she whispered, alarm stirring in her belly.

A funny, melting sensation swirled down her spine. Her vision blurred, making the stones ripple as if reflected in a disturbed pool. The sun that she had loved so well all her life, suddenly left her cold, as if it passed through her without stopping to warm her skin. *The sun cannot see me any more.* The odd notion crossed her mind, leaving her feeling lost and alone.

The stones groaned again.

Her heart thudded wildly in her chest. A hiccup caught in her throat as she tried to rise from her seated position, but her limbs refused to obey.

The distant rumble of ocean waves suddenly sounded as if they were rushing in all around her; the spring's pleasant trickle rose in her ears until it resembled a waterfall that threatened to crash over her head. Water droplets dripping off the stones thudded like hammers. Even the ever-present mist had a voice, an icy hiss that raised bumps on her skin.

She clamped her hands over her ears and cried out.

Dark, squatty shapes lurked at the edge of the circle. The reek of stale breath and unwashed feet assaulted her nose, instantly identifying the creatures.

"*Màthair!*" she screamed. But her mother, she recalled suddenly, was down by the sea shore collecting kelp, well out of hearing range. Instinct commanded her to run, but weakness overtook her body. She had the odd notion that her bones were melting. These creatures were not her friends, like the tender flower Faeries, the night-dancing stone Fae, and the wild Equillians. These were trolls. Trolls! *What are they doing here? Máthair told me none could cross the sea to these shores...*

"Hello?" A new voice, masculine and somehow promising safety, flowed easily through the cacophony assaulting her ears. Her peripheral vision picked up a tall figure, dark-haired, which abruptly dropped a rucksack and hurtled toward her.

"Hey!"

The unmistakable creak of a taut bowstring. Her body felt as if it were falling...falling. Hands came out of nowhere to push her to the ground. The stone depression seemed to mold itself to her body—or was it her body molding itself to the stone?

Cold...cold...

She looked up at the sun, its image slithering about like a reflection off the surface of water in a madly sloshing bucket. Her vision darkened.

The bowstring twanged with release and she knew no more.

CR§∞RO

Finally. Someone who can tell me where the hell I am.

Michael Craig, jet-lagged and a little seasick from his rough ride in the *curragh*, rested a hand on one of the standing stones. Its solid grey bulk, along with the head of white-gold hair on the girl seated at the circle's center, assured him this place was real.

The fishermen at the Kilmore Quay had thought him mad, and had no qualms about telling him so, when he'd inquired about hiring a charter to take him to an island of which no one seemed to have ever heard. He'd even shown them the name of the island on the hand-scrawled map, which had arrived with the last shipment of fine Irish woolen thread, the lifeblood of his family's textile business.

This thread, which had begun arriving several months before in unmarked crates, was so fluid, so soft, that handfuls of it dripped through his hands like water, yet never tangled. Fabric woven from it was delicate enough to pass several square yards of it through a wedding ring, yet strong enough to lift a small car. Samples that his idiot cousin had leaked to clients had stimulated a flood of orders, offering any price for the scarce material. Within months, the mill had gone from the brink of closing to the center of a thriving niche market.

Now, the problem was simply one of supplying the demand. Without even a tracking sticker on the crates, Michael's search for the wool's source had been fruitless—until a single scrap of parchment paper had turned up in a crate, marked with the crudely scrawled words: *Isle of Inisghriann.*

In the end, he'd bought a *curragh* right out from under one fisherman's rubber boots, clambered in and set off on his own.

His father would have called him a fool.

Michael called it going to any length to save the family business and the workers who depended on the mill for their living.

The girl within the circle sat with her back to him, motionless as the stones that sheltered her. Something about that hair, hanging loose but riddled with tiny braids... Maybe he had seen her before on one of his previous buying trips to Ireland.

Perhaps if he saw her face, her name would come to him.

Deep inside, the boy that had long ago fallen asleep under the demands of adulthood now stirred, pushing and shoving at a thick, heavy barrier that seemed to blanket his memory on all sides. His head throbbed with the effort.

"Hello?"

She remained still, as if she had not heard him. Somehow reluctant to enter the circle, he skirted along the outer rim, focusing on the curve of her cheek as it came into view. The upturned nose. His gaze dropped, startled, to the curve of breast that showed clearly under the plain green fabric of the dress she wore. This was no child. He moved his gaze up to her eyes, an impossible color of green that...

...blinked slowly, wide with terror. For the first time, he noticed the panicked sound of her breathing.

Michael blinked hard, but her image wavered, as if surrounded by heat waves off a hot pavement. Suddenly she clamped her hands over her ears and cried out.

"Hey!" He dropped his rucksack and took a few steps toward her.

The hairs stood up on the back of his neck. From between the stones appeared what looked like a garden gnome gone bad. Brown and squatty, with stick-like arms and twiggy fingers that clutched a primitive bow and arrow. Its black marble eyes met his, and it leered a smile that didn't improve its looks. Michael froze in his tracks and stared it.

"What the hell are *you*?"

It didn't answer, but nocked the wicked-looking black arrow, aimed it at Michael's chest...then swung it toward the woman. Michael launched himself toward her, eyes riveted to the tip of the arrow, which dripped some nasty looking green goop.

The woman gave a strange, watery gasp as he closed his hands over her shoulders and shoved her down.

Thwang!

Michael rolled, grunting as his body impacted the rocky ground. The arrow whined past him to crack harmlessly against another standing stone, with a sound that oddly resembled a yelp of pain.

The ugly garden ornament took off down the hill on spidery legs, surprisingly fast for something that barely reached Michael's waist. It breathed hard, a noise somewhere between a stuffed-up Pug and a coughing hog.

"Stay down!" Without looking back, Michael took off after the creature, fury pounding in his ears so loud that a splash of water behind him barely registered.

It was a short chase. A hundred yards down the hill, the creature slipped through a break in a drystone wall. By the time Michael caught up, the thing had vanished down a hole, its snorting breath echoing from somewhere far below.

"Damn," he muttered.

Pain stung the pack of his hand, and he glanced down, flexing it. Blood oozed from a long straight scratch. That arrow must have nicked him.

That's just great. No telling what was on the tip. Already, a sickly shiver rippled across his skin. Ignoring it, he launched himself back up the hill, concerned the arrow might have nicked the woman, too. Tiny as she was, a miniscule amount of the stuff could harm her.

The late morning sun beat down on the back of his neck, humidity plastering his shirt to his body. Gaining the top of the rise, he jogged through the stones and halted just inside the circle.

She was gone.

Michael searched, dodging in and out among the stones. He ended up standing near the center, still alone, his heart racing.

A faint voice called from down the slope. "Abhainn!"

Ah-vawn...

The word tugged ferociously at the thick barrier covering his memory, but still let no light of recognition through. Far down the slope, an older, greyer woman stood in the whitewashed doorway of a neat, thatched cottage, shading her eyes from the sun.

Another shiver ran under his skin, and his mouth went dry. The ground tilted, just enough to send him backward a step, and his ears began to buzz. He looked down at his hand. Swollen, already twice its normal size.

He turned in a slow, careful circle, trying to find the rucksack he'd dropped earlier, which held his water supply and first aid kit. But his eyes wouldn't quite focus. Sun on water flashed near his feet. Blue, then gold. Dropping to his knees, he crawled toward it.

He plunged his injured hand in first, seeking to cool the fire burning under the skin. Instantly, warmth spread through his body, chasing away the shiver and quieting the buzz in his ears. He took a deep breath and sat back on his heels, examining his hand with interest as the swelling deflated and the seeping cut sealed on its own.

Whoa.

He rubbed the water experimentally between his fingers and paused. Had the water just *sighed*?

He shook his head and leaned forward again to scoop some in his hands. It smelled of fresh rain and soothed his parched lips. He closed his eyes in relief and opened his mouth to drink.

He felt pressure against his mouth, entirely too soft for the roughness of his work-hardened hands and too firm for mere water.

And it moved against his palms, just like the jaw line of a woman.

Warm breath, like a woman's sigh, caressed his lips. He opened his eyes and lifted his head.

There, cupped in his hands, was an elfin face framed in wild, white-gold hair. Eyes the color of sun on green water, wide with wonder, glowed above her slightly open mouth, still wet from his kiss.

36

A similar face leaped up from his memory, though still unnamed. It was pale and child-round; the one before him now was contoured with womanhood, though not much larger. The only feature virtually unchanged was her mouth, a study in curves and naturally upturned at the corners, which made her look like she was always on the verge of blurting some delicious secret.

She sat just as he had seen her before he'd taken off after the ugly lawn gnome—in the center of the stone circle, as if she'd never left it. Before he could think about how she'd gotten there, she reached up to touch his hair, reverently, as if it were he who had suddenly appeared before her, instead of the other way around. Her lips moved.

"*Mícheál.*"

Chapter Three

Mih-hahl.

As a boy, he had thought her name for him amusing, though it was his own name in her language. Joy rushed through Abhainn's veins, temporarily sweeping away the weakness, terror and confusion. The face she held in her hands was larger, harder and scratchy with a man's stubble. But above the man-grown angles of his face, the wet-granite grey of his eyes was the same. The unruly mop of curly black hair she remembered on the boy was now clipped so short her fingers glided over it, not through it. And it was lightly salted with silver.

The joy inside her died a little. His eyes, hovering so close, held no spark of recognition. Worse, they held no spark at all. Then, slowly, he blinked. The hard line of his mouth relaxed slightly, and his eyebrows knitted, as if memory warred with disbelief.

"A... A... *Ab—*"

"Abhainn! What in the Lady's name..."

Abhainn tore her gaze away and found her mother frozen in shock just inside the circle. She blinked the blurriness from her eyes and found her voice.

"*Màthair*, look who has come! Remember? It's Mícheál, the boy who—"

But her mother's gaze flicked downward. "Don't...move," said Nuala, hushed.

Confused, Abhainn looked down and bumped foreheads with Mícheál as he did the same.

"You're sitting in a puddle," an older version of Mícheál's remembered voice rumbled in her ears. He rolled onto his feet, crouching, preparing to help her up.

"No!" cried Nuala, rushing forward and falling to her knees beside them. "Did you not hear me, you silly man? Don't move her!" Her gaze moved rapidly back and forth between them, an expression of panic on her face Abhainn had never before seen.

She reached toward Abhainn, but stopped short, as if afraid to touch her. "Your legs. Look at your legs, child."

Abhainn looked down again and hiccupped. Near her knees, her lower legs disappeared into a puddle of water in the stone depression. She tried to lift one out of the water. The water rippled, but nothing emerged.

"She's in a *puddle*." Mícheál's calm tone held a note of impatience. "Let's get her out of it."

Nuala's hands gripped both his and Abhainn's arms, holding them still.

"*Màthair,* what has happened to me?" Abhainn whispered, touching the water's surface and drawing back in surprise, for she felt the touch *in the water*, as if she had touched her own skin.

"Tell me exactly what has happened here," Nuala said slowly.

Abhainn cast a quick glance at Mícheál. He was looking down where her legs should be, confusion slowing giving way to alarm in his face.

"I came up here to play with the Equillians and the ponies. I began to feel a little funny so I sat down, right here."

"Funny? How so?" asked Nuala sharply.

"Weak...like water lying in a bowl. My eyes blurred, but I think...I think I saw a troll."

Nuala drew in a sharp breath.

Mícheál's eyebrows drew together in a frown. "A what?"

"Was it about this high," Nuala held a hand about three feet from the ground, "squat and ugly, brown, with arms like sticks?"

"A troll." Mícheál repeated flatly. "Like in a kid's storybook."

"Quiet," Nuala snapped. Then, to Abhainn, "Did it hurt you?"

"No... I couldn't see clearly, but I think it hurled something at me."

The reassuring touch of Mícheál's hands left her shoulders, and he commenced pacing about the stone circle, gaze on the ground. She tried to turn her head to follow his movement, but Nuala caught her chin and brought her back round. "How many?"

"Only one," said Mícheál, striding toward them, holding something in his hand. "This is what the guy fired at her."

"Careful with that tip!" scolded Nuala, snatching the arrow away from him and examining it, then nodding. "Troll, no doubt. That they've returned to Inisghriann after all this time..."

"Troll, my eye," Mícheál said in a hard voice. "It was a midget with a dark tan. Trolls don't—"

"—exist?" Nuala interrupted. "Did it outrun you?"

Mícheál snapped his mouth shut. Nuala smiled in triumph.

"I thought as much. It's a troll, my boy."

Mícheál's eyes narrowed. "There's no such thing as trolls."

Nuala rolled her eyes. "And I suppose in your world, a girl's legs never dissolve into a puddle of water."

Mícheál opened his mouth, glanced down at Abhainn's missing legs and frowned. Abhainn would have laughed at his expression had her own heart not been beating like the wings of a butterfly trapped in a jar. Nuala turned her back on him.

"Then what happened, child?"

Abhainn swallowed, feeling as if she were on the verge of crossing some invisible threshold. "It was like the dream I had a few days ago, the one I told you about." *And after which,* Abhainn thought suddenly, *you began watching me like a hawk.* "Like I was under water, looking up at the sun. The next thing I knew," she felt her face flush, "Mícheál was here and I was..." She gestured down at the puddle around her hips.

"You." Nuala turned on Mícheál. "Tell me what you saw. What you did."

Mícheál crouched down beside them again, running a hand over his hair, leaning his head on his palm for a moment. For the first time, Abhainn noticed the weary circles under his eyes, the lines framing his straight mouth. He looked as if he hadn't truly smiled in a long, long time. *Oh, my Mícheál, where have you been? What has been done to you?*

"Well, it was like she said. I found her sitting here, but looking like a deer in the headlights. She looked...strange. I can't explain it. Then this midget guy—"

"The troll."

"Whatever. It drew a bow and arrow on her. I pushed her down and ran after the thing. Only it—" his jaw worked "—it got away. I came back up here and she was gone. I scooped up some water from this puddle to drink it, then suddenly she was just...here." He held out his hands, staring at them, then raising his eyes to meet hers. "Abby, how did you do that?"

Abby. His eyes held no hint that he realized he had just remembered his old nickname for her. "Oh, Mícheál," she whispered sadly, "do you not remember the magic of that time you were here before? As a boy?"

Silence descended. Mícheál stared at her as if she had spoken a foreign language. Then something changed on his face. "I thought I had...memories," he said slowly. Then he seemed to catch himself. "I don't know what you're talking about. I've never been here before in my life. I only came looking for a new source of wool for my family's textile mill."

For one crystalline moment, when she looked into his eyes, she thought she saw a hint of the missing spark. Then it was gone. Abhainn's heart ached for him.

"No time for this nonsense right now." Nuala's impatience cut through the moment. Her thoughtful gaze traveled back and forth between Abhainn and Mícheál. Then she set her jaw and nodded, as if coming to a decision.

"You were kissing her when she reappeared." It was a statement, not a question.

Abhainn smiled at the slow flush that crept up Mícheál's neck.

He had the grace to stammer. "It wasn't what it looked—"

"Kiss her again."

Mícheál blinked. "Say what?"

"Kiss her, fool! Do I need to tell you twice? Do it quickly before the trolls catch us out here again!"

Abhainn hiccupped and felt her skin blush. Mícheál's flush also deepened as he went to his knees before her and cradled her face once more.

Then he drew back. "I can't believe I'm buying into this."

Nuala sighed. "Can you males do nothing as you're told? Kiss the girl, fool!"

"All right, all *right!*" Mícheál snapped. "This isn't something I do every day."

Abhainn's heart sped up as his face floated closer, and she closed her eyes. In the next instant, his lips, warm and firm, touched hers and held. And held.

And held.

She thought she heard Nuala say something, but the blood sang in her ears so loud, she couldn't hear.

Abruptly she felt hard stone under her knees.

"You did it." Nuala's voice, weak with relief.

Abhainn looked down. Mícheál swore softly in his own language. Her legs were back, folded neatly beneath her, just as she had left them. She looked up at him and found him staring at her, his wet-stone eyes flickering with the bare beginnings of belief.

"Hurry, to the cottage," urged Nuala, helping Abhainn gently to her feet while not so subtly inserting herself between them. "Two Selchies are here; they must be told of this. They will carry word to the Lady."

Abhainn found herself being hurried down the long slope.

"To where?" Mícheál caught up and supported her on her other side. "What lady?"

Nuala made an impatient sound. "The Lady of Avalon, you dolt. Know you nothing?" She seemed to catch herself and muttered, "Ah, well, you wouldn't, would you? Not after..." She paused, and once again she couldn't quite meet Abhainn's eyes.

The three of them maneuvered through the low-linteled cottage door, and Abhainn winced at the sound of Mícheál's head making solid contact. Two Selchies rose from their task of bundling up Nuala and Abhainn's load of spun wool to take away as they always did, somewhere beyond the mists. She found herself settled near the peat fireplace. Nuala began conversing with the Selchies in rapid *Gaeilge*, and Abhainn took the chance to observe Mícheál without her mother hovering.

Mícheál's gaze darted everywhere, missing nothing, brows knit as if trying—and just barely failing—to make connections between dream and reality in his mind.

I left a tear on his finger. That much I remember. Perhaps it prevented my mother's spell from working completely. Please Mícheál, remember! she willed silently. *Remember!*

As Nuala continued talking, the Selchies looked his way and seemed none too pleased to have him here, either. Abhainn touched his hand, and his gaze swung to her, softening as if relieved to find one friendly face. He crouched close to her, his mouth opening, then closing on a short exhalation.

"This is going to sound strange. I think I've seen this place before."

Abhainn wanted to shake him to jog his memory, and shake Nuala as well, for casting the spell that had separated him from her, in body and in mind, but apparently not in spirit. She touched his face lightly, hoping the physical connection would help.

"You were just a boy, Mícheál. Lost in your boat. By chance you washed up here on Inisghriann, and we kept you safe until your people found you. For those few days," her breath hitched in her throat, "you and I were friends." She glanced at Nuala, who was ushering the Selchies out the door, one of whom cast a jaundiced eye at Mícheál.

Mícheál was studying her. "How old are you?"

Abhainn blinked. "Old? What do you mean?"

"I mean...when were you born? How many years ago? If I were just a boy, you couldn't even have been born yet. Just look at how young you are..."

"Would it surprise you to know that Abhainn is actually older than you are?" Nuala's voice cut in. She brushed past him on her way to a trunk in the corner of the room, as if he were of no more consequence than an annoying fly.

"Time passes differently here," she reported curtly. "Your kind tries to tame time by dividing it into little pieces you think you can hold in your hand. This place is out of your time."

Mícheál rose to his feet, pacing after her as she extracted a small leather pouch from the trunk, let the lid slam shut and headed back in Abhainn's direction, making a sound of annoyance as she had to walk around him again.

"That makes no sense at all," said Mícheál, dogging her heels. "It's been over twenty years since I came with my parents to visit relatives in Ireland. Twenty years since I went out on that boat and got lost." He waved in Abhainn's direction. "Look at Abby, she looks barely more than a child. It's basic science. It's the same time here as it is back on the mainland. It's not out of anything."

Abhainn's heart swelled with grief, and her eyes filled with tears. If he couldn't remember, he was lost to her. Worse, something precious was lost to him—his ability to see and believe in magic. And, by association, in her. He would leave this place again, where his memory of it, and her, would again fade like an inconsequential dream.

Mícheál continued, relentless. "Everything else aside, the fact is someone tried to kill her. And it wasn't just something random, not in a place like this. This guy was hunting her. Why? And how did she manage that puddle illusion..."

Nuala whirled on Mícheál, waved her hand in front of his face three times, and chanted in an irritated rasp, *"Ardaím an chaille ó d' intinn."*

Mícheál fell silent, blinked twice and sat down hard on the floor. His eyes stayed open, but stared inward.

"That should keep you quiet for a while," muttered Nuala as she turned to Abhainn and seated herself on another spinning stool next to her.

"What did you do to him?" Abhainn asked, curious.

"I simply gave him access to his memories of this place. Now he should stop asking pointless questions."

Abhainn watched his face with interest, a slow smile stealing to her lips. "But, *Màthair*, he is right to ask these things. You told me long ago that trolls couldn't cross the ocean to these shores. Why are they here now, trying to hurt me? I've done nothing to make them hate me."

"Hear me now, child." Nuala took her hand. "By your very existence, your life has always been in danger. Until now, I thought you safe as long as you stayed hidden behind the mists of Inisghriann, hidden until the right time. But something, or someone," she scowled at Mícheál as if he were to blame for everything, "has tipped the balance just as you have become your most vulnerable."

A nameless fear crawled into Abhainn's belly, similar to what she had felt up on the hill, with the troll. Small, helpless and, for the first time in her life, unprotected. She turned toward Mícheál, who still seemed unable to speak just yet. But now he watched her and Nuala, this time with recognition dawning in his eyes.

Nuala pulled her back. "This human cannot help you, child. In fact, he could be your greatest danger."

"He is my friend!"

Nuala shook her head. "He *was* your friend. But all children of his kind grow up and forget our world, Abhainn. Look at him. Even now, he remembers, but I can assure you that his mind is busy trying to plug what he remembers into some formula he can grasp. He will not succeed. Only a rare few manage it. I know." She hesitated and drew a long breath. "I was one of his kind."

Chapter Four

Abhainn tore her gaze away from Mícheál and looked at her mother. She reached for her mother's head wrap and lifted it, revealing the older woman's ears. They were pointed, just like her own. "That can't be true... Look, your ears are like mine! You must be Fae."

Nuala gently took hold of Abhainn's hands and held them. Through her fingers, Abhainn felt the other woman's pulse racing in distress. "These were a gift from the Lady, when I was given charge to care for you in the Fae realm. I swore I would defend you with my life, and with that vow, the Lady made me one of you."

Abhainn glanced helplessly at Mícheál. In his eyes, she saw the confusion, the memories warring with disbelief. He caught her gaze and quickly rolled to his feet, his brow furrowed in concentration. She pulled her hands away from Nuala and shrank back in her chair.

"I don't understand. This is all so... What do you mean, I am in danger? What is it about me... Who *am* I? If you are not my mother, then who?"

Nuala swallowed, as if fighting the urge to give in to emotion. "This will explain everything. Take it and hold it in both hands." She upended the pouch into Abhainn's open palms and closed them over a pale blue crystal that appeared to have clouds swimming in its depths.

The cottage around her disappeared into darkness, and in the next instant, she found herself standing outside on a tall hill, near the ashes of a dead fire. She cried out. She still felt the stone between her palms, and Nuala's hands clasped over her own.

"It's all right, child," came Nuala's voice, faint and far away. "I will not let you go. Keep your eyes open and watch. This is your history...and your destiny."

Another pair of hands, larger, warmer, closed over her shoulders. Mícheál's voice murmured something, and Nuala answered in an annoyed tone, but Abhainn couldn't discern the words. It didn't matter; the timbre of his voice calmed her pounding heart as the scene unfolded before her mind's eye. She leaned back, into his arms, and let the vision come.

C3§0&)

A slender young woman, dressed in ceremonial robes of every color of blue and trimmed in gold, stood on the top of a mountain surrounded by sea. The stone circle in which she stood was deserted in the pre-dawn light, the ashes of the Beltane fire at its center long burnt out.

Hooves thundered, closer and closer, until a lone knight reined his horse just outside the circle. He flung himself out of the saddle, his face pale, his armor streaked with blood.

"Afon! Thank the gods you are safe."

He strode toward her, and she ran to him.

"Blaen! What has happened?" she cried, drawing him with her to the side of a stream, where she used the edge of her own

garment to wash the blood from his face. *"I arrived for the Great Gathering, but no one is here!"*

Blaen caught her hands and held them still, his eyes bleak as they stared into hers.

"After I left you, I rode to join the others to prepare for the battle." He paused a moment to catch his breath. *"They were gone. Their campfires were as cold and dead as this one."* He nodded toward the empty stone circle. *"The battle was nearly over before I tracked them down. Afon,"* he choked, *"Arthur is dead."*

Afon gasped. *"How can this be? We were together only a few hours... Then you were to go to Arthur, and I to my place in the Great Gathering, the circle of power that was to ensure Arthur's victory!"*

"Something must have...happened...when we came together. Remember after we loved the first time, you made a wish upon the moon? That this night would last until we could love no more?"

Her face paled. *"Yes, of course. But they were only words spoken on the wings of the moment..."*

"I am a man, Afon, but you are Fae, and High Mother of the Asrai, at that. Your wish held more power than either of us imagined."

Afon covered her mouth with her hands, her eyes wide with horror.

"The Great Gathering is over, and I was not in my place!" Her voice broke. *"The circle is broken and my people...oh, Goddess, my people are cursed and will suffer because of me!"* She stumbled away a few paces, into the stream whose waters had always given her refuge and comfort. She stood there now, shivering.

Blaen followed her into the stream, sloshing in his armor, and gathered her into his arms. "I, too, am cursed," he choked. "Had I been by Arthur's side, he would not have died." He looked out over Avalon, glistening in the rising dawn. "Some foul work is afoot here. I feel it in my very bones."

The sun broke over the eastern horizon, and he closed his eyes against the glare. Afon stiffened in his arms, making an inarticulate sound in her throat.

When he opened them again, his last vision of his love was her horrified face before she turned into a column of opalescent water, and dissolved with dreadful silence into the running stream.

"No!"

She had said her people were cursed, but not this! He waded along the stream, frantically trying to scoop up her bright essence, but it slipped through his fingers. He stood, frozen in shock, as the last of her colors raced down the hill, swept along by the stream and out into the retreating tide, where it quickly faded into the grey sea.

Bone-chilling cold finally drove him out of the stream, stumbling, his mind blank with grief and anger. Breathing hard, he found his horse, withdrew his battle-axe from the saddle and barreled toward the sacred altar stone within the Great Circle. He raised the axe over the stone as the wind rose and howled around him.

"By my blood and this stone, I will seek out and reveal the one who has done this to my love—and to my king! No foul Fae magic will ever again cloud my eyes, nor the eyes of my kin! By my blood and this stone, I swear it!" He sobbed and chanted a third time, sealing the vow. "By my blood and this stone!"

He heaved the axe, breaking off a chunk of altar the size of his own fist. His tears fell upon it, and the blood on his hands *stained it, as he flung himself into the saddle. Leaning low, he rode out of the circle and into the gathering mist.*

Cʒ⁊ʘ⁊

Michael caught the blue crystal, now the color of dull midnight, as it dropped from Abby's limp fingers. Nuala promptly snatched it from him and attempted to shoo him aside, but he would not be shooed. His memories were not all in the right places yet, but he clearly remembered that Nuala had treated him no differently back then; tolerating his presence rather than showing true hospitality. But he was a man now and wouldn't be shunted aside so easily.

"Abby, what is it?"

She didn't answer, appearing still lost in her vision, her eyes gleaming with a feverish light he had never seen before. He looked at Nuala.

"What did that rock do to her?"

Nuala snorted. "That *rock* was the keeper of the memory of Abhainn's people."

"This is why I am afraid of the sea," Abby murmured, blinking back to the present. "I am an Asrai. We are the Fae of the All Waters. Who was Afon, *Màthair*? Was she…"

"An ancestor of yours, my child," said Nuala softly. "She had already borne many daughters for the Isle of Avalon before she fell in love with the human man, Blaen of CraighMhor. On the night of Beltane, there was to be a Great Gathering of all the Fae peoples as a show of support for Arthur's crown; but Afon, the high mother of her people, never came to take her place in the gathering. The circle was broken; without Blaen at his side in battle, Arthur fell. In his bitterness, Blaen of CraighMhor struck a piece off the altar stone and disappeared forever. From that moment to this, the Asrai dare not show themselves in the light of the sun, or... you saw what happened."

"Incredible," whispered Michael, the boy inside him listening with rapt attention while his adult self scoffed at the wild story. Yet, he found himself rising to his feet, drawn to stand beside Abhainn with one hand resting on the back of her chair. Nuala's expression plainly told him she wasn't impressed by his protective stance, but he found himself grinning, enjoying the chance to challenge the older woman's self-proclaimed authority.

She pointedly ignored him and continued. "Your mother was a descendant of one of those daughters. I am not your true mother. But one day I will tell you of the day you were born."

Abhainn drew a breath to speak, but Nuala put up her hand to stop her. She ducked her head to hide the sheen in her eyes. "Not...today."

Wordlessly Abhainn rose from her chair and approached Nuala, extending her hands toward the old woman's face. When Nuala would have turned away, Abhainn caught hold of her face and held it. With one finger, she touched the wetness at the corner of Nuala's eye.

"There is a memory in this tear," she said quietly. "I would have it."

"No..." moaned Nuala, her voice breaking.

As Michael watched, his finger tingling with the remembrance of the child-Abhainn's tear on his skin, Abhainn closed her eyes as her mother's tear ran along her finger. She gasped. "My mother died birthing me..." She opened her eyes and smiled. "You saved me."

The strain on the old woman's face almost made Michael feel sorry for her.

Abhainn spoke again, with a steadiness in her voice he had not heard before. "You raised me. You are the mother sent to me by the Goddess so that I should live. That is all I need to know."

"No," said Nuala, recovering her composure. "That is not all you need to know. You are an Asrai, yes. But you are the last of your kind, Abhainn. Until now, a birthspell cast by the spinner of your lifethread, a Stone Maiden, has kept you alive. Her magic allowed you to walk in the sun, and kept you hidden from those who would seek to harm you. The earth is sick and suffering, child. Men cannot hear her cries as they blindly destroy it. They have forgotten us, forgotten the Fae who used to teach them how to live gently upon it. Only you have the power to heal the Great Circle, Abhainn. Heal the Great Circle, and we have a chance to join together to heal this world. Without you, hope is lost—for both men and Fae."

Abhainn, her customary fidgeting gone, stood perfectly still for several moments. Michael thought he sensed a fine tremor pass through her body. Fear? Or something else?

"What happened to me," she reached up and laid a small hand on Michael's where it rested on the back of the chair, "to us...up on the hill today?"

Nuala sighed. "Your birthspell has worn off, as the Lady foresaw. I had hoped it would hold until you came of age, when you would take your rightful place in the Great Circle. But..." She shrugged in an it-is-what-it-is attitude. "Fortunately for you, I suppose," she lifted her nose in his general direction, "this human appeared at the right moment and you drew from him the strength to withstand the sun. Though why you would draw strength from the likes of him is beyond me. By the Lady's grace, you were in a place that kept you from draining away into the sea."

He felt Abhainn tremble. "Like my ancestor," she whispered.

"Your fear of the sea is born within you. Now," Nuala's tone shifted from gentle to brisk, "before they left, the Selchies told me there is to be another Great Gathering in Avalon at the next full moon. The original plan was to bring you there under the protection and guise of the Selchies; but thanks to this bumbling human for letting that troll get away, it won't be long until Queen Berchta sends more trolls to finish the job. You must leave at once."

"*Berchta.*"

Michael felt Abby hiccup. "You're scaring the hell out of her, woman," he growled.

Nuala turned on him with surprising vehemence. "Good. She needs to be frightened. Fear may keep her alive long enough to reach Avalon."

"Or paralyze her long enough for those Mr. Potato-Heads to find her," he shot back. "Who the hell is this Berchta, anyway?"

"Merely the queen of the Dark Fae. She who would tip the balance of power irrevocably to the side of darkness and destruction. Long have the mists hid this island from her eyes. But the troll somehow found its way here under the ground. As you were too slow to catch it, it won't be long before it brings back its friends."

Michael leaned toward her, growing more irritated with her by the moment. "Excellent! Evil queens, armies of garden gnomes gone bad. How do you plan to get her across open water to the mainland?"

"The Selchies…"

"How are they going to help Abby? If she sets one toe in the open sea, we could lose her."

"'We'?" Nuala scoffed as she bustled about in a sudden frenzy to make ready for the journey.

Michael followed her around the room, keeping one eye on Abby, who still looked stunned and none too steady at the moment. "If there is no 'we', then why are you packing only one bag?"

She hesitated. "I am old. Whatever magic the Lady granted me in order to protect this child faded with her birthspell," she said reluctantly. "She will be safer with those who possess the power to shield her."

A quick look at Abby. Her hands were over her mouth, eyes distressed. How much more bad news could this fragile-looking woman take?

"She can't go alone," he barked, then caught himself. What was he saying? He had responsibilities in his own world. A business. Workers who depended on him. Obligations... He shrugged offhandedly. "I have to get off this rock anyway. I'll take her with me."

"You! You?" Nuala hooted. "To Avalon. That's rich. Selchies are the stuff of fairy tales, remember? Trolls don't exist, remember? And Avalon is just a legend." Sarcasm dripped from her tone.

"I know what I saw with my own eyes," he retorted. "I saw what happened to Abby. The arrow that bloodied my hand was real; the poison that could have killed me was drawn out when I touched that water." His own scalp prickled at the realization. "*Her* water."

Nuala's breath caught. She dropped the loaf of bread she'd been stuffing into a sack. Abby rose out of her chair. She and Nuala exchanged glances. Michael plowed on. "Abby looks okay now, but what about later? What if the spell wears off again?

She'll need..." He trailed off as the two women stared at him. "What?"

Nuala sat down on the long bench by the trestle table. "Your blood...mixed with hers?"

Uh oh. What other Faery Commandment have I broken now? "Uh, I guess you could say that..."

Clunk. "You! Get out of there, you little thieves!" Abhainn's cry brought them both up short. She was busy shooing something away from his upended rucksack. "'Tis well," she said, scooping up the scattered contents one by one. "They were only naughty Pixies looking for food."

Michael frowned, looking around the floor. "Uh, I don't see anything."

Abhainn gave her mother an accusing look. "I thought you said you had given his memories back!"

Nuala threw up a hand. "That doesn't mean his eyes have the power to see what's right in front of him, child."

Abhainn's fingers stilled when they closed over the bluish lump of granite that he had carried with him from home. She held it up for her mother to see.

Faint red streaks marked its surface, and several dark patches showed dampness.

Nuala snatched it and turned it over and over, examining the finely hewn corner and the rougher, broken side. She fixed him with a glare. "Where. Did. You. Get. This?"

Michael held out his hand, and when she did not give it up, he made an impatient sound and took it from her, plucked his rucksack from the floor, and dropped the stone inside. "My grandmother said it came from 'the old country', which I assume is Wales, since that's where her family came from. On her deathbed she asked me to return it to the place where it had come from. She called it a 'weeping stone' because it never quite dried up. If you left it in a dry bowl at night, by morning the bowl would be full of water. She used to think it was lucky, but before she died she told me whatever luck it had, had worn off. She wanted to be rid of it." He felt his face flush, remembering his father's ridicule when the man had discovered his son had fallen for the old woman's fanciful tale.

Nuala's eyes narrowed at him. "Remind me. What is your second name, boy?"

The question caught him blind-sided. "It's...Craig. Why?"

Nuala groaned and buried her face in her hands.

Abby's face began to glow. "Craig, *Màthair*. 'The rock'. This is why the Old Mother Goddess must have sent him. He is of CraighMhor blood."

Nuala waved for silence. "This is the reason you came here?"

His patience wore thinner. "I came because of this." He unbuttoned a shirt pocket and drew out the slip of paper and a swatch of the incredible woolen fabric. "I'm looking for whoever makes this thread, because it may be the key to saving my company. The other thing...was just a promise to keep for an old woman, nothing more."

Nuala's forehead creased as she took the articles from him. Abhainn crowded close to read over her shoulder.

Isle of Inisghriann.

"Who sent this to you?" she said sharply, eyes narrowed.

"No clue. All I know is, if I can't find more of it, my family's mill will close."

Nuala and Abhainn gave each other a long look, then they commenced a rapid, whispered conversation in some language he couldn't have understood anyway.

Abruptly Nuala threw up her hands. "But he's a male. A shiftless male."

Irritation flared in his chest, but Abby's small hand on his arm stayed his retort. He looked down into her elfin face.

"In our world, the males of most Fae peoples don't amount to much," she said softly. "They spend most of their time feasting and lazing about." Her eyes twinkled. "But they are at heart a chivalrous lot and can sometimes be moved to go to war for a lady's honor." The complete trust in her eyes left him speechless for a moment, then he grinned.

"I guess it's safe to say some things don't change from one dimension to the next."

For a split second, their gazes locked, and something moved in him. A memory. Of he and Abhainn as little children, heads together, planning what game to play next. Deep in his belly, a long-forgotten sense of anticipation tightened, the sense that he was on the verge of an adventure.

I don't have time for an adventure, damn it.

Then he looked down at her tiny hand on his arm, so slender it looked like he could snap it without even trying. Whatever it was she had to do, she surely was not strong enough to do it on her own.

As if she read his thoughts, she straightened in defiance and turned to Nuala. "*Màthair*," she said firmly, "he is going with me. I think he already has a plan, don't you, *Mícheál*?"

Nuala's raised eyebrow loosened his tongue. Yes, he *did* have a plan, as it happened. One that could serve both their purposes, and his.

"I'll get her to Avalon. By taking her out of this realm and hiding her in mine. They won't be able to track her as easily on the other side of the mists."

Chapter Five

Mícheál's guttural growl of frustration crescendoed in time with a solid kick to the hull of Nuala's decrepit *curragh*. Its lone mast lay splintered across the gunwale, tattered sail flapping forlornly in the freshening night wind.

"Trolls!" Nuala spat.

Mícheál immediately started toward Abhainn as if to shield her.

"Not now, fool," Nuala said, exasperated. She pointed up, toward a circling flock of gulls. "If there are any about, the gulls will warn us."

Mícheál eyed the sky with suspicion. "If you say so," he muttered.

Abhainn huddled, shivering, near the bow of the little boat, which lay beached well out of reach of high tide. Even so, at the slap of a big wave hitting the shoreline, she squeezed her eyes shut, hiccupped and edged her bare feet still farther inland. She clutched her cloak about her. The magical wool normally kept her warm as a tea cozy on the coldest of nights, but now, closer to the sea than she had ever dared step before, she felt as if nothing would ever warm her again.

How am I to journey all the way to Avalon when I cannot bring myself to go near the ocean? Her hand closed over the small pouch that held the Asrai crystal, keeper of her people's memories. She hiccupped. *I must.*

"My boat's in pieces," Mícheál gritted out. "And this one's not much better. Now what? I don't suppose you have a magic wand or a spell to fix it?"

Nuala ignored him with a visible effort. "We will call for aid from the Selchies," Nuala decided.

Mícheál ran a hand over his hair. "They left hours ago to carry a message to...your leader. Whatever her name is."

Nuala stretched up on her toes and whacked him soundly on the back of the head. Despite her terror, Abhainn stuffed her fist into her mouth to keep from giggling at Mícheál's annoyed expression.

"Try to show a shred of respect, fool. Think you the Lady would have left this island completely unguarded? The Selchies have aye better things to do protecting this island than listen to you blether on. Who do you think will guide you back through the mists?" She turned to Abhainn, her features softening in something very like pity.

"Come, child. Told you I have the ways of the Selchies. I am old and have no tears left to shed; at least, none strong enough for them to hear. It is yours we need."

"Tears?" Mícheál queried, eyes narrowing.

Nuala's work-worn, leathery hands enveloped Abhainn's cold ones and pulled her to her feet. Shards of fear rattled clear down to her bones as the older woman led her, step by unsteady step, toward the water. *Hiccup.*

A warm, solid arm slid across her upper chest, effectively barring her way. "What the hell are you doing?"

Abhainn gripped his arm and pulled free. "No, Mícheál! I must shed seven tears into the water. Then the Selchies will come for us."

Mícheál turned on Nuala. "And you're going to let her risk her life for a few tears?"

Nuala drilled him with a scornful look. "Do *you* have them ready to shed?"

Mícheál's mouth snapped shut, his jaw tight. His arm fell away.

Nuala sniffed. "I thought not. Come, child."

The world tilted and Abhainn found herself swept up in Mícheál's arms. His voice rumbled in his chest, next to her ear. "The next big wave will knock the both of you down. Stand aside, woman." He waded into the surf up to his knees. She felt Nuala's hand still clinging to one of her feet, just in case.

Against the side of her face, Mícheál's heart thudded. She closed her eyes and listened.

Oh yes, Mícheál, *there are tears unshed in this heart. Enough to raise this ocean. You won't miss a few.*

Abhainn silently drew seven tears from his soul. When they trembled on the edges of her lashes, she turned her face to the sea and released them into the water.

In moments, three grey-brown seals popped their heads out of the water. They dove under the surface, and when they came up again, three tall, brown-skinned Selchie males rose from the sea and stepped smoothly to shore. To the casual eye they now looked like any other human-like Fae, save for the smallish ears and the liquid-black eyes of their sealish form.

"Whoa," murmured Mícheál, wonderstruck.

As he carried her back up the beach to the boat, Abhainn felt his fingers moving experimentally on the soft woolen cloak she wore. After he set her on her feet, his hands lingered on it, testing a corner of it and bringing it closer for examination.

"This is the same stuff that was sent to my factory..." he began, then paused, searching her eyes. "Did you send it to me?"

"No. The Selchies come with each moon to take away our spinning work. I have never known where it goes. The Lady is wise. She must have known that one day we would have need of you." Abhainn looked into his eyes and saw another piece of his grown-up armor chipped away. She slid one hand over his. "It seems you have been part of this from the beginning," she whispered.

Nuala, who had been negotiating with the Selchies, turned to them and beckoned. "Come," she called. "They will take you through the mists on one condition. That *you*," she jabbed a finger at Mícheál, "swear on pain of death to say nothing about what you see." The Selchies, tall, silent and imposing, looked down their long noses at the human in their midst.

"Whatever. Let's get this show on the road." He lifted Abhainn into the *curragh* and shoved the broken mast clear. She huddled on the hard wooden seat. Panic squeezed her heart as the Selchies brushed him aside, lifted the craft and began carrying it toward the water. She saw Nuala pull on Mícheál's arm to get his attention. Over the pounding surf and her own fear, she strained to hear what her mother was clearly admonishing Mícheál to do.

Nuala thrust a bulging sack and a long bundle into his hands.

"I need not tell you," she said, her voice low and urgent, "to keep her away from running water. Don't look at me like that, boy. Abhainn knows nothing of the world outside this protected island. She is used to having her freedom, like all Fae peoples. Keeping her safe is going to be more difficult than you think."

With an uneasy glance at the retreating boat, in which Abhainn looked even smaller than she was, Michael took the sack from Nuala and opened his own rucksack to stuff it inside. She thrust a much-folded piece of parchment at him.

"This is a map that shows you where the Holy Isle will appear out of the mists at the next full moon. I have not been in your world for many years, but I assume the island of Holyhead is still there?"

Michael opened the map and examined it briefly, nodding. "Once we make landfall, all we have to do is get to Dun Laoghaire and catch a ferry."

Nuala scowled. "I put no faith in the contraptions of men. If it comes down to it, summon the Selchies again."

He refolded the map and stuffed it in his shirt. "Mmm, yes, I'm sure they'll enjoy that," he said sarcastically.

"The sack contains bread and water."

"Thanks. I haven't eaten since..."

"It's not for *you*, fool!" Nuala snapped.

"Of course it isn't," he agreed dryly, holding his palms up in a hands-off attitude.

"The water is from the spring at the base of the circle's head stone. Should she become ill, use this to cure her. The medicines of your world will do nothing for her. The bread is made with fennel seed."

Michael sniffed and coughed. "It smells like mothballs."

She helped him finish fastening his pack closed. "It will repel all manner of nasty little dark Fae. Use it wisely and don't get it wet."

"Yes, Mother."

She ignored his remark and shoved the long bundle into his hands. "Do your best not to hurt anyone with this."

Michael unwrapped a corner of it. Dull, rusted metal gleamed dimly under the overcast skies. "A sword?"

"Don't thank me. It's probably almost as useless as you are. But it may come in handy if you manage to muck things up, which you probably will." Nuala sniffed and turned away to say goodbye to her daughter.

Michael caught the unmistakable sheen in her eyes before she turned away.

He touched her arm, stopping her briefly. "She'll be safe with me. I promise."

Nuala drilled him with a stare. "You know nothing of what awaits you, human. Try to pay attention now." She began ticking off on her fingers. "We do not know how long the strength you gave her through your kiss will hold. You should kiss her before sunrise each day, until you reach Avalon."

He grinned. "Not a problem, ma'am."

"When you get to Avalon, keep your clumsy human feet out of the Sacred Circle. If you get swept away in the Faery dance, you will be of no use at all. Not to mention that if you lose yourself in the dance yet somehow manage to escape, centuries of your time will have gone by before you return home. Everything you know will have passed out of memory."

"Not a problem there, either. I can't dance worth a damn."

For once she had no retort for him. Only tear-filled eyes. She pulled his ear closer, her voice low so Abhainn wouldn't hear. "You must reach Avalon before the next full moon, when the gathering is to take place. If Abhainn...if she does not live to see the full moon, take the crystal she wears to the Lady. Perhaps the Old Ones will be appeased and agree to continue their efforts to heal the human world." She released him and Michael thought he heard her add, "Though I doubt it."

C3♥80

The eerie wails and screeches began moments after their *curragh* emerged on the other side of the mists. Starlight glinted off the glossy heads of the Selchies, who towed the boat so hard the ropes they held in their mouths groaned with the strain.

From her position secure under Mícheál's left arm, Abhainn felt him lean back and look up. "I could have sworn it was barely noon when we left the island," he said, loud enough to be heard over the thumps of the hull on the choppy water. "Look at the horizon...it's almost dawn."

"Time is different on your side," she answered, trailing off as the unearthly noises pierced the wind.

"What the hell..."

The lead Selchie turned its head and squealed at them between teeth clenched around the rope.

"What did it say?" said Mícheál as his hands strayed to the wrapped sword. He edged it out of her line of sight, but slight movements of his shoulder told her he was attempting to unwrap it without her noticing.

"*Hic.* Tempestaries! *Hic.*" She tried to control the hiccups that always accompanied any stab of fear, but despite clamping her hands over her mouth, the annoying spasms worsened.

"What are those?"

"You will find out soon enough," barked a new voice, right behind them.

Abhainn squeaked and Mícheál sprang up, ripped the rusted sword from its wrapping and whirled, his momentum almost carrying him over the side. The voice turned out to be the lead Selchie, who clamped a web-fingered hand onto Mícheál's arm, simultaneously protecting himself from the blade and keeping Mícheál from falling out of the boat.

"Sit down, human," it growled. "Before you hurt yourself."

Abhainn clutched his arm. "Listen to him, Mícheál!" She felt tension vibrating through his body. "This is no game like we played when we were small! The dragons are real this time!"

Before her last words were out of her mouth, the waters around them heaved, then tossed up a half dozen green-black, bat-winged creatures with long claws and even longer teeth. In the next instant, dozens of Selchie-seals, orcas, dolphins and other finned and scaled creatures formed a shining-wet wall of defense around and over-leaping the *curragh*.

Abhainn found herself squashed in the bottom of the boat, her back pressed down by Mícheál's chest, one of his arms clamped tight around her and the other jerking savagely as he stabbed out with the sword, fending off something shrieking and smelly. Out of the corners of her eyes, she saw the lead Selchie's feet on either side of them, shielding them both.

Water poured in from all sides. She sputtered and coughed as the *curragh*, incredibly, picked up even more speed, bobbing wildly as the Selchies pulling it dodged and rolled.

Thump!

The *curragh's* forward motion stopped so abruptly, she and Mícheál flew forward and out over the bow, helped along by the lead Selchie, who had handfuls of their clothing. His grip prevented them from grinding their faces into the stony beach when they landed.

"Go!" he roared, shoving them. "Get above the tide-line! You'll be safe there!"

Mícheál picked her up under his arm like a child's toy and took off at a dead run up the beach, no questions asked. Abhainn, her breath bumping in and out in time to Mícheál's stride, risked a glance backward.

She shut her eyes against the sight of red-stained water and the upended *curragh* sinking into the sea, with a huge bite out of the hull right where she and Mícheál had been crouching.

As quickly as the attack had erupted, all fell to silence, leaving her and Mícheál alone in the grey light of dawn.

He sat down hard on the sand, staring at the rusty and now bloody sword in his hand.

"I swore to myself I'd never do anything like that again," he said quietly. "In my world or any other."

He drew a deep breath and looked up at her, eyes dark. "Are you all right?"

She went to her knees beside him, pushing a handful of errant hair out of her eyes. She opened her mouth to assure him she was well, but only a watery gurgle came out.

As one, their gazes turned to the brightening horizon. A sliver of sun peeked above the rim of the world.

"Uh oh." Mícheál dropped the sword, pulled her into his lap and kissed her hard.

She forgot to close her eyes. And so, she observed, had he. He kept one eye on her and the other on the rising sun.

Her heart beat faster and faster, and she wondered if it was because of the change trying to take place within her, or because of the heat of his body pressed against hers. His face blurred and she hiccupped a mouthful of water. Her insides weakened and sloshed with every breath. She tore her mouth away and gasped his name.

He swore, cradled her head in his hands and kissed her again. Deeper this time. Angling his head to open her mouth and delve deep with his tongue, as if he could somehow use it to pull her back from the brink. She wrapped her arms around his neck and held on tight, toes digging into the gravelly beach that would not hold her if she dissolved.

There!

His strength flowed into her, filling her being and setting everything to rights. She drank him in, kept on, even after she was sure the danger was past. Something wild took hold of her, set a fire low in her belly that she'd never felt before.

She squirmed against the feeling, and Mícheál's deep groan of response reverberated in her delicate ears. Suddenly he took her by both arms and set her away. A protest sprang to her swollen lips, but it changed to a slow, awakening delight as she watched his face.

He seemed to be having trouble opening his eyes.

As surely as she felt his strength and calm settling into her bones, she sensed more than a little of her Fae magic seeping into his being.

And he didn't quite know what to do with it yet.

Chapter Six

By the time they reached his rental car, still parked on a side street near Kilmore Quay, Michael had a firm hold on Abhainn's hand to keep her from wandering off for the hundredth time. Every other step, it seemed, she was darting off to look at some new wonder that in her world she had never encountered.

His first stop had been a tourist shop, and she now sported a pair of child-sized jeans and a garish green sweatshirt with EIRE emblazoned across the front, sleeves rolled up several times over so her hands would be free. She'd turned her nose up at shoes entirely. He was beginning to wish he'd bought a child leash along with the clothing.

Though he had hidden her bright hair and pointed ears under a Carolina Panthers baseball cap from his rucksack, there wasn't much to be done to disguise her sun-on-green-water eyes, which sparkled with relentless curiosity and smiled at everyone they passed on the village streets.

Wherever she cast her brilliant eyes, a spell seemed to fall. By the time they had reached the end of the single street with its rainbow row of neat buildings, the local shopkeepers had them well supplied with food. A few extra scones here, a bag of apples there. In their wake trailed a horde of entranced children who would not be shooed until Abhainn had kissed each one on the forehead.

He marveled at her ability to completely put aside the gravity of her quest and simply enjoy the moment.

Finally, at the car, he let go of her hand, placed his hands on her shoulders and held her still. "Do you think you can manage to stay in one place for thirty seconds?"

Her brow furrowed in confusion. "Of course I can! Oh, look..." She touched the front of his shirt. "You've got Spriggan spit on you."

He looked down at a new brown stain that he was pretty sure hadn't been there before. It didn't smell too pretty, either. Any other day, he would have assumed he'd dropped food on himself.

Out of the corner of his eye, he caught a movement near the car's front tire. But when he turned his head to follow the movement, it was gone. He shook his head. Ever since dawn, when he'd kissed her a second time, he had been plagued by these edge-of-peripheral-vision flickers.

Muttering to himself, he opened the passenger door, threw his rucksack in the back seat and got in, scooting across to the driver's side. "Get in," he called as he started the engine.

Abhainn jumped backward, eyes wide, hiccupping. He leaned over so he could catch her eyes. "It's all right! It's called a car. It will take us where we need to go a lot faster than the Selchies can swim. Believe me."

Her face brightened. Pulling her cap down more securely over her ears, she stepped forward and placed a hand on the door frame.

Instantly she cried out and jumped backward again, holding her hand as if it had been burned.

71

Simultaneously, the engine died.

Ignoring the engine for now, Michael scrambled out of the car. "What's wrong?"

Whimpering a little, she showed him her hand. A large red blister scored her palm.

"It is made of iron!" she cried. "Faeries cannot abide it!"

"You mean you're allergic to metal?" *Oh, great. Now what?*

"Not all metal," she said, "Not copper or bronze. But iron..." she shuddered. "Still have you the flagon of water Nuala gave you?"

He brought it out and poured some over her hand as she directed. The blister quickly faded.

She shivered and looked around. "This world is full of wonders," she murmured. "But it feels...wrong. The air smells...thick. The earth feels tainted under my feet. And the water..." She reached down and touched a puddle of fresh rain water, rubbing it between her fingers and grimacing. "The water stings my skin. Is there something in it?" She raised her fingers to her mouth.

"I wouldn't do that," he said, catching her hand before it reached her lips, then using the edge of his shirt to wipe it off. "It's probably polluted with something that will make you sick." *How am I going to keep her safe and healthy long enough to get her to Avalon? Everything she comes in contact with here is tainted...*

"What does 'polluted' mean?" she asked, head tilted to one side.

"It, uh, means tainted. Dirty. Poisoned."

She went pale and wrapped her arms around herself. "Why?" she asked to no one in particular.

Leaving her standing there looking around with new and worried eyes, he rounded the front of the car and popped the hood. "What in the *hell* got in here? A cat?" he muttered, reaching in and pulling up a variety of shredded hoses and tattered wires. Under the car, pebbles scattered noisily as something small scrambled away. By the time he dropped to his knees to look for it, it had vanished.

He got up and Abhainn appeared at his shoulder, peering cautiously at the mangled engine. "Spriggans," she announced. "They like to chew things."

Michael slammed the hood shut. He ran a hand over his hair and looked at her, but not really seeing her. His mind was turning over the next step. "Okay. Apparently you can't touch a car. I assume that means planes and trains are out, too. Can't hitchhike. Walking's too slow." He focused on Abhainn who, now that her hand was healed, was cocking her head to one side, as if listening. Then she brightened.

Clop, clop, clop, clop.

At the end of the street, a small draft horse and a brightly painted gypsy caravan trundled by. On the side a phone number for a rental stable stood out in bold white against red paint.

He looked from the caravan to Abhainn's mischievously tilted chin. And back. "You've got to be kidding me."

She raised a brow in a perfect imitation of Nuala. "You've a better idea, fool?"

ೞഌ

Late afternoon sun slanted low across the little brown-and-white draft horse's briskly swaying haunches as Mícheál guided it northward along a narrow, deserted farm lane.

"You don't have to do that, you know?" she said, trying and failing to suppress her mirth.

He looked at her from under drawn-down brows. "Do what?"

"Use those..." she gestured, pretending to flap a set of long leather reins like the ones he held in his hands. "I told the horse and its Equillian where we wanted to go and that we needed to go there as quickly as he can manage. They know the way."

"What's an Equillian?"

"The Fae creature that tends to horses." She pointed toward the horse's shaggy mane. "See there? Those braids?"

Mícheál leaned to one side and looked, brow furrowed. "Those weren't there before. I remember having to mess with the horse's mane while we were hitching up." He turned to look at her. "You didn't do it?"

She smiled and shook her head. "Look at it with soft eyes," she said helpfully. "Just off to the side a little, not directly at it. You'll see it then."

Mícheál grunted noncommittally, and Abhainn sighed quietly. She had been afraid there would be no one like herself on this side of the mists, but she had been pleasantly wrong. Faeries abounded, everywhere, even here. Humans had simply forgotten how to see them. Mícheál was no exception. Oh, he could see the Selchies and he could certainly see her; no doubt he, like other humans, had seen Fae all his life without realizing what they were. But he still could not see the smaller, quicker little creatures that populated the landscape, all around, just beyond the edge of normal vision.

The only difference in these Fae and those on Inisghriann was that they all seemed beset by gloom and grump. Well, no wonder, she observed. The Fae continued to do their workings in the human world, *for* humans, and never got any credit or acknowledgement. It was enough to depress the most cheerful and helpful of creatures. *No wonder the Fae world is drifting farther and farther away...*

The late sun caught the side of Mícheál's face, and for the first time, she noticed the dark circles under his eyes, the fatigue that dragged at the corners of his mouth. It occurred to her that he had not slept since the previous day. And this time of year, the days lingered long. Still, he drove doggedly on, determined to fulfill his promise even if he didn't quite believe everything he had thus far heard and seen. In the slope of his broad shoulders, she sensed the burden of responsibilities that he carried.

The sun slipped behind a wall of incoming clouds. A shiver ran unexpectedly down her back and she moved closer to Mícheál. Night was approaching, and this world was different from her world on Inisghriann. Usually, at this time of early evening, Nuala would be preparing supper, and the cottage would be warm from the peat fire and full of the rich smells of fresh-baked bread and apple tart.

Feeling small and alone, she closed her eyes, leaned into Mícheál's solid body and tried to think of something else. His scent enveloped her as he let her fit naturally under his arm, as if that space had been made just for her.

"Mícheál, what is it that you swore you'd never do again?"

"Hm?" His gaze never stopped moving, always on watch. There was no point in telling him that, all along the way, she had seen signs that they were well guarded by a wide variety of Fae—creatures of the rocks, the meadows, the deep trees.

Everywhere she sensed their watchful gazes, but Mícheál, human as he was, could not.

He shifted and breathed deeply, his chest rising and falling against her cheek. "Years ago, I was in something called 'the military'. An army. Do you...know what that is?"

"The Fae have their warring tribes, that much I know," she volunteered. "And Avalon fought alongside the knights of Arthur long ago. I may have been sheltered on my island, but have heard all the stories."

"Yes, well...I was in a few battles. War is nothing like the pretty stories they tell. It is ugly, dirty, painful...bloody. I swore when I went home I would never draw blood again. Unless," he looked down at her, a slight smile tugging at his lips, "it was in direct defense of the ones...I care about."

She tilted her head back to look up him. "I would expect nothing less of a knight, Mícheál."

He cleared his throat and looked away. "Nuala gave me back my boyhood memories of the time I was marooned on the island. The memory of you. But it's...it's all detached, somehow. Like I read it as a story in a book somewhere, not something that really happened. I'm not sure all *this* is really happening, that it's not some jet-lag-induced dream—or nightmare—that I'll wake up from. Something that a psychiatrist will give me a pill for." He shifted his shoulders. "A big part of me wants this to be real, the way all dreams used to be real to me. The way every new day was a new adventure, playing make-believe out in the woods. But," he shook his head, turned away and slapped the reins, "another part of me is telling me I have work to do. People are depending on me. I should wake up, shake this off and do just what I came here to do—find the fabric for my family's mill, take the stupid rock back to Wales, and get home."

Abhainn refused to give in to the sadness that threatened to swamp her at his reluctance to finally, irrevocably accept the Fae world and his part in saving it. She rose up onto her knees and put her arms around him, pulling his face around to make him look into her eyes. At the bleakness she saw there, she made a distressed little sound and stroked his cheek.

"I vow to you Mícheál CraighMhor, that when this is over, you will have accomplished those small tasks...and so much more. And I will seal this promise—"

"—with a kiss," Mícheál finished for her, his slight smile and tilted head telling her that this was one memory of her that had not grown fuzzy with time.

She threw her head back and laughed. "With a kiss!"

Her laugh turned to a gasp when she felt his warm lips on her exposed throat.

This was different from the kisses they'd shared before. Those had been out of duty, to keep her from melting into a sunlit puddle.

This kiss was because he *wanted* it. Wanted to taste her. Just for himself.

Faery bells rang in her ears and she forgot she had ever been chilled. Heat flooded her small body as he worked his way up her throat, nipped at her jaw line, then found her smiling mouth.

A muted, leathery clatter told her he had dropped the horse's reins at last, and his hands pulled her into his lap and roamed up and down her back, molding her closer to him. Small peals of delighted laughter shook themselves out of her belly, and he took advantage of her open lips to slip his tongue inside.

Her laughter melted into sighs and she gave herself wholly into the sensation of tasting the rich flavor of his wet, warm mouth. She let her fingers play with his curiously human-round ears, his hair, and slide inside the collar of his shirt where his skin was hot.

Finally he broke away, breathing hard, once again having to struggle to open his eyes. When he finally managed it, he focused on something over her shoulder, then nearly jumped out of his seat, grabbing her before he dumped her onto the road.

"What is *that*?"

She turned around and saw nothing unusual. "Where?"

"On the back of the horse! See it? It looks like Tinker Bell, only bigger."

She threw her arms up in exultation. He could see! With their third kiss, he could really *see*! She hugged him hard.

"That, my fine fellow, is an Equillian. Her name is Eoth."

In response to hearing her name, Eoth grinned and waved at them both.

"Hail and there be Arthur's man!" A new voice boomed off to their left.

Mícheál went still, eyes sliding sideways as if not daring to look in the direction of the voice. "I think that wall just said something to me."

Sure enough, the carved face of a Green Man leered out at them from a garden wall. It chuckled, sighed and went back to its snoring nap.

Abhainn leaned close to Mícheál's ear and whispered, "Welcome to the world of the Fae."

Chapter Seven

How had it come to this?

He stood rooted to the spot, watching a black-sailed funeral ship fading away into the mists. Far below, on the rocky beach below the cliff on which he stood, the members of the funeral procession began to trudge away, leaving their banners stuck in the ground.

Banners bearing the symbol of the house of Pendragon.

He looked down at the shiny and unbloodied sword in his hand. He shook his head in confusion. How had he managed to miss the battle entirely? The enormity of it hit him square in the stomach, and he sank to his knees with a cry that had a few of the people far below him turning their heads to look.

I was not at Arthur's side, and now he is dead!

An empty stone circle, it too abandoned and long silent... A woman crying... The mighty clash of axe on stone... An oath.

Eyes all around. Staring. Accusing. Pleading. One pair of eyes, sun-on-green-water, beckoning. Return...return...

A spinning wheel, endlessly clicking, clicking, clicking. Desperate. Grim.

Michael awoke sitting straight up and sweating in the compact bed in the back of the caravan.

He rubbed his face hard and muttered, "Keep your bloomers on, people, I'm returning her as fast I can."

The caravan was still and quiet, not rumbling, bumping and creaking along as it had been when Abby, after nightfall, had beckoned him into the back of the vehicle. Though he thought it safer to pull off the road after dark, the horse showed no sign of tiring from its brisk trot. Now that he could better see and sense the number of friendly Fae along their route, guarding their progress, he gave in to his sagging eyelids and went willingly.

Her beckoning smile hadn't hurt, either. But when she had taken off his shirt and trail boots, and unbuttoned his pants, she had done something totally unexpected. She had drawn him to the bed, all right, but she had cradled his head and stroked his eyelids with butterfly fingertips, and in seconds he was gone.

Now, sitting upright, her fresh rain scent lingered and her taste, of cool spring water, rested on his tongue. Uncertain morning sunlight, mostly blotted by clouds, streamed in through the caravan's single window. *The sun is up. Where is she?* His hand automatically reached out to feel the spot where last night Abhainn had lain down with him. But she was gone.

He grabbed his shirt and pulled it on without buttoning it. He was halfway to the caravan door before he realized the taste on his tongue wasn't just part of the dream. She must have kissed him in his sleep before slipping out. Still, she had no business being out there alone, no matter how many friendly Fae surrounded them.

The familiar tinkle of her laughter drifted in through the caravan's half open door. He stepped quietly outside and settled on the driver's seat to watch the scene before him. The horse, unhitched, grazed nearby; Eoth lay draped across its back, sound asleep. Michael's gaze swept the stone-littered meadow, and at last he found her.

She sat on a boulder, legs folded beneath her, arms thrown wide. Unabashedly naked as the day she'd been born. His groin tightened as, unobserved, he let his gaze pass over her body. Tiny as she was, there was no doubt that Abby was a full-grown woman, all slender curves and high, firm breasts. The morning light glowed on her pale skin, so fair as to be translucent, traced with river-maps of blue veins, flawless from the tips of her toes to the delicate points of her ears.

All around her flitted a cloud of tiny, winged Fae, who tended to her as if she were a queen in waiting. Which, he realized suddenly, she was. As the last of her kind, she by default was the Queen of the Asrai.

Humming like a swarm of honeybees, the Faeries combed and braided her white-gold hair, washed a smudge of dirt from her nose, handed her damp handfuls of moss with which she cleaned herself, rubbing it over her skin—all her skin—in slow, sensual delight.

More Faeries brought her sips of water and a sticky substance that looked like nectar, cupped in spring flowers. She tipped her head back and accepted their offerings on her tongue, smiling and licking her lips after each taste, catching stray droplets on her fingers and licking them, too.

The ache in his groin hardened into a painful knot. Blood pounded in his ears so hard that for a second he couldn't trust himself to move. Despite the lust that roared through his veins, he remained conscious of the delicacy of her small, fragile body. *She's like porcelain. Like one wrong touch could break her.*

Yet for that second, he understood what had driven Blaen of CraighMhor to risk everything for one night with a Fae.

And he lost it all, Michael reminded himself.

As if she sensed his eyes upon her, she turned her head and looked at him. She blinked once, slowly, and the smile on her face grew brighter. She held out her hand.

Abruptly, the attending Faeries screeched and scattered. Only one stayed, hovering above and just behind her golden head. Its buzzing grew into a snarl, and before Michael's eyes it changed from a thimble-sized thing to a fox. It bared its fangs and bunched its muscles to spring at Abby's unprotected back.

With a sickening lurch that took him back to his combat days in the Marines, time slowed to a crawl. Every detail of the scene sprang into sharp relief. Before Michael could do more than shout a warning, Abby's face went blank.

Then, as the fox sprang, she changed into a statue of clear, hard ice.

The fox yowled in frustration as it clawed and bit at the back of her neck, but managed no more than a few superficial scratches.

Michael took advantage of the time she had given him by lunging into the caravan to retrieve the rusted sword. He lay hands on his rucksack and threw himself out of the caravan, pulling the sword out and dropping the bag on the ground as he ran, spilling the contents.

He sprinted the few yards that separated him from Abby, a hoarse cry in his throat and the sword raised to strike. The fox saw him coming, issued a series of short, harsh barks, then shapeshifted *again.*

Michael found himself looking up into the face of what could only be described as a vampire-like woman, complete with glistening fangs and black wings sprouting from her shoulders. With a hiss she flew at him, driving him back. He let her come, knowing it would draw the creature away from Abby.

"Come on, come on, bitch! What ya got? Come on!" he growled, goading her with the sword.

The vampiress closed in, and with moves too quick to see, she knocked the sword away then hit him square in the center of the chest with the leading edge of a black, leathery wing. Michael caught his heels on the rucksack and landed on his back, flinging his arms wide to break the fall.

His hand fell on his grandmother's precious stone, which must have rolled out of the rucksack when he'd dropped it.

Wrapping his fingers around it, he waited, heart speeding to dangerous levels as the vampiress closed within striking distance. Waited, sweating, until her hot breath blistered his face, until he could count the veins in her bulging eyes. Then he swung at her head.

Instead of spurting blood, the broken skin on the side of the creature's face erupted with huge horseflies the size of golf balls. In moments, the thing had completely dissolved into a cloud of the droning black bugs. Abby's attending Faeries chased them all away, leaving the morning eerily quiet, as if nothing amiss had happened at all.

Panting, Michael hauled himself to his feet.

"Well done."

He spun and found a tall, Tolkienesque elf lounging against the side of the caravan, idly examining his fingernails, longbow thrown casually over one shoulder.

Michael relaxed and straightened. "Thanks for the help," he said dryly.

The elf raised an eyebrow, as if he were actually offended. "You did well enough on your own. Had you needed it, I would have intervened. The Lady chose well." With that, the elf sauntered away into the trees.

"I will never get used to these people," he muttered, turning toward Abby as thunder rolled overhead.

Abhainn still hadn't changed back from the block of ice. It was a perfect replica, captured just as she had been sitting on the rock.

He crouched by the rock, afraid to touch her. "Abhainn. Abby, can you hear me?"

Huge, fat raindrops began to splat the ground.

Maybe she can't change back.

His mind kicked into gear, looking for a way to keep her from melting and running in rivulets down the side of the rock. But as the first drops of rain struck her head, she shifted back into normal form and fell, shivering and blue with cold, into his arms.

"Jesus, you scared me, woman," he said, gathering her closer, rubbing her arms. The bare skin under his hands felt like the ice from which she'd just shifted. He quickly lifted her hair to examine the back of her neck. Relief flooded through him. Her skin remained unbroken.

"I...I...knew not...I c-c-could do that," she managed through clattering teeth. "I-I-I sensed the Mei was behind me and-d-d it j-just happened!" Then, incredibly, she began to laugh. "I wonder...w-w-what else I can do?"

Before he could stop it, anger flared white hot in his chest. How could she laugh? She had come within a hair's breadth of death, and yet she laughed!

Shaking, not trusting himself to speak, he scooped her up in his arms and strode toward the caravan.

"Mícheál?" she gasped between giggles and shudders of cold. "W-what is it?"

"The fate of your people depends on you," he gritted out. "And you sit there laughing when your quest almost came to nothing."

She leaned back in his arms, her laughter fading to a gentle smile. "But it did not," she said simply. "I have you to protect me. All is well. And I have found that I have powers I knew not I had. Why not enjoy the moment?"

He stopped dead in his tracks, light rain tapping on his head. He had no answer for her.

"Mícheál," she said gently.

He shook his head, surprised at his inability to speak, jaw clenched tight. *She could have died. She could have...*

"Mícheál." This time her lips touched his ear.

At the touch of her breath on his skin, he drew her to him tighter still, buried his face in her hair, inhaling the fresh-rain scent of her. He could find no words to say other than her name.

The skies let loose with a torrent of rain.

Michael staggered a few steps into the shelter of a tree, then sank to his knees on the soft grass. She shifted, wrapping her slender legs around his waist, grabbing handfuls of his shirt and pulling it off his shoulders.

"Warm me," she demanded, throwing back her head and offering to him her throat.

He rubbed his open mouth over the smooth skin, feeling it heat under his lips. The cool tips of her breasts brushed against his chest, and he covered them with his hands. His fingers felt big and clumsy on her small frame. She exhaled sharply, arching her back to thrust her breasts more firmly into his palms.

Would it surprise you to know that Abhainn is older than you?

Nuala's off-handed question drifted across his mind as Abhainn finished removing his shirt, tossing it aside onto the rain-soaked grass, and her hands boldly explored his bared skin. The Faery child he had known as a boy was now full-grown liquid fire in his arms, weaving her magic all through his senses. He forgot to be worried about hurting or frightening her. It was clear Abby knew exactly what she wanted.

He sought out her mouth with his own, but she drew away, a mischievous sparkle stealing into her eyes right before she shifted into a cloud of blue mist. He held perfectly still, imprisoned by an assault of sensations, as she moved all around him, caressing every inch of his bare skin, front and back, sides, head to foot.

Between his legs.

He forgot to breathe.

She condensed behind him, laughing into his ear as she slid her arms and legs around him again. She teased his chest with her fingers, then slid them low under the unbuttoned waistband of his jeans. He groaned, his body hard and aching, as he swept his hands along the smooth thighs locked around his waist.

"I wonder what else I can do," she said low in her throat.

He flipped around and bore her toward the ground, but *poof!* she misted once again. Though his body was taut with desire, he sat back on his heels and, finally, laughed out loud.

"That's better," said her disembodied voice. She condensed, on her knees before him, but she held up her hands when he reached for her. "Move not," she warned. "I am new at this kind of play."

She touched his eyelids, bidding them close.

He spent the next several minutes immersed in Abhainn's version of a Faery hot tub, all steaming and bubbly, complete with cock-stiffening games that featured ice cubes applied to his nipples, traced from his lips down his throat, on down his torso to the very tip of his erection.

Near to bursting, he managed, "Damn, woman, you learn fast."

He opened his eyes to find himself enveloped in licks of blue-green tongues of mist. It flowed all over and around his naked body. At some point he'd lost his pants, and he didn't even care that he was lying stark naked under a tree, flat on his back, writhing in pleasure, ignored by a dozing horse and its napping Equillian.

Fascinated, he lifted his hands, running them through the Abhainn-mist, spreading his fingers to stroke and play with the swirling colors dancing around him. She sighed and giggled, dripping playful drops of alternating hot and cold water all over his body. He heard her breath catch when he extended his tongue to taste the part of her hovering just above his face. In a swift, silent shift, she condensed back into her solid form, already wrapped tightly around him, trembling with need, taking him inside her warm, wet passage before he had a chance to prepare for the intensity of the sensation.

One hand wrapped in her hair, the other pulling her pelvis tight against his, he rocked into her hard, shouting his release into her mouth as she shuddered and sobbed with her own.

In the aftermath, Michael found the strength to lift his hand to capture the single tear that traced a path across her nose. As he watched, it turned to silver, then sank into his skin. Abhainn, still lying on his chest, propped her chin on her hands, and for just one luxurious moment he let himself drown in her sun-on-green-water eyes.

"What amuses you?" she said, her voice sated and husky.

He laughed. "Your tear tickled my finger. I remember now... It did that once before. Long ago."

In the distance, cows mooed, bringing Michael back to the present. A little of the joy faded from Abhainn's eyes.

"We mustn't linger," she murmured. "Already the sun is high. Eoth told me if you let her drive this time, we will reach Dun Laoghaire by nightfall."

He rolled them both to their feet, setting her off to gather her clothes with a playful pop to her backside. In a wink she dodged his hand, hopped up lightly and nipped his ear.

"Ow!"

"Start not what you cannot finish," she cooed.

"I'm way bigger'n you, sugar."

"I have way more friends in the immediate area than you, fool," she laughed. "We may be smaller..." Pinch. "But we are quicker!" Another pinch, too quick for him to retaliate.

Then his grin faded as realization struck him. "You mean we had an audience?"

She shrugged into her clothing, apparently unabashed. "I doubt it not that every tree, rock, and Fae creature within earshot found us more interesting than yon kye." Right on cue, a shaggy-haired cow looked up from a nearby pasture and mooed.

A strangled noise crackled from inside the caravan. Before their eyes, a waist-high creature, with blue- and brown-mottled skin, dull yellow eyes, dressed in odd bits of birch bark and sporting an oak leaf cap, appeared in the door. It coughed and grabbed its throat.

"That thing doesn't sound too healthy," Michael said, observing that the random appearance of odd Fae creatures no longer alarmed him.

Abhainn had different ideas. She grabbed his arm and dragged him backward. "It's an Utchin!" she cried. "Touch it not!"

The Utchin went limp and fell headfirst out of the caravan, hitting the ground with a solid thunk.

Its fist opened, and out rolled a half-eaten piece of the fennel bread Nuala had sent with them from Inisghriann.

All her gaiety gone, Abhainn shuddered. "If the Mei and this dimwitted creature both found us so quickly, it won't be long until word reaches Berchta and others come looking for us," she said. "We must fly! Now!"

Michael ran his hand over his hair, trying to think. Even with Fae magic, the sturdy little draft horse wouldn't be fast enough to stay ahead of the trolls and whatever other foul creatures allied with Berchta's army. Not far away, he picked up the whisper of early morning car traffic. "Where are we?"

Abhainn, her nose wrinkled in distaste, was using a stout stick to roll the Utchin away from the caravan. "Eoth told me a village called Rathdrum lies just over the hills."

"Tell Eoth to take the pony home. We're going to have to find some way to get you inside a car."

Chapter Eight

"Are you burned anywhere?"

"*Hic.* Just here." Abhainn showed Mícheál a small spot on her left ankle.

He drew breath through his teeth and fished in his rucksack for the flagon of stone-spring water. "When did that happen?"

What seemed like mere inches outside the ferry's main cabin window, the Irish Sea rolled under threatening skies. So much water. So much *open* water. She turned her face away and tried hard not to shake. The other passengers on the last ferry out of Dun Laoghaire bound for Wales were beginning to stare. "*Hic.* When you picked me up and put me in the car. My foot brushed up against the metal door."

Mícheál's brows drew together. "You sat there for two hours and didn't tell me?"

She dropped her voice to a whisper. "I wanted not to alarm the beast's driver, *hic.*" Rain splashed against the glass, and she flinched. "Are you sure this *curragh* is seaworthy?"

"I won't let you fall into the ocean, darlin'. Don't worry. Besides, if the worst happens, remember that ice floats. Just turn yourself back into an iceberg and I'll push you home." He slipped the water back into his rucksack, then grimaced and pulled out a battered loaf of fennel bread. "I could use this as a float."

She allowed herself a giggle. Vibration from the ferry's engines thrummed rhythmically against her back, almost as soothing as Mícheál's warm fingers that continued to caress her ankle long after the spring water had had its effect.

But he looked not at her. His granite-grey eyes scanned the cabin without being too obvious about it. Surreptitiously she followed the path of his eyes. It struck her that save for herself, she was the only Fae creature of any substantial size on the vessel. Oh, here and there a creature poked its bony face out of a handbag, a pocket, or a slipped-off shoe, but nothing anywhere near her size.

We are unguarded.

Her and Mícheál's gazes met. The smile he gave her didn't quite reach his eyes.

"*Hic.*"

He tweaked her nose, then his attention was drawn to something outside the window. This time his eyes crinkled with a real smile and he pointed. "Look out there."

"*Hic.* I don't want to look at the water," she whispered.

"If there's one thing I've learned about Selchies, they're a snobby crowd. I'd acknowledge their presence if I were you."

She quickly twisted around and pressed her hands and nose against the glass. There! A safe distance from the ferry's wake, one, three, then seven slick, dark heads surfaced, snorted, then dived under again.

"No trolls or tempestaries will get you out here." He leaned close to her ear. "Your Lady has not forgotten you."

Yet even as he said the words, he continued to scan their surroundings, never resting.

Fog closed in, enveloping the churning ferry in a curtain of grey, obscuring everything within inches of the window. At least, blessedly, she was spared the constant reminder that the open sea lay just a few feet away.

Mícheál leaned back on the bench and stretched out his legs, lifting one arm so she could curl up under it. Nearby, a nosy matron eyed them over the rim of her glasses, then went back to her knitting.

She curled into the curve of his body, and she observed that he somehow felt different. Gone were the lines of tension that bracketed his mouth and creased the space between his brows. A new light glowed deep in his dark eyes, the light of a man looking forward to the next twist or turn of events. His body rested in a relaxed position; yet a fine, alert tension hummed just under his skin. Like a man who would not welcome battle, but neither would he run from it.

A true knight, she thought with a secret smile.

She leaned her head on his chest. The heartbeat that thudded there was quicker, lighter. Unburdened by the old walls set there by the harsh lessons of his world. The world that had tried to drum into him the idea that magic wasn't real.

Ah, but now he believes. I feel it.

Mícheál murmured into her hair, "This will all be over soon. Then I can take you home. Your mother'll be glad to see you. Although," he chuckled, "I doubt she'll be particularly happy to see me. I'm sure she's hoping I get some vital part of me lopped off by one of Berchta's finest."

Abhainn's belly clenched. She drew away and sat facing him, drawing her legs underneath her.

"Nuala didn't tell you."

"Tell me what?" The wary darkness returned to his eyes, dimming the boyish light of a few moments ago.

She released a little sound of frustration from her throat. *Oh Màthair, what have you done?* The old woman had told her much of what would be expected of her once she reached the Great Gathering, but apparently had left deliberate gaps in Mícheál's knowledge.

"Once I take my place in the circle, I can never return." Aching, she watched his face for a reaction.

He leaned forward, propping his elbows on his knees, and let his head drop forward for a moment.

"One representative of a race must stay on Avalon at all times," she continued, "or the power of the circle will not hold. I am the last of my kind…"

Mícheál sat back. "She did tell me. Nuala warned me not to set foot inside the circle. She told me you must go in alone, and my human presence would 'contaminate' it."

"Ahhhh," she whispered, letting a new smile widen her mouth. *She knew Mícheál would not listen. She knew he would stay at my side until the end. Just because she had told him not to.*

"She just wanted to pound it home that I was to keep my paws off you, so not to distract you from your task," he muttered, brows drawn together. He patted at his shirt pockets. "Damn, I wish I still smoked."

"No, no!" she insisted, moving closer. "When she saw the stone you carried, she knew you had your own destiny to fulfill. Don't you see?"

He frowned in confusion and opened his mouth to speak, but the unmistakable sound of a seal bark shattered the drowsy quiet inside the cabin compartment.

Their eyes met a split second before the ferry lurched violently, its port side rising up, up, up. The fiberglass hull and superstructure groaned under the strain.

93

"It's going over!" someone shouted.

Only Mícheál's arm shooting out at the last second kept her from sailing headlong to the far side of the cabin along with the rest of the passengers. He'd managed to snake his other arm around a steel support pole and wrap an ankle around a leg of the bolted-down bench. Swinging from his arm, Abhainn glanced out the window. She hiccupped so hard, the pain of it stole her voice, but only for a moment. She managed to sob out one word.

"Larvae!"

Unearthly screeches filled the cabin, drowning out the cries of the alarmed passengers. The ferry's hull slapped back down onto the water with a sickening crunch, and the engines died. Wind and rain whistled in through broken windows.

Sounds that might have been mistaken, by inexperienced ears, as a strong storm, Michael recognized for what they were. The Selchies were once again battling for their lives. The eyes that Abby had magically opened for him with her kisses now revealed the creatures of the dark underbelly of that world— long, bulbous, pasty white wormlike monsters, armed with rows of tiny needle teeth in deceptively small mouths, rose and plummeted in the waves just outside the window, flinging Selchie bodies in every direction.

He took one quick scan of the other people in the cabin, who were just beginning to pick themselves up off the floor. Crew members shouted directions, something about donning life jackets, that no one was to leave the cabin just yet.

Abby clung to him. He tightened one arm around her and groped for his rucksack. *Got to keep her out of the water, no matter what.*

Then in a crash of violence, the large grey-brown body of a seal and a shower of broken glass rocketed through the main cabin, landing lifeless and bloody against a bulkhead.

He felt rather than heard Abby's scream, for her face was buried against his chest. Pandemonium ensued, and crew members began attempting to organize stampeding passengers to evacuate on lifeboats.

"We have to get out of here," he said in a low voice. "If they make us get on the lifeboats, we're dead."

Abby clutched his arm. "I...I can't go out there! The water..."

"We're not going in the water, sugar. We're going up top. Quiet now, we don't want the crew to catch us slipping out, okay?"

Within moments they had managed, in the confusion, to slip out the rear bulkhead door. The waters around the boat suddenly quieted. No Larvae broke the water's surface. Tellingly, no Selchie heads did, either.

"Where did they go?" Abby whispered.

Dead, most likely, he thought, but did not voice it.

"Up you go," he said, hoisting her easily over the chain blocking the stairway to the observation deck, then bounding up the stairs himself with ease fueled by the adrenaline pounding through his veins.

"Get under the bench," he directed as he dropped the rucksack on another bench and pulled out the wrapped, rusted sword.

"I will *not*," she said.

He turned and found her standing on the bench rather than under it, which brought her head almost level with his.

She stood defiant, holding in her hand a tiny, wicked-looking knife he'd never seen her wield before.

He drew out the sword, still stained with the blood of the tempestaries of a few days before. "Don't be a ninny, woman," he growled. "I can't protect you if you're exposed."

She lifted her chin. "I am not a ninny," she quavered. "I am a queen!"

Wind and heavy mist plastered her hair against her face, bedraggling her clothes until they hung limp from her fragile body. But this time, she thrust out no petulant lower lip as she had so long ago. She looked like something wild, something beautiful. Something not to be trifled with.

She almost pulled it off, except for the slight tremble of her chin, the way her gaze flicked to the waters rolling and slapping against the hull. The way her chest jerked with suppressed hiccups.

He scowled at her, hoping to mask his admiration with ferocity. "This is not a game, woman."

"No knight goes into battle without someone at his back! Or are you the fool Nuala takes you for?"

A loud popping noise, and they both crouched between the benches as, below them, the passengers and crew evacuated in rapid-inflate life rafts and rowed away, locator beacon lights flashing until they had disappeared in the enveloping mist. Within minutes, they were alone and adrift on the disabled ferry.

He rose from his crouch, his own heart thudding hard in his ears as he grasped Abby's arm and backed her up against the bulkhead that formed the rear of the wheel house. Along the way, he snagged the rucksack and swung it onto his back, his warrior instinct telling him it might give him an extra millisecond to react if he were attacked from behind.

Her eyes searched his, the sun-on-green-water irises standing out from her pale face like two beacons that burned with love, hope and a healthy dose of terror.

He managed a grin and crouched down before her, holding her shoulders. *Her bones feel like a bird's under my hands.* "I would have a kiss before I go into battle," he said.

Something shifted in her eyes. She threw her arms around him in wild abandon, planting her mouth on his with such ferocity that he almost tipped over backwards. Liquid fire flowed into him, and for a moment he forgot where he was. Almost forgot who he was... The warmth filled him, turned into something almost solid in his bones, something fortifying in his muscles.

She is giving me back the strength she drew from me!

He tore his mouth from hers, took her by the arms, and barely managed to peel her away and set her back.

"Stop it," he gasped.

She sank back against the bulkhead, a faint smile on her face. "Now," she said with satisfaction, "you will move with the speed of Faery fire."

The waters to the port side of the boat exploded.

With a loud, wet slap, a Larva landed like a flopping fish on the upper deck, then began to shapeshift.

"Stay down," he commanded, raising the sword point before him. From behind him, he felt Abby thrust the hilt of her small knife into his other hand. Not daring to take his eyes off the horridly shifting creature, he took it and flipped it so that the hilt rested in his palm, point down.

The Larva transformed from a wormy sea-going creature into a ten-foot-tall, naked warrior female, with shark-like skin, wiry arms and legs, and wings that resembled those of a sting ray. Its dragon-like head sported a long snout and rows of jagged teeth.

Michael sank into a crouch, the world around him compressing down to this moment, this enemy. He wished like hell he had something more potent than a rusted sword in one hand and little more than a pocket knife in the other.

Behind him, he heard Abhainn breathing fast. "Don't let it bite you," she said through clenched teeth.

"It's not the teeth I'm worried about, sugar," he said, baring his own in readiness to fight. "I can fight anything with two arms and two legs. It's what's coming out its ass end that's got my attention."

A long, whip-like tail lashed out from the base of the creature's spine, complete with a glistening razor tip.

The thing finished shifting with a series of sickening snaps as bones locked into place, then it thrust its head forward on its long neck until it loomed inches from Michael's face and screeched. Michael took a swipe at it, but it danced backward, taunting him with its longer arms tipped with needle-sharp claws. It tried to reach around him to stab at Abby with its dagger-tip tail.

Michael found himself thrusting and parrying with both arms, faster than he had ever managed to do even at his top form while in the Marines. Abby's magic flowed through his body, lending lightning and fluidity to his movements.

And, to his amazement, the creature fell back. He followed, intent on driving it over the edge and back into the sea.

Somewhere behind him, he heard Abby scream.

He risked one glance over his shoulder. Another Larva had landed on the deck and was in the process of shapeshifting. He had been drawn away from Abhainn deliberately. And damn him, he had fallen for it!

As quick as that, the Larva's whip tale snaked around and sliced through his shirt, through skin, down deep into the muscle of his left arm, knocking him sideways. White-hot pain and rage blanked his mind. Using that momentum, he spun halfway around and used all his weight to thrust the sword backward into the creature's soft underbelly.

The blade gave way, leaving him holding only the hilt as the Larva fell into the sea, trying frantically to shapeshift back into the seaworm before it hit the water. It failed and sank like a stone.

"Mícheál!"

Breath coming hard and aching in his chest, his wound stabbing with pain, Michael turned and staggered across the deck toward where Abby stood at the bow, backed up against the safety rail, clinging to it tightly with both hands while hurling Gaelic invectives at another fully-shifted Larva. It loomed triumphantly over her, raising its tail to slash.

Michael tried to switch the blood-slippery knife to his other hand and failed. It skittered away across the deck. He left it, put his head down and charged like a linebacker, ignoring the logical part of his mind that measured the distance and his speed and told him he wasn't going to reach her in time.

The Larva's tail sliced down.

Abby vanished.

A cloud of white mist hung where she had just been, and the dagger end of the Larva's tail passed harmlessly through it. It backed off a step, head cocked, as if confused.

Abby condensed, once again clinging to the railing, this time with one foot on the bottom rung. Michael vaulted over the bulkhead.

Another sideways slash.

Abby misted and tried to condense farther away. She only managed a few inches.

It took yet another swipe at her.

Abby cried out and misted, but slower this time. Michael heard fabric ripping. As she condensed this time, she scrambled over the railing and prepared to jump. A metal-on-metal screech issued from the Larva's mouth, a victory cry. It poised its tail to strike once more.

Abby threw back her head, her face straining, and screamed with the effort it took to shift one last time.

Michael threw himself the last few yards, plowed into the Larva's midsection, and carried it—and himself—over the side.

It sank as the other one had sunk, except this one tried to wrap its taloned hand around Michael's foot to take him down with it.

He'd been dragged down at least three fathoms before he managed to wrench his foot free. He fought his way back toward the surface, lungs bursting, twisting his arms free of the rucksack and its added weight. He let it sink without a backward glance.

Abhainn...

He broke the surface with a mighty gasp and looked through salt-stung eyes at the bow of the ferry.

He caught sight of it just as it slipped below the churning surface, on its way to the bottom of the Irish Sea.

Treading water madly, he twisted around, trying to find her in the water, in the air, anywhere. The grey fog that had enveloped the vessel was rapidly clearing, revealing the Welsh coastline less than a half mile off. Michael refused to think about how far the ferry had been pushed off course by the Larvae. The map had gone down with the rucksack.

There.

He caught sight of a patch of mist that drifted slowly against the wind, fanned along toward the shore by some kind of nearly transparent wind Faeries.

He put his head down and pulled for shore, ignoring the pain in his wounded arm. He swam for Abby's life.

Because he realized that his own would be nothing without her.

Chapter Nine

The wind died as Michael staggered onto the rocky shore, stepping foot on the Welsh coast just as the moon broke through the ragged edges of the last of the Larvae's fog.

First things first. He bent over and unceremoniously got rid of what had to be a gallon or so of seawater he'd swallowed, narrowly missing a scurrying flock of surf Faeries that had ridden in on the last wave with him.

"Holy shit," he muttered, wiping his mouth on his soaked sleeve. "They're freakin' everywhere."

Random patches of mist floated in and out among the rocks, in the cliff crevices, and the clumps of trees that crowned it. He called Abby's name, even though he knew she may not be able to answer.

Fruitlessly he chased one blob of mist after another, his wounded arm throbbing with the sting of salt water, and his heart thumping with dread. *It can't end this way, dammit. I won't let it...*

He got hold of his galloping thoughts and forced himself to slow his breathing. *Watch the mist. See how it moves. If I were in Abby's place, what would I do, where would I go? Look for some mist that isn't behaving like it should...like...*

There! Just before it disappeared above the cliff edge, he saw it. The patch of mist floating against the wind.

The cliff wasn't much of a cliff, as cliffs go, but it was dark and slick, and bisected by a stream that tumbled down to the ocean.

Hang on, Abby, stay out of that stream if you can.

Finally he gained the top of the cliff, having left a few patches of skin behind along the way. A single, giant willow tree, surrounded by hundreds of saplings lining the bank, hung heavy branches across the stream.

"Ho, Arthur's man! Over here!" squeaked a tiny voice.

It was coming from somewhere in that tree. He batted his way through the saplings, ending up standing in the middle of the stream, looking up into the towering willow's feathery branches.

Snagged in the branches, trying to wrap itself around the willow's proffered fingers, she floated.

Abby's face appeared inside the ball for a few precious seconds, her lips moving in a silent litany of his name.

His stomach dropped. *She doesn't have the strength to change back. She gave too much to me...*

"Hurry! We can't hold onto her much longer!"

He ran forward a few steps and blinked. The tree was filled with twig Faeries, nearly invisible, so like their host were they. Dozens of them swarmed around Abby, trying their best to anchor her.

A drop of water fell from above and hit his nose. Alarm reared its ugly head. *Dew point. The mist is condensing.* The water droplet fell off his nose and into the running stream at his feet. *I'm going to lose her in the stream.*

He ripped off his shirt and tried to hold it under her, but he quickly realized it was too wet for what he needed. It would never hold all of her. He looked around but found nothing of use.

Think, you idiot, think.

Nothing came to mind. He balled his fists in helpless rage and roared to the sky. Never in his life had he *not* known exactly what to do.

No, don't think. Just look, but do what Abby said and look with soft eyes...soft eyes...

His peripheral vision picked them up, two red-capped Pixies poking idly under a rock, paying no attention to him. Careful not to look directly at them, he waited until they were both looking away, then shot out his good hand and snagged them both at once. They shrieked in protest, searing his ears, but he shook them until their knobby little heads rattled together.

"You," he pointed at one. "I know all you people can shapeshift to some degree. I need a bucket. Can you manage a five-gallon size?" Not waiting for an answer, he jabbed his finger at the other one. "And you. I need...uh...I need...an umbrella. A big one, like they use on the Auld Course St. Andrews."

"What makes you think we're going to just snap to for you, human," they snarled in unison.

He brought them up very close to his face, risking a nose bite.

"I have a nice piece of fennel bread with your freakin' name on it, that's what. And I'll shove it right up your snotty little noses if..."

Snap!

"Whoa! One bucket, one umbrella, at my service."

He set the bucket aside, opened the umbrella, and flipped it upside down, catching the first drop just in time as Abby began to condense in earnest.

CB&OBO

The full moon was riding high by the time he tipped the contents of the umbrella into the bucket for the last time. Arms shaking with fatigue, wound no longer bleeding but throbbing relentlessly, he plopped down beside the bucket and stared at the water within. It rippled and swirled, throwing the moonlight back in wild patterns.

"You're trying to shift, aren't you?" he said, to himself as much as to her. She'd expended so terribly much energy on the ferry, defending herself, that now she was too weak to change back. All he knew to do now was what he had done the first time he'd seen her. Plunge his hands in the water, so she could draw strength from him.

Waves of dizziness washed over him, and he examined the Larva cut on his arm. Whether Larvae tails were venomous, he didn't know, but he was pretty sure this wound couldn't be healthy. For himself, or for her. He hesitated, hand hovering over the water's surface.

A glimmer of light out to sea drew his attention. He blinked and squinted, then drew in a slow breath as an island appeared, shimmering with white light under a cloak of mist. At the top of the island's tallest mountain, a huge fire blazed, surrounded by a ring of standing stones. Ethereal shapes moved in and out among the stones.

Avalon.

He turned and without hesitation plunged his hand into the water, and immediately felt Abby's pull on his soul. In a few seconds, she stood before him, safe and whole.

The bucket and the umbrella shifted back into the two Pixies, which ran off, flinging a stream of unintelligible insults over their shoulders.

Michael tried to push himself up off the ground, but failed. The Fae magic Abby had given him was holding off the worst of the Larvae sickness, but cold realization told him he had done all he could do.

The rest was up to her.

Then she was at his side, parting the shredded fabric of his shirt to examine the wound. Her breath hissed between her teeth.

He tried to give her a smile. "So, am I going to live?"

She grimaced. "Yes, but for a while you will wish you had not. Remember when you ate that fennel bread instead of the scone?"

He blanched. "That bad, huh?"

"No," she said regretfully. "Worse, I'm afraid."

He groaned, but turned away her effort to throw her arms around him. "You're running out of time, Abby," he gasped, pointing out to sea. "Avalon has appeared. The fires are lit. You have to get to it somehow."

"I'm not going without you!" she cried.

Michael laughed. "It's what Nuala wanted," he gasped. "For me to keep my polluting kind out of the Great Circle."

"No, you do not understand! *You have to be there, too!*" she said, frantic.

He ruffled her hair. "You don't need me any more. I've taken you as far as I can go."

Her brow wrinkled, and tears threatened at the corners of her eyes. He took hold of her face and turned it toward Avalon.

"There is where you belong. Call your Selchies, woman. If there are any left alive, they'll carry you on their backs, and I'm willing to bet they won't let you get a toe wet. It's not far. They can get you there before the Larvae know you're in the water. Call them."

She got up and walked to the edge of the cliff, looked down at the sea, and called with her tears. Nothing responded but the crash of the tide, which had now risen to the base of the cliff, covering the beach in heaving water.

Michael managed to get to his feet and walked, weaving, to her side.

"They're not coming," she said, sounding truly hopeless for the first time since he'd known her. In the distance, Avalon's brilliance grew. Tantalizingly close, yet so far. Too far for Abhainn, even if she were not afraid of the open sea.

He tried not to think of the reasons why none answered her call. If any were left alive within hearing distance, they would have come - unless their wounds were too great.

"You're going to have to swim for it, Abby," he said gently.

She shuddered and wrapped her arms around her waist. He grabbed her shoulders and turned her to face him.

"You can do this. You're strong now—I've given you almost all the strength I have." He looked out over the water and an idea formed in his mind.

She saw it on his face and was already shaking her head vigorously before he spoke his next words.

"I can give you the rest, Abby. I'll hold onto you. Take what you need from me and use your powers over the waters. We can do it together."

She shook her head wildly. "No...no! I'll lose strength before we get there. The water wi...will take me, and you'll drown out there alone!" Her fear sent her into a violent spasm of hiccups.

"Abby, you don't have a choice! You have to go *now!*"

"No! I won't sacrifice you for a silly Gathering." She threw her arms around him, trembling.

He squeezed her tight to him and sighed. "Aw, Abby. I hate to do this to you, but... I love you."

Another hiccup. "What?" She drew back and stared at him.

He grinned at her and tucked her head under his chin.

"I love you."

And he launched them both over the edge of the cliff and into the sea.

Even before they hit the water, Michael felt her turn them over so she would hit the water first. Hitting the surface of the ocean from that height should have broken a few bones, but her springy Fae body absorbed the shock. When their heads broke the surface, he hauled in great breaths of air and discovered she had already towed him well beyond the dangerous breakers.

"See?" he shouted above the crashing waves. "Your people are the Fae of the Waters! This is where you belong!"

Stunned surprise warred with mortal fear in her eyes. She glanced back at the cliff, as if she were contemplating trying to scale it and get back to dry land. "Oh no, you don't!" He grabbed her and turned her toward Avalon. "There it is, Abby. We can make it. I'll hang onto you so you can have your arms free—just remember to let me breathe once in a while. Okay?"

She could only manage a quick little nod in answer. And a hiccup.

The fires of Avalon flared brighter, and the sound of deep-throated drums throbbed on the air. He wrapped both arms around her waist.

"Now, Abby! Go!"

He wondered if taking off in the space shuttle felt anything like this. He could never have guessed she would swim so fast underwater that he had to close his eyes to keep his eyelids from turning inside out.

As she became accustomed to the water, she swam faster and faster, surfacing every few seconds to let him breathe, then diving under again to race like a torpedo, dead-on for Avalon.

We're going to make it, he exulted to himself. *We're going to...*

She faltered.

He buried his forehead into the back of her neck, pleading silently, *Hang on, Abby. You can do this. You're almost there.* He held tighter to her waist, silently willing more of his strength into her.

No, stop it, Mícheál. You will have none left for yourself.

Take it, Abby. Drown me if you have to, but take it. No matter what, you have to make it.

No!

Don't let them win! Do it!

The ocean, the air around him dimmed, compressing to one pinpoint of light somewhere deep in his brain.

When he opened his eyes, he found himself lying on a silver shore—alone. Above, up on the mountain, the fires burned and the drums throbbed.

Michael looked down at his hands.

The only thing clutched in them was Abhainn's crystal necklace.

CRRO℘

His heart heavy, Michael's feet dragged to a stop just outside the biggest, widest stone circle he had ever seen. It resembled Stonehenge, only this structure made Stonehenge look like a playpen.

He leaned against the nearest stone. It vibrated with the beat of the drums, as if it, too, wanted to join the dance going on just in front of it. Too weary and heartsore to stand it any longer, he pushed away from the stone and lifted a foot to step inside the circle, Nuala's warning be damned.

Someone shouted, and the drums stopped, their thunder echoing away down the mountain. Every eye turned toward him. Thousands of Fae—thousands upon thousands. In every shape and size, no two alike. One of each race, just as Nuala had said. Some looked like they had just stepped out of a Tolkien novel. Others looked like nothing even the maddest artist could dream up.

"Abby, you should see this," he whispered. He took another step, but found his way blocked by a troll. Two of them, in fact. Michael's gaze sharpened. There seemed to be an inordinate number of trolls in the crowd, despite the fact only one of them was supposed to be here.

"Ye are no' welcome here, human," the troll sneered, the words dripping with contempt as thick as the snot dripping from its nose.

A tall, magnificent woman approached. Her eyes flashed many colors, and she wore robes of shimmering green. Her hair shone silver above a face of indeterminate age. "The last time I looked, troll, you were not in charge here."

"Open your eyes, Old Mother," came another voice from across the circle. Another woman, equally as tall but imposing in a way that made Michael's skin crawl, glided into the picture. More trolls escorted her, rudely knocking bystanders out of her way. "The high hour approaches, and the Great Circle is incomplete."

The Old Mother lifted her chin. "There is still time, Berchta. We will be patient a little longer."

Berchta laughed, a sound not unlike the stuffed-up-Pug breath of her minions. "The Asrai will not come. They are no more. Hiding their cowardly selves in the darkness for so long, they shriveled and died out long ago."

"No," Michael stated. "There was one."

All eyes turned to him once more. He closed his fist around the crystal pendant, feeling the edges dig into his palm. Drawing a deep breath, he took another step into the circle.

"Stop," snarled Berchta. "He is contaminating these proceedings. Remove him!"

The Lady raised one graceful hand. "He will be allowed to speak. You bring us news of the Asrai, human?" Her eyes twinkled expectantly. He steeled himself to give the news that would certainly extinguish that spark.

Emotion choked his words. "I bring word...of her death." He raised his hand and let the crystal pendant dangle from his fingers, its facets catching the firelight.

Cries of dismay filled the air from the Old Mother's side of the circle. She closed her eyes, but no grief marked her face. She seemed to be listening for something far away.

Michael plowed on.

"She disappeared into the ocean, within a hundred feet of these shores, trying to reach Avalon in time to heal the circle.

111

To heal," his voice broke, "the earth, and the rift between our peoples. I was told that if she did not live to see this night, that I was to bring this token."

In the silence, Berchta began to laugh. "The balance of power has shifted at last, Old Mother. Your time is done."

The Lady opened her eyes and, incredibly, she smiled. She looked up at the moon. "The high hour has not yet come."

"It does not matter!" The evil one snarled. "The Asrai are finished. This human has seen the last of them die. It is your turn, Lady, to leave your high place by the altar stone, just as you ousted me two thousand years ago."

As if she hadn't heard, the Lady held out her hand. Reverently, she took the crystal from him and laid it on the flower-covered altar stone. She glided smoothly around to the corner of the stone, and laid her hand on a chipped-off corner. Her strong gaze penetrated clear to his heart.

"You carry with you another stone. Where is it?"

For a second, his mind blanked. Then he remembered. "You mean...my grandmother's weeping rock?"

The one that sank into the sea when he'd shrugged out of his rucksack.

"That 'rock', as you call it, belongs here," she said, touching the broken edge again. Many generations of your time ago, a human man with a broken heart struck this altar. Through treachery, he had lost his king—and the Asrai woman he loved. He vowed with his blood and upon this very stone that he would reveal the one who had led them astray, so that it appeared they both had betrayed their people."

The Lady reached out and touched the cut on his arm. The wound sealed, but not before a puff of black smoke issued from it, taking with it all traces of sickness and pain. The puff rose into the air and flew toward Berchta. The dark queen flinched,

112

but the smoke angled away from her head and disappeared into the blood-red stone at the head of her staff.

"And by your blood, it appears that vow has been fulfilled," said the Lady. The Faery host murmured in surprise.

Berchta's face purpled.

Blaen of CraighMhor's blood and mine. It is the same. The revelation brought him no joy. Instead, his heart fell into his stomach. "But the stone is...is lost, ma'am," he said in a low voice. "It fell into the sea during an attack by the Larvae."

A treasure now lost to him, to this Circle, just like Abhainn.

He dropped his head and whispered desolately, "I'm sorry, Lady. I have failed you, and I have failed Abhainn. I swore to bring her safely to this place, no matter what the cost. In the end, it was she who saved me. She paid the highest price."

Still unable to meet the Lady's eye, he held his arms out from his sides, palms up in supplication.

"I offer myself in service to Avalon."

A collective gasp was followed by a growing din of exclamations and chatter, all in languages he couldn't understand. Apparently this kind of thing didn't happen every millennium.

He sneaked a peek out of the corner of his eye. Berchta looked none too pleased with his announcement and was watching him closely, shushing the trolls that chattered around her.

The Lady's quiet voice cut through the chatter.

"You realize that no human has set foot on Avalon for over a thousand years?"

"Yes."

"That for a thousand years, no human has believed—*truly* believed—our world exists right alongside theirs? That no living human has memory of the time when we walked together?"

"Yes."

"Why should you be any different, then?" She leaned forward conspiratorially. "Is it not possible that you think you are simply lost in a dream, or suffering from some obscure mental illness?"

He had to laugh, in spite of his grief, at his own words coming back to haunt him. He winked back at her and shrugged, letting his hands fall to his sides. "It's possible, I suppose. But then why did I haul that rock around with me all those years, if some part of me didn't believe...didn't hope...my grandmother's stories were true?"

Creases wreathed the Lady's face as she laughed and held out her hands to him.

"Come, *Micheál CraighMhor*. You have brought the Asrai talisman that proves Abhainn's good intention. The altar's missing piece is lost, but you offer yourself in its place. This does honor to the memory of Blaen of CraighMhor, and his oath. Come now. Join the circle. Dance with us."

Berchta laughed. "Old One, you are a fool. He will never agree to such folly! And even if he did, one puny human will never repair what is broken."

The Lady ignored her and continued to hold out her hands toward him. A slow smile spread across his face, in answer to hers.

"I know this legend," he said quietly. "Once I join the dance, I can never return. Or if I do, I may find several generations have come and gone while I danced."

"Perhaps," she acknowledged. "But at least those generations will have an Earth to call home. A healthy one.

Come. Dance for her," she urged, a strange light leaping into her eyes. "Dance for Abhainn."

He felt something release inside him, and the boy within him bade him throw up his arms and call for the drums.

The music thrummed through his body, moving him without his consciously having to think about it. He forgot about the fact that he couldn't dance, not in his own world. But here, it didn't matter. He turned his face up toward the moon, closed his eyes and abandoned himself to the beat, feeling the brush of other dancing bodies close beside him, hearing the laughing voices of the Fae cheering him on.

A drop of cool water landed on his face. Then another. And another.

The boy in him allowed him to pretend that each drop was a kiss from Abhainn. That the scent of it on his skin was the scent she had left behind on him after their lovemaking.

He clearly saw her in his mind's eye, laughing in that way he had once thought silly and foolish. She had known it all along. It was he who had been foolish, for not seeing the world through her eyes sooner.

It didn't matter now. Soon he would see a new world unfolding, a healing one, and he would see it through eyes she had opened.

A pair of small arms clamped around his neck. A pair of small hands pulled his face down from its tipped-back position.

"Open your eyes, fool." *Her voice.*

He opened them. Abhainn's face, plastered round with wet hair, laughed up at him.

The rain continued to fall from the clear night sky. Water puddled then rose up to form small, slender Fae, all with Abhainn's wild pale hair and green eyes. More and more of them rose from the water, until Berchta and her minions were pressed aside. One by one, the trolls disappeared down various cracks and crevices of the earth. Finally, only one remained, crowded out to the edge of the circle along with his fuming dark queen.

Abhainn leaped into his arms. He fell to his knees, more from sheer emotion than the force of her weight. He clutched her to him, eyes squeezed shut against the tears, afraid this was all a dream and she would disappear if he let go.

"I thought I had lost you," he choked. "I thought you were dead."

She laughed through her own tears and leaned her forehead against his. "My people found me," she rejoiced, motioning to the large number of Asrai now filling out the jolly circle. "Some of us learned to survive. They found me and taught me that though we were at the mercy of the waters, by banding together we could avoid the oblivion of our kin. We have been waiting for this night, they tell me. The night that a human would take the first step toward healing the earth—by simply believing."

The Lady pulled them both to their feet.

"We needed more than just the Asrai to heal the Great Circle," she said. "Berchta knew this. That is why she cast her foul spell upon Ardaith and Blaen. In one stroke, she planned to eliminate the Asrai and tip the balance in favor of evil, and also sever the last fragile bonds between our worlds. But the Asrai were not as weak as she thought. As long as one human retained the ability to dream, there was always hope."

Michael frowned in Berchta's direction. "But if she's the one who caused this mess, she should be banished."

The Old Mother smiled. "Stay your wrath, knight. She has her place in the Circle. Her place in the delicate balance between dark and light. Berchta will have, as your people say, 'her day in court'. Worry not."

Michael hugged Abhainn closer and shrugged. "All right. We won't. Now. Where do we start with this 'healing the earth' thing?"

The Lady threw back her head and laughed. "With a kiss, fool. Know you nothing?"

Epilogue

Looking through the portal, Cadwyn smiled as she watched the dance of the Great Circle. Between her busy fingers, Abhainn's lifethread swelled with joy...and some new energy Cadwyn had never before felt.

On her right side, the spinner of Michael Craig's lifethread looked up at her and grinned. It had taken some doing, but she had managed to work his strong thread across the gaping split between the human and Fae webs, where it readily intertwined and held fast to Abhainn's anchor. Encouraged by her success, more spinners were winding out their threads across the gap, both Fae and human. Cadwyn could see that it would not be long before the rift would be fully healed. Already, all over the web of life, colors brightened and lifelights shone cleaner.

She heard another wooden stool scrape up beside her. She glanced over her shoulder, surprised to see a new spinner settle at her left side.

"I was told to come sit by you," said the young spinner anxiously. "I am told there is a new lifethread to spin." In her lap, she reverently cradled a bowl of Sunrise.

Abhainn's lifethread leaped in her hands, curving strongly toward the bowl, bulging outward like a pregnant belly. Michael's spinner whooped in surprise as his thread almost pulled her off her stool. The bowl of Sunrise grew bright, almost blinding.

Cadwyn's breath caught. *A child is to be born.*

She held out Abhainn's thread toward the new spinner and pointed to a particularly bright spot upon it.

"Begin here."

About the Author

To learn more about Carolan Ivey, please visit www.carolanivey.com. Send an email to Carolan at books@carolanivey.com or check out her blog to join in the fun with other readers as well as Carolan! http://www.carolanivey.blogspot.com. To get the latest news about Carolan's upcoming releases, and to be automatically entered in all her prize drawings, join her mailing list at http://groups.yahoo.com/group/wild-ivey.

The Heron's Call

Isabo Kelly

Dedication

For my husband Brian, my own personal hero. Thank you for always supporting my mad ventures and being patient with me when I'm not particularly patient back.

For my funny little dog, Eddie Monster, who always knew when it was more important for me to play with the ball instead of work.

And for Mom, Pop and Jenny because I would never have gotten this far without you guys.

Chapter One

Rowena twisted in her bedroll, restless and uncomfortable on the hard-packed earth. Frustration gnawed at her. It was that blasted dream again. The dark bulk of him rising above her, the scrape of callused fingers over her nipples, the feel of his hard cock thrusting into her. She rolled her eyes at the memory and a groan escaped between her clenched teeth. She hated the dream. Especially when she had no chance of experiencing those sensations in real life. Thanks to *him*.

She'd been having the same dream nearly every night for the last week. *Him* kissing her mouth, her breasts, her pussy. *Him* fucking her while keeping her gaze locked to his. His tongue, his teeth, his fingers, his come spurting hot inside her. She'd barely been able to sleep since she set out on this mission three days ago. And when she had slept, her dreams had been so erotic and so...demanding she woke up as exhausted as when she'd stretched out on her pallet the night before.

She turned again and the bedroll bunched beneath her. In a fit of irritation, she finally threw the blanket off and sat up. And saw the shadows closing in around her.

She surged to her feet, sword in hand, with a speed and grace she hoped the robbers would recognize. She hated to kill people just for being stupid enough to attack someone like her.

As the shadows stepped into the faint light from the crescent moon, she realized they weren't ordinary robbers. Their linen shirts were too clean, their leather trousers and bracers too well repaired, their weapons and steel breastplates too well made and maintained. Seven of them in all. Mercenaries, she guessed, noting the rough look of them despite the high grade of their gear. She turned in a small circle as they surrounded her, gauging their movements.

"I give you fair warning," she said, studying their faces. "Put up your swords and leave. Now. And I won't kill you."

As she'd expected, the standard warning was met with derisive laughter. She shook her head. Mercenaries, of all people, should understand what it meant to face a sword sworn of the Aleanian Temple. "Very well." She lifted her sword. "Shall we?"

And she grinned.

If her movements hadn't given her away, her grin should have. Still they came at her, an all-out attack, seven at once. Not the best tactics, she thought as she danced away from them and into the clear, using only the briefest flicker of mind-hazing. The mercenaries got in each other's way, too many swords in too tight an area. They adapted quickly though. When they turned on her this time, they attacked two or three at a time.

She laughed as the fight got underway, rejoiced in the feel of her muscles moving, her skills being tried, her mind sharp and focused. Seven opponents was a good number—enough to make her work and stretch, not too many for her to handle. She twisted away from an awkward swing by one man, countered a blow by another, and disarmed a third with a back swing. As the disarmed man scrambled for his sword, another took his place. She didn't rush to incapacitate them. She was having too much fun. But she knew she'd have to take care of them soon. No point in exhausting herself. She still had a long way to go before she reached Dorjan's lands.

She hated to kill them, though. They were just doing a job. A job she had no doubt Dorjan had funded. But she couldn't afford to have them at her back either. Maybe if she gave them a thorough enough beating... She disarmed two men and faced the four converging on her.

Suddenly, the air around them darkened, inky blackness too solid to be real. Rowena and the seven mercenaries stilled and looked around. A flash of blinding light, a crack like thunder. And a dark figure rose up in front of Rowena.

Even with his back to her, he was obviously male. His broad, thickly muscled body was encased in leather trousers and vest. His dark blond hair hung just above his collar in a tempting disarray of waves. What she could see of his pale skin gleamed silver in the moonlight.

The stranger raised a sword in front of him. From her position, Rowena watched the long blade come up over his head. The steel glowed purple.

The mercenaries backed away from the man, their weapons at the ready. Rowena kept a tight grip on her own sword in case the stranger turned. A moment later, the fine hairs on the back of her neck stood up. She heard the soft rumble of the stranger's voice, chanting, quiet, vibrating through her bones. She sucked in a breath and it felt as if the air had thinned.

Another blinding flash of light and power rolled over her in a heart-stopping wave. She dropped to one knee, ducking her head to brace against the storm winds of his spell. For an instant, all air was sucked away and she couldn't breathe. And then as suddenly as it happened, the light faded, the air calmed, and the dark night fell quiet.

Rowena dragged in a lungful of air, blinked to clear spots from her eyes and raised her head. All seven mercenaries lay unmoving, their swords blown beyond their grasp. She looked up at the stranger just as he turned around. Their gazes locked. It took a second, no more, before she recognized him, before the jolt of his presence ricocheted through her body.

She rose slowly to her feet, never taking her gaze from his green eyes. When she stood at her full five-foot-ten height, she straightened her shoulders, flicked a glance at the downed mercs, and said, "Kael, you bastard. You ruined a perfectly good fight. What the hell are you doing here?"

Dark eyebrows rose and his sexy mouth twitched at one corner. "Rowena," he murmured in a voice that made her thighs clench. "It's good to see you again too."

She cursed, long and eloquently, as she snatched up her scabbard from beside her bedroll, sheathed her sword and strapped the scabbard diagonally across her back. Her stomach danced giddily, and the sensation disgusted her. She didn't want her body to react, not to Kael Zyhn of Heron's Deep. She hated that she couldn't control the heady roll of lust pumping through her blood. "Answer my question," she said. "What are you doing here?"

"I came to help."

"I don't need your help." She propped her hands on her hips and glanced at the mercenaries. "Are they dead?"

"No. Unconscious. They won't wake for two days. At which point, we'll be long gone."

Her eyes narrowed. *We? I don't think so.* "Some strong spell, Heron. To leave me out of it."

He dipped his head, accepting her reluctant compliment with an arrogant grin.

"But I still didn't need your help."

"There were seven of them."

"Ha! I only have to worry when there's more than ten. Anything less, I'm perfectly capable of handling."

He smiled and her body responded. Her womb clenched, her stomach danced, and her heart beat an erratic dance. Damn him. What the hell was he doing here now? She hadn't seen Kael in twelve years. Not once since that first meeting, the first and only kiss. Not so much as a note. She'd spent years convincing herself he was just another man, no one special. Because if he'd really been her *raynei* he would never have abandoned her. That logic hadn't stopped her from dreaming about him. It hadn't stopped her longing for him.

But it had guaranteed she was so royally pissed off at him, she never wanted to see him again.

She glared at his smiling, gorgeous face and stomped past him. "You can go," she said over her shoulder, bundling up her gear. She couldn't stay here now. Might as well move down the road a bit and hope she could find a safe place to settle for the last few hours of darkness. She doubted she'd get any more sleep though.

Her heart thudded loudly as she packed. She could feel Kael's gaze on her back, burrowing into her. The intensity of his stare made her movements stiff and uncoordinated. She had never, in her entire life, felt uncoordinated. That pissed her off even more. She slung her pack across her shoulders so it crossed her back opposite to her sword, then stood without looking at him. She glanced down at the nearest mercenary. He didn't look comfortable with his legs folded under him and his head wrenched into an awkward position. He was going to hurt when he woke up. He groaned a little in his sleep, but otherwise didn't move.

Rowena shook her head. "Ruined a perfectly good fight,"

she muttered. She started to walk away, past the other unconscious bodies, still without looking at Kael. But his voice stopped her.

"I couldn't have my *raynia* killed."

Her shoulders stiffened. Her stomach tightened. Her eyes narrowed and her jaw clenched. Anger so hot it nearly suffocated her flowed through her. How dare he call her that? After all this time. How dare he use that excuse!

"Don't you call me that again," she said, her voice harsh and low. When the man nearest her made a slight noise, she turned and kicked him in the stomach. He rolled away slightly but didn't wake up. She stomped off, cursing under her breath.

So much for Aleanian compassion, she thought with an inner cringe. All her years of training and in a fit of anger she kicks an unconscious man. That outburst was as good a sign as any that she did not need Kael Zyhn in her life.

Kael watched her stalk away, his body so tight he could barely draw breath. He actually shook with his need to touch her, pull her close, bury himself inside her. His *raynia*. His soul twin.

She was a lot angrier than he'd expected. He didn't quite understand why. But the fact that she actually kicked an unconscious man, she a training Aleanian priestess, only proved how furious she was.

He frowned at her retreating back, his gaze drawn against his will to the curve of her ass, the long sweep of her legs. He could practically feel those taut legs wrapped around him. His cock throbbed. He adjusted his trousers to accommodate his erection, but it didn't help. Nothing would help until he was buried deep inside her, bonding them together.

He waited until she was just out of sight then spelled

himself into her presence again. He didn't bother with a dramatic appearance this time—his earlier entrance had been fed by his anger at knowing his *raynia* was in danger. Now he simply materialized next to her. Her surprised gasp incited his hunger. Without thinking, he wrapped his arm around her waist and pulled her tight. The feel of her curves pressed against his overheated body made him groan.

He'd denied himself her touch for too long. He lowered his head, intent on tasting her lush, wet lips, but stopped short when he felt the edge of a blade against his throat. He raised his head, frowning.

"Back off, and back off now, Kael," she hissed. "I don't want anything to do with you anymore, so you can just bugger off."

"You're my *raynia*." And that should have been enough. He couldn't understand her resistance. She should be feeling the same fire as him. They wouldn't be completely bonded until they made love, but even now their souls were entwining, meshing together. He could barely see straight for wanting her.

She laughed, a harsh, unpleasant sound. "I don't care what you think I am—"

"I don't *think* you're my *raynia*," he interrupted. "I know it, Rowena. You know it too. You can't deny it."

"I don't want this, and I don't want you. Run on home to Heron's Deep, mage, because I'm not having anything to do with you."

His arm flexed around her, tightening, pulling her closer. But her knife pressed sharply into his throat, a reminder she was serious. Slowly, he loosened his grip and stepped away. She edged the knife from his neck then sheathed it at her hip. With a final glare, she spun around and continued walking. He fell into step beside her.

"What the fuck are you doing?" she shouted, turning to

face him. Anger made her cheeks flush pink against the golden tan of her skin. "Go away. You think I want to see you now? After twelve years? Well, I don't. I've been doing just fine without you."

He watched the flash of pain in her dark eyes, the barest hint of an emotion other than anger, before she managed to mask it. His eyes narrowed, and he studied her more closely.

She'd changed in the last twelve years. She was only fourteen when they'd met. At twenty, he'd been too old for her. But she was his *raynia*, and he hadn't been able to stay away from her. He met her in the city, the day she came with her family to begin her apprenticeship in the Aleanian Temple. That day had changed his life.

Then, as now, he couldn't resist her. He'd had to kiss her, even knowing she was much too young. He couldn't stop himself. And that single kiss had shifted everything. He couldn't remember much after that, not for several months. His trance hit him prematurely, and he hadn't become aware of himself and his surroundings again for a long time. When awareness finally returned, he was in the middle of forging a mage sword. The next six years were subjugated to the sword.

He'd waited too long to claim her, he realized now. His reasons had all seemed logical before, but with her glaring at him, those black eyes snapping with temper, he knew he'd made a mistake. But how to fix it?

"I'm here to help you," he said. "Dorjan is a powerful warlord. He's got a wizard working for him. You aren't a mage. You can't fight the wizard."

Her brow furrowed. He had her, and they both knew it. Despite her stubbornness, she wouldn't sacrifice the life of an oracle, or anyone else for that matter, in the name of her own pride.

There was a reason she'd come so far and was so close to taking her vows.

After a moment, she sucked in a deep breath. He couldn't stop his gaze dropping to the rise and fall of her breasts, pressing against the fitted, light blue tunic of her uniform. She'd grown in the last twelve years, her curves filling out. Despite the constant sword training, she'd still developed a nicely rounded pair of breasts, a neatly tucked waist and a very feminine flair of hips. The tightness of her ass made his mouth water.

When he raised his gaze, caught the moment of breathless desire in her expression, he smiled. She might try to deny it, but she was his soul twin. She wanted him as badly as he wanted her.

Her nostrils flared and her eyes narrowed. "It's not good for you to be near me for long," she said. "We'll bond, and I might be killed. Go away. If you're worried, send another mage. Another Heron if you like. But not you."

His smile deepened at the tone of her voice, logic fighting against anger, and under it all, concern. "I'm afraid you're stuck with me, Rowena. I'm not going anywhere. I *want* us to bond."

She rolled her eyes and stalked away again. He kept his chuckle too quiet for her to hear. "Will you walk the rest of the night?" he asked.

"No. Just far enough away from the ambush."

"I can move us farther away, quicker than walking. So you can get some sleep. There's still hours until sunrise."

"No, thank you." The polite words belied the bite in her voice.

They walked in silence then, giving him time to contemplate her, and her anger.

Once he'd finished forging the mage sword, he'd needed several years to recover. Only one or two true mage swords were ever forged in a generation. Sometimes not even then. His parents' generation had seen no mage swords formed. The process was demanding, physically and mentally. It drove the smith to the limits of endurance. For six years, he hadn't been able to do or think of anything beyond the sword, the magics being poured into it, the spells, the power, the skill. He'd barely slept, barely eaten. And when it was done...

One of the most magnificent creations in their world was born.

He'd needed the better part of three years to regain his full strength, heal his body completely. But once recovered, all he could think about was claiming his *raynia*. She would have been twenty-three and old enough by that time. But his family insisted he wait.

The sword needed to be claimed, they said. His newfound mage skills had to be trained—the early inducement of trance had brought about an increase in his powers. Rowena was still sword sworn, his parents said, not yet a full priestess. Until she took her vows, her life was forfeit to the Temple. If they bonded and she died, Kael would follow her. Wait, his father coaxed. Just a bit longer. You'll have your entire lives together, his mother said, why rush into the bonding?

He heeded their advice to an extent. He waited. He trained his powers. He honed his strength. But he couldn't stay away from Rowena altogether. Every trip into Malyk, he contrived a way to see her, from a distance so she wouldn't notice him. He snuck into the Temple to watch her train. He even followed her into town one night when she went with some of the other sword sworn to a pub. She laughed and talked and seemed to enjoy her evening. And to his infinite relief, she turned away any man brave enough to approach her—even when some of her friends went off with other men.

But he wanted more. Each time he saw her, watched her, it fed his hunger. Until all he could think about was having one intimate moment with her. One stolen minute alone. So he snuck into her room, in the darkest hour of the night a week ago, just to watch her sleep. His skills made it easy to materialize in her room quietly to avoid disturbing the Temple guard. He stood in a shadowed corner and stared at her, sleeping on top of her sheets. His body burned, his cock so hard it hurt.

When her dreams took her, made her shift restlessly in the bed, he opened his senses enough to feel the nature of the dream. The eroticism, the sheer sexual heat he felt nearly brought him to his knees. He wanted her so badly he came close to climbing into bed next to her. Willpower alone kept him in the dark corner, watching.

He rode the surging heat of her dream, couldn't stop himself from taking his cock in his hand and stroking as he watched her breathing quicken. When her back arched against the bed, he came, his orgasm so powerful it left him weak. He cleaned himself using one of her towels, a towel he kept because it was hers, and watched her now relaxed body sleep soundly, her breathing even. Some of his tension had eased, but it wasn't enough. The experience left him feeling...lacking. He didn't just need an orgasm, he needed her.

Despite his better judgment, he went back to her room four nights in a row. Each night he rode her dreams, wanting to wake her, knowing he shouldn't. She was one year away from taking her vows. His father still insisted he wait. Once she finished her time as sword sworn, took her vows as a priestess, her life would no longer be in danger. They could bond without risking Kael's life.

But the wait had gone on too long, the need had become too great. He had to have her. Fully and finally.

And the night he arrived to claim her, he discovered her gone, sent out on another mission.

He'd spent so much hidden time near her they were more tightly bound than she realized. He could feel her, even at a distance, and had tracked her without much difficulty. Seeing her surrounded by seven well-trained swordsmen had stopped his heart.

Logic abandoned him. He came to her aid, using the mage sword to protect her without thinking about his actions. He'd seen her training, knew she was one of the best swordswomen among the Aleanians. But all he'd been able to see was four men converging on his *raynia*. He didn't regret his actions. He'd do the same again. But as he glanced at the hard line of her jaw now, he realized he had robbed her of a good fight. The sword sworn were trained to feel compassion for those they fought, to cherish the lives of others. But they were also trained to enjoy the moment, to savor a life well lived. And so most of them enjoyed the play of battle, the art and act of combat. They never killed easily, but they did get a rush out of the fight.

And he'd denied Rowena that joy.

He glanced at her again, the curve of her breasts, the sway of her hips. Before the night was out, he intended to make up to her for denying her the fight by providing her with another rush. A rush they could both enjoy.

Chapter Two

Rowena fumed as the bulky sword mage glided along next to her, not taking any notice of her anger. She couldn't believe he was here. After twelve years! And he thought they could start up again where they'd left off? *Not in this lifetime, Kael.*

Her traitorous body wasn't cooperating very well, though. She was so wet and needy, so weak-kneed as his scent filled her, she could barely walk straight. He had changed some over the years. His frame filled out with thick cords of muscles. His jaw was harder, more sharply defined, and faint creases framed his beautiful green eyes and firm mouth. But his face was still stunningly gorgeous, maybe more so now, with the hard cut of life etched into it. And his more mature, thickly muscled body did outrageous things to her libido. She tried to blame her earlier dream for the frantic pull of lust, but she knew better. Like it or not, deny it or not, Kael was her *raynei* and her body wanted his.

Her heart, on the other hand, was still too bruised from his rejection twelve years ago. She wasn't about to risk that pain again.

She forced herself to study the trail, her surroundings. They needed a place to rest. And she needed some space.

The appearance of the mercenaries so early in her journey only proved how determined Dorjan was to keep the Valen horse clan's oracle. The poor oracle had probably told him a sword sworn was on the way. It didn't matter. Rowena knew her approach wouldn't be a surprise.

She also knew she couldn't fight Dorjan's wizard. The priestesses had given her as much protection as they could. But it wouldn't be enough. On missions like this, she envied her mother the mage sword, Ba'nari. Ba'nari blocked magic. With Ba'nari in Rowena's hands, nothing the wizard threw at her would matter. But Ba'nari refused to leave Kellyn until Kellyn's death, and because Rowena loved her mother, she was happy Ba'nari was still in her possession.

She sighed and studied the scarce trees lining the rutted road. Not much cover, but the night was clear, the stars bright. Anywhere would be as good as anywhere else. She was tired now. The rush of adrenaline from the fight, the sudden appearance of her erstwhile *raynei*, the loss of sleep over the past week left a toll on her body. She needed rest. When they neared a grassy clump, she stopped.

"I'll bed down here. Feel free to go somewhere else. In fact, please go somewhere else." She ignored Kael's raised brow, his sardonic expression. She dropped her pack on the grass and pulled out her bedroll and blanket. When the pallet was made, she hit the release on her chest for the strap holding her scabbard across her back, set scabbard and sword next to her makeshift bed and crawled under the blanket. She wrapped a hand around the hilt of her sword, letting its familiar touch give her comfort. Then she closed her eyes, trying her best to ignore the still looming Heron.

And because of her exhaustion, she succeeded in ignoring him for all of three seconds. Then he moved, sitting on the grass next to her. A moment later, she felt the heat of a fire. She frowned, glanced at the glowing ball hovering just in front of Kael. With a grunt that could have been interpreted as a thank you if he were feeling generous, she turned her back on him and his magical fire and shut her eyes.

She had to suppress a moan when he stretched out behind her and spooned up against her back. "What do you think you're doing?" she demanded, but her voice sounded breathy, not dismissive as she'd intended.

"Keeping you warm." His hot breath brushed across her neck, making her shiver.

"I'm not cold."

"You're trembling."

Damn. How did she explain the trembling without admitting her desire? "I can't sleep like this," she said instead.

"Then we'll find something else to do to pass the night."

His hand slid across her waist. The feel of his big palm spanning her stomach, his thumb nearly touching the underside of one breast, made her entire body flush with hot need. Gods, he felt fantastic. His hips pressed up against her bottom, giving her a tantalizing feel of his erection—a hard, thick bulge encased in tight leather. Her eyes rolled back in her head, and against her will, she found herself grinding her ass against that bulge.

"Rowena," he groaned into her hair, and the hand on her stomach flexed, inching lower.

Oh no. She lurched up and scrambled a few feet from the pallet. This was not going to happen. Not now. Not ever. She'd rather die a virgin. Even if the very idea pissed her off as much as anything else Kael had ever done. "I told you no," she hissed, backing farther away as he eased into a sitting position. "I don't want you."

"Liar."

"Fuck you." She spun around and stalked off into the trees. She hadn't gotten more than a few feet before she remembered her sword. Still cursing she returned to the bedroll, snatched up her weapon and stomped away again, ignoring the look in Kael's beautiful green eyes—a combination of amusement, confusion and hurt she didn't care to know about.

She strapped her scabbard onto her back absently as she wandered in the dark. She kept near the road, using the dusty track to avoid getting lost. She could feel Kael anyway, so she wasn't worried about going too far. Her biggest worry was going back.

Years of hurt welled up and clogged her throat. Twelve years! She'd been young when they met, only fourteen, but she'd been positive Kael was her *raynei*. At the time, she couldn't have been happier. He was tall, handsome, a gifted smith of the famous sword mages, the Heron, he was nice and sexy. And he gave her a sense of safety. Like nothing in the world would ever hurt her so long as he was near.

So much for that fantasy.

She rubbed a spot on her chest beneath the cross strap of her scabbard. She hadn't been prepared to see him again. Now her emotions were all over the place. She didn't know how to deal with his presence. Especially when she had a mission. A woman's life, an oracle's life, depended on her. And like it or not, to save the woman Rowena needed the blasted Heron's help. But how could she spend the next few weeks of travel with him when she could barely stand to be around him for a few minutes?

She wandered until the sky lightened, too numb to do much more than walk. She came back to where she knew he still waited and packed her gear without a word. When she started down the road, he fell into step beside her.

"You're tired," he murmured.

"I'm fine. I don't need much sleep."

They walked in silence for a while before stopping to break their fast. From out of nowhere, Kael produced a handful of apples and a round of cheese. She raised her eyebrows in question.

"There are advantages to being a sorcerer," he said with a grin that made her heart hammer. "For one, you can travel light."

She grunted but accepted the fresh fruit and cheese. Her rations, a bundle of hard oatcakes and a last chunk of fresh cornbread, seemed sad fare in comparison. She didn't even have any dates left. She hunted for food along the way so she could travel light. As she took a bite of the juicy, crisp apple, she decided Kael's method had definite advantages.

She glanced up from her next bite of fruit to see him staring. "What?"

He didn't answer. Instead, he leaned close and wiped a drop of juice from the side of her mouth with one long finger. Her breath hitched at the brief contact. She looked away from the heat in his gaze and concentrated on her food.

"Tell me about your family?" he asked, quietly.

The question startled her. "I suppose you didn't get to meet my parents last time, did you?" she said, more to herself than to him. Her parents had been there, but by the time they'd arrived...

She inhaled, let her breath out slowly until she could think past the old terror. "My mother, Kellyn, was a sword sworn to the Aleanian Temple when she was young. But she forsook her vows to follow her *raynei*."

"That doesn't happen often with the sword sworn. She was to be a full priestess?"

"No." Rowena smiled at the often-told tale of her parents' first meeting. "When she went to the Temple to undergo the testing, a priestess had a vision. She gave my mother a prophecy about the way she'd meet her *raynei*. It meant she wouldn't be...suitable to become a full priestess. But she was sword sworn to the Temple for a year before she met my father."

"And your father?"

Now she grinned. "He's Gryphatar." She watched the surprise shift across his face, his eyes widening, his mouth opening. She loved seeing that reaction when she told people about her father. She didn't tell many, only very close friends at the Temple. Having a shape-shifter for a father, especially one of the legendary Gryphatar, had its disadvantages. But it was worth telling Kael to see his shock.

"That's why your mother followed him," Kael said. "He couldn't move away from Gryphaldin."

She nodded. Gryphatar lost control of their ability to shape-shift when they stayed away from Gryphaldin for too long. Their gryphon form would take control, overpowering any human thoughts with the rage and territoriality of the beast. "I grew up in Gryphaldin," she said. "I missed the aerie for a long time after I moved to Malyk, to the Temple. But Malyk is my home now."

Kael nodded, as if digesting the information she'd given him. Then his head snapped up, his gaze sharpened. "Kellyn? She's Ba'nari's owner, isn't she?"

Now it was Rowena's turn to be shocked, although she wasn't sure why she was so surprised. There were so few mage swords in the world, of course the Heron would know who they were and who they'd claimed as owners. She nodded at his question.

"Strange," he muttered, looking away, his brow creased.

"What is?" She leaned to the side, trying to see his face. When he looked back, she straightened.

He shook his head. "It's nothing. I just didn't expect... Doesn't matter." He tilted his head, his gaze sweeping over her face. "You're obviously not able to shift like your father or you wouldn't have been able to stay away from Gryphaldin for so many years."

"My younger sister and older brother are both Gryphatar. That trait skipped me. But I got my mother's sword skills and my father's eyes." She didn't mention the other things she'd inherited from her father.

Kael reached out and brushed a finger over her cheekbone. "Very beautiful eyes at that."

Her stomach quivered. "My mother's eyes are really beautiful. Blue and big. Her best feature, she used to say. I always wished I had eyes like hers."

He shook his head. "No. Your eyes are perfect."

His big hand cupped her cheek, and it was all she could do not to rub her face against that callused palm.

A brief, unwanted image flashed through her mind of those thick, rough fingers rubbing up the inside of her thigh, gently parting her nether lips, slipping into the wet heat of her. She could nearly feel his hand on her, his finger inside her and the sensory impact of the fantasy made her lightheaded. She shook herself and eased away from his touch. "We'd better go. There's a lot of ground to cover before we reach Dorjan's lands."

Kael walked beside Rowena, trying his best to keep his lust under control. There'd been something in her eyes when she'd run away last night, something that had stopped him from chasing after her. She was more than just angry. More than hurt. Last night he'd seen another emotion beneath it all.

Fear.

But it didn't make sense for her to be afraid of him. She'd proven as much by holding a knife to his neck. And he'd seen her face in the midst of that fight with the mercenaries. While *he* might have panicked, she'd enjoyed the battle. Now, she traveled into a dangerous land to rescue an oracle from one of the most vicious warlords in the east. And she never showed a hint of fear.

So what scared her when she looked at him? Why did she keep running away?

To further complicate matters between them, her mother had a mage sword. The weapons were so rare it was unheard of for two people in the same family to be claimed by more than one. Oh, a mage sword might pass from parent to offspring or grandchild, remaining with one family for generations. But two in the same family was... Well, it had never been recorded in all the centuries of Heron history.

He frowned, glancing off into the field they skirted so Rowena wouldn't see his expression. He'd been positive the mage sword he'd forged was meant for her. He knew it in his soul. And yet...

He'd expected Ca'laez to claim Rowena immediately. The sword hadn't. Ca'laez had remained silent, leaving him in the difficult position of not being able to explain his long absence to Rowena. After finding out about her mother, he was starting to doubt his instincts. Maybe the sword wasn't meant for her after all. Maybe it had been forged for someone else.

Damn, that would make things difficult. The mage sword had to be claimed.

He glanced at Rowena, her beautiful face set and distant. She was thinking. Hard enough that a little line had formed between her brows. He smiled, unable to stop himself. Being near her made him feel whole. Not quite settled, though. They'd have to complete the bonding for that. But even now he found it hard to imagine being without her. Unfortunately, until the mage sword claimed her owner, Kael didn't have much choice about being with Rowena.

She didn't stop for a middle meal, which surprised him. Instead, she took out a cloth-covered stack of oatcake rations and nibbled at one while they walked. When she wordlessly offered him one, her gaze open as she held the cakes out to him, he felt something in his chest pull tight.

She'd seen him pull food out of mid-air—a mage trick only one of his power could accomplish—yet she offered some of her own food without thought. He had no doubt her rations were sparse. The pack she carried wasn't large enough for much food. And still she offered him a share. Openly. Easily.

"Thank you," he murmured as he took one of the hard biscuits.

She nodded and color tinted her cheeks. She turned back toward the path, scowling at the fields as she munched her food. He smiled and bit into the dust dry cake. She might try to deny it still, but their bond intensified with each moment they spent together and their souls intertwined.

She offered her water skin as casually as she'd offered her food. As he took a drink, he tried not to think about the fact that her mouth had been in exactly the same spot only moments before. He could still taste her, the hint of her, and it was all he could do not to drop the skin and pull her into his arms.

They stopped for the night inside a copse of trees at the

edge of a yellowing wheat field. Rowena laid out her bedroll, collected twigs and bits of wood and started a small fire, all without speaking. She'd been quiet most of the day. Oddly, though, he found her silences as comforting as her talk. She was with him, near him. She didn't try to push him away. He had no doubt she'd give in to the need to bond fully soon enough.

She settled in front of the fire and produced the admittedly-filling-but-tasteless oatcakes again, offering him another. This time he shook his head. "Save them. I'll go get us something nicer to eat."

Her eyebrows popped upward, but she nodded, smiling slightly as she gestured for him to do as he liked. She even put the oatcakes back in her pack, which pleased him immensely for some strange reason. He returned with a pheasant fat enough to feed them both.

"Nice catch," she said. Then she formed a spit for over the fire while he prepared the bird.

It was almost more than he could stand, watching her lick fat juice from the roasted meat off her fingers as she ate. To keep his mind off licking her himself, he said, "Have you always wanted to be an Aleanian priestess?"

She looked up, her eyes widening a bit. "No, actually. I mean I was raised to understand the Aleanians, obviously. It was my mother's way of life, her religion and philosophy. She taught that to all of us. But it wasn't until my first trip to Malyk when I was twelve that I decided I wanted to become a part of that life."

Rowena smiled at the memory of that first trip, remembering the tingle of anticipation fluttering in her stomach as she left the aerie. "It was just my mother and me on that visit," she said, half to herself. "My father hated letting us go alone, but my older brother was in the middle of a difficult stage of the Gryphatar's life cycle. He couldn't leave Gryphaldin at all, and my father had to be with him to help him through. I'd gotten very handy with a practice sword by that time, so my mother decided I had to have a proper one. And once she made up her mind about something, there was very little my father could do."

She glanced up, met Kael's gaze over the fire. With a deprecating chuckle, she said, "The Gryphatar are brilliant artisans, but everyone in the freeworld knows the best swords are found at the base of Heron's Deep. Kellyn thought I'd proven myself and deserved a good blade. It wasn't until later she admitted to hoping I'd choose the Aleanian path. Probably to make up for only serving a single year of her own time as sword sworn."

"Why only a year?"

"She went to rescue my father. After that, she moved to Gryphaldin and had to break her vow."

"She was sent to rescue your father so young? Did she swear her sword late?"

"No. She was only twenty-two when she went to rescue him."

"But..." He set aside his food and his brow creased.

Rowena couldn't help but study his face. The strong jaw, the high cheekbones, the temptingly firm lips. She had to shake herself when her mind dipped into a fantasy of licking grease from his chin.

"But," he continued, "I thought you swore your swords at fourteen, during the Choosing."

"Ah," she said, understanding his confusion. "No. That's when we begin the apprenticeship. We don't swear our swords until we're twenty-one. Before that, we're taught the skills, trained, and given a chance to have a bit of fun. The life of a sword sworn can be short. They like to give us time to enjoy our youth before they start sending us into danger."

He nodded. "In keeping with Aleanian philosophy. I'd just never realized."

"I'm surprised. The Heron have such close dealings with the Temple."

He smiled wryly when he said, "And the Aleanians still keep much of their inner workings to themselves. There's a lot those outside the Temple don't know. Not unlike the Heron."

She laughed. "I've never thought of that before. But you're right. There's a lot we don't know about you."

His expression stilled and his eyes darkened. The sudden change had her heart thumping. "What?" she asked, swallowing to wet her suddenly dry throat.

"You should laugh more often."

The intensity in his voice, his expression caught her breath. "I do," she said as her heart squeezed tight. "Most of the time." She couldn't explain to him that his mere presence made her ache for something she didn't want, something she knew would break her heart. The hurt she couldn't seem to control around him bit sharply and made it harder to laugh.

He nodded at her statement. "I saw you once, in the city. You were in a pub with friends. You laughed a lot that night."

Her gaze narrowed. "You saw me? You saw me, and you didn't say anything?" Her throat closed against the punch of pain to her chest. He really had been avoiding her. For twelve years!

Chapter Three

"Damn you, Kael," she muttered, turning her head so she didn't have to look at him. As the pain swept over the top of her anger, she wondered if she could really blame him for avoiding her. After the way their first meeting ended, she probably would have avoided her too.

"I wanted to talk to you," he said quietly. "I couldn't. Not then."

"Why?" She refused to face him. She hated that he might see her hurt instead of her anger.

"I can't explain." She caught his shrug from the corner of her eye. "It's to do with our ways. The Heron."

"Can't explain? Even to your *raynia*?" She snorted, not even trying to hide her disbelief.

"The Heron are as secretive as the Aleanians. As the Gryphatar. We have our reasons." He was silent for a moment. Then said, "That's the first time you've admitted to being my soul twin."

She rolled her eyes. "It's hardly worth denying now, is it? We both know it's the truth. But that doesn't mean we have to..." She trailed off, felt her cheeks heating.

"To what?"

Humor crept back into his voice, making her shiver despite the heat from the fire—a fire that had continued to burn even though she was no longer feeding it wood.

"You're maintaining the flame, aren't you?" she asked, changing the subject to avoid answering him. His wry look told her he knew what she was doing, but she didn't care. She didn't want to talk about sex. She was too angry. And too hurt. He'd seen her in Malyk. And he'd avoided her.

"I am," he answered her question. "There's not much wood here."

"I'm going for a walk," she said abruptly, lurching to her feet. "To that hill." She nodded behind her to a field that overlooked their copse. "I don't want another surprise like last night."

She didn't wait for him to respond before hurrying away from the fire. She stayed away long enough she thought he'd be asleep. To her infinite irritation, he wasn't. He leaned against a tree, his thick arms crossed over his chest, watching her as she returned.

"Feel better?" he asked.

"No." She tried to pass him, determined to crawl into her bedroll and ignore him until exhaustion made her sleep. He stopped her with a hand on her arm. She glared at the hand, then at him. He didn't even flinch.

"You're angry with me. For not coming to you sooner."

"Damn straight I am. And that surprises you?"

"Actually, I was surprised at first. But I understand a little better now. What I don't understand is why you keep running away from me? You can feel our bonding as well as I can. You can't stop it now. Why deny it?"

"Because. I. Don't. Want. You." She bit off each word.

"Yes. You do." He pulled her against him, catching her off guard with the sudden jerk. "And obviously," he ground his hips against hers, "I want you too."

Her stomach danced. There was no denying the very large erection pressing against her belly. Her breathing sped as his gaze held hers, forcing her to acknowledge the attraction. Her heart thumped so hard she thought it might burst. A full out fight with seven armed men hadn't made her blood pound this hard. But Kael, just looking at her, took her breath away.

She didn't protest when he backed her up against a tree, didn't pull away when he ran his hands down her arms and settled his big palms on her waist. His thumbs stroked over her belly, and she was instantly wet and ready.

It would be so easy to give in, so easy to let him strip off her trousers and thrust that thick, hard cock into her. She tried to remember why she kept denying this, why she kept refusing him when she wanted nothing more than to fuck him until dawn. There was a reason...

His abandonment, her logic tried to tell her. *He ignored you, avoided you for twelve years. If you give in now, you'll never be free of him.*

But would that really be so bad?

His gaze dropped to her mouth and his head followed, slowly, easing closer as if he couldn't stop himself. His breath brushed hot against her lips, and a sensory memory flashed. Kael, twelve years younger, his face not etched so hard as now. He'd been much taller than her then—she hadn't had her growth spurt. He had her backed up against a building, away from the crowded market streets.

His eyes, so green and intense, fascinated her. He was a lot older, but she didn't care. He was her *raynei*. She knew it, felt it with every fiber of her being. And she wanted him to kiss her, there in the alley. She didn't care who saw.

He leaned in close, seeming to struggle against his urge. Bold and eager, she rose onto her toes and brushed her lips against his. He groaned low in his throat, and his mouth crushed down on hers. His arms cinched around her waist, nearly pulled her off of her feet. Her young body hummed with sensation, thrilled at the feelings he stirred. She wanted more. She wrapped her arms around his neck, tilted her head, let him deepen the kiss.

Then, suddenly, he wrenched away. He took a step back, his muscles tightening as he blinked rapidly. She reached out to him. "Kael?"

He looked at her, his eyes rolled back into his head, and his body began to convulse as he collapsed to the ground. She screamed and called mentally for her mom and dad. They found her crouching over Kael as his body jerked violently.

"Turn him on his side," her mother said. "And keep him that way. Cushion his head so he doesn't hurt himself." Her father helped her roll Kael's body onto his side. Then Rowena knelt to cushion Kael's head in her lap while her father kept a gentle pressure on Kael's back. As they worked, her mother unsheathed Ba'nari, murmured something Rowena couldn't hear, and dropped to one knee, driving the sword deep into the ground through the stone slabs lining the road.

Rowena wasn't sure how much time passed. Tears streamed down her face as she held Kael despite the rhythmic jerking of his muscles. She petted his hair, kept saying his name. She looked up when two Heron materialized at Kael's feet. They took him from her arms and an instant later the seizure ended, leaving him limp and unconscious.

"Will he be all right?" she asked, struggling to her feet.

The Heron exchanged a look. One, an older woman with

blonde hair, said, "He'll be fine. We'll take care of him." And they disappeared.

Rowena hadn't seen Kael again until he'd appeared in front of her last night. At least, she hadn't seen him in person. She'd dreamt about him constantly since that day.

The memory of that first kiss shot terror through her. She couldn't face that happening again. She had no way to call the Heron this time. Panic blinding her, she struggled out of Kael's arms before his lips touched hers and stumbled away from the heat of his body. The moisture on her cheeks surprised her. She wiped it roughly away as she sucked in deep, calming breaths. Slowly, the panic eased, but she kept her back to him as she tried to regain her control.

"Rowena?" His voice was soft, colored by concern.

Gods, he'd probably seen her tears. Humiliated, she started back to camp, but he stopped her with a hand on her shoulder. She spun around to face him and without thinking, her sword was in her hands. "Leave me alone, Kael. I mean it."

"No. Tell me what's wrong. Why are you crying?"

"I'm not. And it's none of your business anyway."

His eyes narrowed, sparked with a dangerous glimmer. "Yes. It is." He pulled his own sword from the sheath strapped over his back, touched his blade to hers. "Winner take all," he murmured.

"You don't want to fight me."

"You're right. I want to fuck you. You're the one insisting on a fight. So we'll play your way first. Then we play mine."

Her fear morphed to anger. "Arrogant bastard." She spun away then swung back to catch his blade with her own, the sound of steel on steel ringing in the dark copse. There wasn't a lot of room between the trees, but she used what she had, unleashing her anger and frustration, slashing, testing, pushing him to show her just how good he was.

He tried to back her against another tree, she turned the trick on him, had him braced between bulging roots, barely able to deflect her attack as he untangled himself. She laughed at his growl, let the energy rushing through her wash away everything but the battle. Her muscles bunched and flexed, her feet danced, her blood pumped in time to the rhythm of the fight. "You underestimate me, Heron," she said, swinging her blade to push aside his blow.

"Never."

But on his next attack, he overstretched. She twisted around behind him and slapped him across the ass with the flat of her blade. She laughed, pleased with his yelp. As he turned on her, she continued to grin, enjoying herself, reveling in the play of skill against skill. He was good. Very good. And it made the battle more exciting.

He got in under her guard once and returned her slap, only he used his hand on her ass instead of his blade. She squealed and jumped away. Rubbing a hand over her stinging skin, she glared. It was his turn to grin, but there was something very serious about his grin, something dangerous that made her hurry to put more distance between them. Despite herself, her body reacted to the gleam in his eye. And she found it hard to think for a moment beyond the way his palm had felt on her butt.

She returned to the matter at hand with a jolt when his blade swung toward her again. He wasn't much taller than her anymore, but he was easily twice as thick, his muscles honed in the smithy. She couldn't take many of his blows directly on her blade, but she knew how to counter superior brute strength. She knocked his blade to one side, stepping in close to keep from taking his full power on her shoulders.

But getting that close to him was a mistake. He used her move, grabbed the strap of her scabbard where it crossed between her breasts and pulled. Before she could protest, before she could gasp, his mouth closed over hers. His tongue plunged between her lips, taking, dominating. For a breathless moment, she fell into the kiss and savored the taste of him as their tongues tangled. Gods, she'd wanted this for so long, the feel of his firm lips covering hers, the heat, the need. She pressed closer, demanding more, and he groaned into her mouth.

Her eyes snapped open. Panic flushed through her system. With a strangled sound, she jerked back and stumbled away without ever taking her gaze off him. Her heart raced, her hands started to tremble. She raised her sword more out of habit than in self-defense and stared. Waiting.

Kael's gaze narrowed as he studied her. Her face was pale beneath the golden tan. Too pale. Her eyes were so wide and dark they dominated the planes of her face. She was breathing hard and her mouth hung open. But instead of anger, he saw panic. That same damned fear he'd seen earlier. But fear of what?

He brought Ca'laez down to his side, relaxing his stance. She kept her sword up. In fact, she didn't move a muscle. A minute ago she'd been laughing and enjoying their battle. Now, she stood like a terrorized statue, staring at him. He didn't understand such a dramatic change just because he'd kissed her.

After a few quiet heartbeats, her grip relaxed, and she straightened. Her brow creased. "Are you okay?"

His eyebrows shot upward. It was the last question he'd

expected her to ask. He frowned. "Of course I'm okay. Why wouldn't I be?"

Her cheeks puffed as she blew out a pent up breath and let her sword drop to her side. She blinked a couple of times then shook her head. "You're not going to...? I was afraid... After last time, I thought..."

He could actually see her swallowing. She rubbed a hand over her mouth and turned away.

"Sorry," she said, and sheathed her sword.

"Rowena?" He took a step closer, watched her shoulders rise and fall with her slow, methodical breathing. And then it hit him. The last time they'd kissed, the only time they'd kissed, he'd had a seizure. The fit hadn't had anything to do with her, at least not directly, not the kiss. He'd entered his trance. The initiation of trance started with a seizure. And his had been triggered early by meeting his *raynia*. Who, until today, he'd been convinced was to be the owner of the mage sword he'd forged.

But Rowena wouldn't have known any of that. Couldn't know any of it. And the Heron who'd come to take him back into the Deep, his mother and uncle, wouldn't have explained. Rowena thought their kiss had triggered his seizure. She thought he'd been avoiding her for twelve years because kissing her had caused a fit.

Hells. "Rowena." Her name came out a sigh. He sheathed his sword and closed the distance between them, folding his hands over her shaking shoulders. "Baby, that seizure had nothing to do with you. It was... Heron biology. Something that some of us go through. But only once in our lives. And it had nothing to do with you. It was just bad timing."

"So...so it won't happen again? You swear it won't happen again?"

The fear trembling in her voice nearly undid him. He pulled her back against his chest, wrapped his arms around her. Her sword pressed across his chest and stomach, but he ignored it. He rested his cheek against her left temple to avoid the sword pommel sticking up over her right shoulder. Rocking her gently, he breathed in her scent, closing his eyes to savor it. "It won't happen again," he murmured into her hair. "I swear it."

She nodded and took a long, deep breath. The exhale shuddered out of her. "Good."

Because he couldn't resist the temptation, he nuzzled her neck, kissed the silky skin. Tasted. Bit down gently. "You taste good," he said and moved his lips up her neck to the soft skin at the base of her jaw. Her head tilted to the side, giving him better access. The unconscious gesture made him smile. "Feeling better?" He nipped her earlobe.

"*Mmm...* Well, I'm not worried about making you ill with a kiss anymore."

The wry note in her voice made him chuckle. "Your kisses do a lot of things to me, baby, but making me ill isn't one of them." He reached up and moved the short length of her hair aside so he could taste the back of her neck. At the hairline, he kissed, licked then blew warm air across her skin. She shivered.

"What are you doing?" she asked, her voice breathless even as she leaned into him.

"Tasting you."

"You shouldn't be doing that."

"Why not? I'm enjoying myself. And we've established the fact that I'm not going to collapse from it. Though I may burn up." The arm he still had wrapped around her dropped lower so he could pull her ass up tight against his cock.

"Kael." Her voice strained now. She brought a hand up and clenched his arm where it circled her waist. He'd anticipated her pushing him away and tightened his hold, but instead she gripped his forearm and held him in place.

"There's no reason to run, Rowena," he murmured as his lips brushed over her throat to the collar of her tunic. He nuzzled the material aside to nibble the skin at the curve between her shoulder and neck. "We're soul twins. *Raynyn.* This is right."

He closed his free hand over her breast without losing his hold on her waist. She moaned, her head dropping back toward his shoulder. The pommel of her sword got in the way, but she didn't seem to notice. He did. And he didn't want the hindrance. "That's a Heron blade you have?" he asked against her ear.

She nodded. He reached to the strap crossing between her breasts and found the hidden release catch. For ordinary Heron blades, anyone could press the release and cause the scabbard strap to open and drop away. If they knew where the catch was. Freeing a mage sword scabbard was more complicated—only the owner could use the quick release catch. But Rowena wasn't wearing a mage sword. He pressed the release, heard her gasp as the scabbard loosened and slipped between their bodies to the ground.

"My sword." She tried to lean down to pick it up, but he gave her no room.

"It's fine." He released his own scabbard, gently setting his sword on the ground with hers. "We won't go far." He rubbed his palm over her ass cheek and patted gently to move her forward. When the two swords were no longer underfoot, he turned her to face him and back her up against a tree.

"You've got the nicest ass," he said, continuing to suck and lick the skin over her throat. He closed both hands over her butt and squeezed. "Very tight. Very curvy. I'm looking forward to fucking you from behind so I can feel this lovely ass of yours slapping against my hips."

"You're very crude," she breathed between panting breaths.

"Because you're enjoying it."

"How would you know?"

"I can feel it. And you're melting in my arms."

"Am not."

He laughed at the blatant lie. "No?" He brought his mouth up to hers, swirled his tongue over her lower lip and dipped inside her mouth with a quick, teasing lick. "You'd rather I didn't tell how good you taste? How hot you feel? How much I want to be inside you? How I'm going out of my mind right now with wanting you?"

"*Hmm.* Okay, you can tell me those things."

He chuckled and took possession of her mouth. Her tongue tangled with his, welcoming, wanting. This time, he could feel her curiosity, her hunger overpowering the fear that had haunted her for years. He drank it in, fed it, urging her need higher, tighter. She ground her hips against his straining cock, and he groaned into her mouth, his hands clenching tight on her ass. "Gods. Rowena, you drive me crazy." And he kissed her again.

His hands moved over her, exploring, teasing. She inched her fingers up under his vest, touching skin, and his head spun from sheer pleasure. "Yes," he muttered, "touch me." He shrugged the vest off, leaving his chest bare, accessible to her exploration. Then he buried his hands in her hair and angled her head to deepen the kiss.

He couldn't get enough of her. The feel of her hands on his skin was like fire, burning lines down his back, across his stomach. When her fingers skimmed his lower abdomen, near the top of his trousers, he shuddered and his hands clenched tight in her hair. If he didn't bury himself in her soon, he might just die.

When he came up for air, he was panting and close to losing control. He drank in the sight of her mussed hair, her red, swollen lips, the dreamy daze in her dark eyes. He loved seeing her this way, just like this, drowsy with desire, too needy to think beyond him. "You're so beautiful," he said, cupping her cheek in his hand.

She closed her eyes, rubbed her face against his palm, the gesture so intimate it made his throat tight.

"No. I'm your *raynia*," she said. "You have to think I'm pretty." Her eyes blinked open, twinkling with amusement as they met his.

"Let me ask you, do you think I'm handsome?"

She rolled her eyes. "Gods, yes."

"And am I handsome because I'm your *raynei* or because I'm really handsome?"

"Any woman with half a brain would think you're handsome, Kael."

He grinned, liking the little hint of jealousy in her voice. "And I think we can safely say you have more than half a brain."

She snorted, trying to hide her grin.

"I feel the same way." He leaned in to brush his lips over her cheeks, across her forehead. "Any man with eyes would think you're beautiful. I imagine a number of men have in the last twelve years."

She shrugged.

His eyes narrowed. "How many suitors have you had?"

She didn't hide her grin so well this time. "One or two."

"One or two?"

"Maybe three. Could have been four."

"So that's what you've been doing while I was...?" He took a deep breath, let it out through his teeth. Her grin was huge now, teasing. And he liked it, but he wasn't about to let her know. "So I've been pining away for you, and you've been flirting with other men. That's very hurtful of you, *raynia*."

"Ha! Pining, my ass." She looked him up and down in a way that made his blood boil. "You kiss too good to have been 'pining' for twelve years."

"Do I?" His voice dropped to a low purring growl as he pressed closer to her again.

She scowled. "Yes." His hand closed over her breast, rubbing through the thin material of her tunic. She gasped and arched against him. "And you know what you're doing," she murmured. "You couldn't have..." Her breath caught when his hand slipped inside her tunic. The only thing separating his palm from her bare skin was the thin wrap of linen binding her breasts. "Couldn't have gotten this good without practicing," she finished.

He watched her eyes darken as he worked the linen wrap loose enough to allow his hand to slip underneath. He twisted a finger around her already peaked nipple, teasing the little bud tighter, then pinched it gently between forefinger and thumb.

She groaned. "Kael." Her voice strained out between her teeth, a plea for mercy.

For her teasing, he intended to show her none. "You think I'm good? You like the way I touch you?"

"Yes." She moved restlessly under his palm, rubbing against him.

He leaned close to nuzzle her neck, still toying with her nipple. "Have you many men to compare me to? Have you let other men touch you this way?"

She shook her head, her hands clenching and unclenching against his waist. "Damn you," she panted. "I met you when I was only fourteen. I haven't been able to stand the touch of another man since." She shuddered as his teeth sank into her skin, biting none too gently. "All your fault," she managed, her voice barely audible.

"You're a virgin." He'd suspected as much, despite the erotic sensations flooding her dreams.

She nodded and her short nails bit into his back. "All your fault," she said again.

Growing more desperate by the moment, Kael pushed her tunic fully open, ripping one of the front buttons off in his haste. The linen binding beneath was pushed up onto her chest, exposing both lush, full breasts to his hungry gaze. He closed his hands over both, squeezed. She inhaled sharply, as if burned, and the sound made his already throbbing cock jump.

"If it makes you feel any better," he said, then trailed off. He watched in fascination as her golden skin flushed, turning her breasts pink, darkening the dusty rose color of her nipples. He licked his lips and leaned down to close his mouth over one hard little nub. She cried out, her hands clenching tight in his hair. He circled the tip with his tongue then pulled her into his mouth again, suckling hard. Her knees buckled. He circled one arm around her waist to hold her upright.

"You were...saying...something about...making me feel better," she said between gasps.

For a heartbeat, he had no idea what she was talking about. Her emotions, her needs were flowing over him, through him, and he knew she was feeling very good at that moment, if a little desperate. Feeling her emotions like this was infinitely better than riding her dreams because now he knew he was the cause of her passion. And he had every intention of making them both feel even better before the night was out.

Then he remembered what'd he'd been about to tell her before getting distracted. He gave her nipple a last lick before straightening. He held her tight, loving the feel of her breasts pressed flat against his chest, skin to skin. "I was saying, if it will make you feel any better, I've been celibate since meeting you, too. And not at all happy about it either."

Her eyes narrowed. "You? You were celibate for twelve years?" Her gaze danced over him. "I find that very hard to believe."

"Believe it." He took her hand and brought it down to his cock, pressing her palm against the hard bulge of his erection. "This is because of you, only you since we met. And I've been this way almost constantly since last night."

Her fingers squeezed, testing. At his urging, she rubbed her palm up and down the length of him, through the barrier of his trousers. He dropped his head against her shoulder, groaning. "Gods, that feels good."

"*Mmm...* Yes, it does."

He released her wrist to clench at her hip as her hand continued to stroke him, gently, slowly. He was going to come in his pants if he didn't stop her soon, but he couldn't quite bring himself to end the agony. When she started to stroke faster, harder, he gripped her wrist and forced her hand away. "You're lucky I've lasted this long," he said when she whimpered in protest. "Twelve years is a long time to wait."

"You really haven't had sex with anyone since we met?" There was a quiet wonder in her voice that made him smile.

He touched his lips to hers. "I really haven't. I've only wanted you since that day. You're my *raynia*."

Her eyes snapped fire. "Then why the hell did you wait so long?"

Chapter Four

The petulance in Rowena's voice made Kael grin. He closed his mouth over hers, tasting her impatience, her desire. Without breaking the kiss, he pulled a part of his mind away long enough for a spell.

It took power, more than just transporting food. More than he should probably use while they still had Dorjan's wizard to face. But he didn't want her first time to be up against a tree or on the hard, rough ground. He wanted to make love to her in a bed. At least this time. Later, he wouldn't feel the need to restrict themselves to beds.

Rowena felt the tingle of something beyond her own desire, beyond the heat of his emotions pouring into her. She could feel his lust, his impatience, his need to please. But for an instant, a part of him moved away from her. She could feel it, like she could feel all his other emotions. She was an empath anyway, but the bonding between them made her particularly sensitive to him. She pulled back to look into his face, to ask what was wrong.

And that's when she saw the bed.

Her eyes widened and her mouth dropped open. It was huge, the mattress thick and covered with white linens that glowed in the deepening gloom of night. Four thick stone pillars in the red sandstone of Malyk and Heron's Deep cornered the bed. The pillars were rounded and carved with exotic pictures of twining animals and plant life. The bed squeezed into the space between the trees at the center of the copse, so tight one tree actually butted up against one of the shorter sides of the mattress. Her bedroll, pack and the remains of their dinner fire were just visible beyond the bed.

"Where did that come from?" she asked.

He chuckled and nuzzled her neck in a way that made her eyes cross. She loved the feel of his mouth on her throat, his lips brushing against her pulse.

"A present," he said. "For you."

"Yes, but..." Her thinking blurred when his lips returned to hers. He walked her backward to the bed, holding her tight, his mouth devouring hers. She felt the mattress against the back of her thighs, then his hands gripped her waist. She gasped when he picked her up and tossed her, easily, into the center of the bed. Her stomach danced at the show of strength.

He stood at the foot of the bed, staring at her, the green of his eyes nearly black. "Undress," he said, without moving.

She swallowed and slipped her already open tunic off. The linen wrap was wrenched up high on her chest, but he'd loosened it enough it was easy to unwind. Still he didn't move, just watched. Because she could feel his emotions, feel the intensity of his desire, she felt luscious and sexy under his gaze. Any other man, any other time, and she knew she'd have felt awkward and self-conscious. But not with Kael.

She sat up and removed her boots, tossing them aside. Then she unhitched her belt, letting the dagger and sheath drop carefully to the ground. She unlaced the leather bindings on the side of her trousers, slipped the butter-soft suede down her hips, watching him, watching the effect she had on him. Naked, she lay back on the white sheets and waited. Her breathing came fast, her pussy flooded with moisture, and her body trembled in the cool evening air. She wanted his heat, wanted the feel of him next to her, the hard length of his cock thrusting into her. But she waited. And he watched.

Finally, he leaned over and took off his boots. His gaze never left her. When he put his hand to the leather straps of his trousers, she shuddered. It was so like her dream. And yet nothing like it. She knew this was real, this was Kael. No illusions, no fantasy. Her *raynei*. All her earlier fear, all the hurt seemed so far away. A part of her still wondered, still worried. But most of her was so centered on him, she couldn't think beyond the movement of his hands as he pushed his trousers down over his lean hips and stepped out of them to stand naked before her.

Her lips parted as her breath left her on an exhale. He was magnificent. Perfect.

Large.

She swallowed. Sex had never hurt in her dreams, but this was going to. Her friends had assured her it passed, and then it was wonderful. She'd have to trust to their experience. But she couldn't take her eyes off the sheer size of his cock, the purple head already glistening with a drop of moisture.

Did all men look like that? she wondered as he moved up onto the bed next to her. She'd touched him through his trousers. Did he feel different, flesh to flesh? Her gaze on his, she reached out and touched his cock, just the head. His eyes fluttered closed and his jaw clenched.

"You like me to touch you?" she asked, genuinely curious. She wanted to please him. When he nodded, she ran her fingers down the length of him. His skin was soft over the hardness beneath. With her thumb and forefinger, she stroked him, fascinated when his cock twitched. "I like touching you," she admitted. She cupped his balls in her hand, squeezed gently, felt them tightening.

His body jerked. He reached down and pulled her hand away, set it against his chest. She could feel his heart racing, matching the pace of hers.

"Twelve years was too long," he muttered, breathing through his teeth.

She smiled, leaned in and kissed him. He met her hungrily, pressing her back into the mattress as he ravished her mouth, her neck. His lips dropped to her breasts, tugging, sucking her nipples until she thought she'd go out of her mind. Her womb clenched, her legs moved restlessly under him. Then his hand slid down her stomach, making her entire body contract.

He ran a finger over her hipbone, just above the thatch of hair between her legs, down the inside of her thigh. She panted, barely able to draw breath. And then his palm covered her mound, and one finger teased between her nether lips where she was slick and ready. He slid along the crease, rubbing gently. With each stroke, he pressed his fingertip against her opening, never actually pushing inside. She barely recognized the needy, pleading sounds she made, only knew he was driving her mad.

"More?" he asked against her mouth. She nodded. And he dipped inside her, his callused finger moving deep. She arched under him, groaning. This was just as she'd imagined, just what she thought his finger would feel like moving inside her. Only she had ever touched herself this way before, but she'd fantasized about his hands, his fingers. And now she knew. Her fantasies paled in comparison to the real feel of him.

"Kael." His name sighed out of her.

"You like me inside you?"

She nodded, arched as his thumb found her clitoris while

165

his finger still moved in and out of her.

"It doesn't hurt?"

"Gods, no," she groaned.

"My cock is bigger."

"Yes."

"It'll hurt at first."

"I know."

"It won't last long. Then it'll be nothing but pleasure. I promise."

"I know." She captured his mouth, threaded her fingers into his hair to hold him close.

"I want you to come for me, like this," he said against her mouth. "I want to make you come just like this, with my hands first."

Her hips jerked, but she shook her head. "No. I want you inside me. Kael, I want us joined."

"Don't worry, baby." He grinned even as her body started to spin out of her control, tightening around his finger. "I want us joined, too."

She tried to hold on, to hold back. But he knew, he could feel when his movements hit just the right spots, held just the right pressure. She couldn't hide her emotions from him, not now. She couldn't control her body's reactions. When the pressure was too much, the intensity too sharp, she gave in and let go, crying out with the force of her orgasm.

She trembled and shuddered in the aftermath, curling into his arms, his warmth. "Gods," she muttered against his neck and felt his chuckle vibrate across her breasts.

He rolled between her lax thighs, lifted them to circle his hips as he settled with his penis poised against her. She was slick with excitement and her own come, but the press of the head of his cock reminded her of his size. He cradled her face between his big hands, kissed her gently. "Fast or slow?" he asked. "Either way will hurt some. I can't help that. But I leave the method to you."

"Fast," she said after considering. She wanted the pain done with so she could go back to enjoying him. A part of her almost wished she'd had sex before so her first time with Kael wouldn't be shadowed by the blasted inconvenience of her virginity. But another part was glad he would be her first, her only. It seemed right. She could feel their bond tightening, their souls so intermeshed now there was no separating them. This one last step would complete the process. They would no longer be able to stand being apart for long periods of time. And if one died, the other would follow.

For a brief moment, her fears rose up again. He was Heron. Heron didn't live outside of Heron's Deep. And she was to be a priestess of the Aleanian Temple. She couldn't move underground, couldn't live away from the Temple. Would they survive living that far apart, seeing each other when they could, but not constantly, not the way her mother and father did?

She reminded herself that her mother traveled without her father to Malyk sometimes, stayed away from him for weeks. And they managed just fine. Maybe it wasn't so much proximity as the knowledge that the other was there...somewhere.

She tried to latch on to the thought, tried to sort through her fears with logic. But then Kael brushed his lips over hers, sunk deep into the kiss, blurring all her thoughts. She wrapped her arms around his neck, held him close, kissed him hard and clenched her eyes tight when he thrust into her in one quick, hard stroke. The pain only lasted a moment before she was distracted by the feel of him inside her, the utter satisfaction of it, the rightness. *This is how he should feel inside me.* Just like her dreams, just like her fantasies. Only better. He filled her, stretched her. And she felt in that instant the bond sealing. Their souls were joined, their lives now one. From this moment on, they would be whole. Complete.

She sighed, smiled against his mouth as she felt his fascinated awe. And she knew he sensed it too, the final melding of their souls. His kiss turned tender. And he began to move.

At first, his thrusts were slow, steady, coaxing her. She clenched around him, loving the way his hard, thick cock felt inside her. Without the distraction of pain, she could fully appreciate the size of him stretching her tight, the friction of his movements. Her hips jerked against him and she shuddered as her sensitive clitoris rubbed against the dark curls nestling his cock. She moaned and thrust against him again. It was almost more sensation than she could stand.

He reached between their bodies, fingered her clit as his thrusts increased, pounding harder into her. Her head arched back against the bed. She bit her lower lip to keep from crying out, but a taut sound still escaped. Her fingers dug into his shoulders and her entire body clenched and jerked until she came with a ragged scream. She barely had time to recover before he was pounding into her, harder, faster. He propped his hands on the bed beside her head so his upper body towered over her. His gaze bore into her, held hers and before she could stop it, she came again, the force so powerful tears leaked from her eyes.

His hips jerked against hers, his breathing harsh above her. Her vagina pulsed with too much sensation, overwhelming her nerves. Her inner muscles clenched around his cock as the aftershock of her latest orgasm shuddered through her. He groaned, cursed under his breath. And then his back arched, his neck muscles straining. With a harsh cry, he erupted inside her, spewing hotly into her core.

He collapsed, covering her as he shuddered. She wrapped her arms around his neck and squeezed her arms and thighs, hugging him with her entire body. The hug didn't have much power in it. She didn't have any strength left. But her emotions overwhelmed her in that instant and she needed him close.

When they were both breathing more normally, he rolled to the side, taking her with him. Their bodies still intertwined, he reached up to the tangled mass of her hair and smoothed it back from her sweat-soaked brow. His smile was tender and heart-wrenching.

"That was worth waiting for," he said.

She laughed, part embarrassment, part pleasure, and buried her face against his chest. She inhaled, pulling in his scent. "Yes," she murmured, placing a kiss on his chest, just above his nipple. "Yes, it was."

ෆ෫෧෨

Kael let her sleep for a few hours before he couldn't stand the wait any longer and had to wake her. She'd surprised him by falling asleep almost immediately, while he'd felt energized by the sex, even in his exhaustion. He'd dozed some. But mostly, he watched her, studying the curve of her jaw, the soft line of her mouth still puffy and red from his kisses, the curve of her lashes against her cheek. Her skin was dark against the stark white of the sheets. He placed her hand on his chest, studied the contrast of her darker skin against his pale flesh. For some reason, her hand looked perfect, right where he pressed her palm against his heart.

She was all warmth and soft flesh now, her toned body relaxed in sleep. He studied the golden highlights in her dark brown hair. At a certain angle, if he wasn't paying attention, the gold looked almost like feathers woven into her hair. An illusion of light and shadow, probably something she inherited from her father. But it was exotic and tantalizing to see. He absently wondered what else besides her eyes and the golden glints in her hair she'd inherited from her father.

Kael slid his hand down to her breast, squeezing the heavy mound in a gentle massage. She moaned in her sleep, stirred a little, moving closer to him. But she didn't wake up. He grinned. Leaning over, he took her already hard nipple into his mouth, tasting the salty sweetness of her skin as he rolled his tongue around her. Her breathing deepened, but she didn't wake up.

She must be exhausted, he thought, feeling a twinge of guilt. He should let her sleep. They'd have the rest of their lives for making love. But his cock was already hard and straining for release. And his mouth watered for a taste of her pussy.

He skimmed his lips over her stomach, savoring her flavor with quick flicks of his tongue. He felt the change in her, heard the shift in her breathing when his teeth skimmed over her hipbone.

"What are you doing?" she murmured, her voice heavy with sleep.

"Something I've been wanting to do for a long time," he said. He shifted, settled between her thighs. Her scent, sharp and feminine, wafted up to him and he growled. He stared at the dark thatch of curls, the faint glistening of moisture already visible, the swollen flesh of her lips peeking out from the curls. He caught her gaze for an instant before he dipped his head and touched his tongue to her warm, wet pussy.

She arched up on the mattress, her fingers digging into the sheets. "Kael."

He loved hearing his name straining out of her. He flicked his tongue over her flesh, parted her lips, delved in deeper. He licked and sucked, savored the musky taste of her as she writhed above him. When he pushed the tip of his tongue inside her, her hands clamped down on his head, her grip tightening in his hair. He played her, fed on her until her body jerked and she came hard. She tried to pull away as her body shook with her release, but he clamped his hands on her hips, held her in place and moved his mouth back to her.

"Kael, no. I can't." She twisted under him. "It's too much."

"You can take more," he said, his breath brushing against her damp curls. His mouth closed over her again. His tongue brushed once, twice and she came again, screaming. He drove her until she begged, pleaded, until her voice was too strained to beg more. Then he rose above her, plunged his hard cock into her and watched her eyes close against the overwhelming sensations.

"Gods, you're beautiful," he murmured. Then lost himself in a hard pounding rhythm. He held himself back long enough to give her one last orgasm then all control shattered. He slammed into her until his balls tightened and he came hard and hot.

When he could move, he rolled onto his back and pulled her over him, blanketing himself with her warm body. She snuggled close, wrapped her arms under his neck. His heart still thumped in his chest. He felt the echoing pound of her heart, and a tenderness he'd never imagined washed through him. He hugged her close and buried his face against her throat.

"That was a nice way to wake up," she murmured, making him chuckle. "But it's still dark."

"I know, baby. Sorry. I couldn't wait for dawn."

He felt her grinning, even if he couldn't see it.

"You're forgiven," she said, the humor in her voice

unmistakable. "In fact, if you have to wake me again before dawn, I'm sure I'd be able to forgive you for that too." She yawned and snuggled closer.

He ran a hand up her back in a lazy caress, wondering if now was a bad time to discuss anything she might have to think about. "Baby?"

"*Hmm?*"

"If I've gotten you pregnant—"

"We don't have to worry about that." Her voice was quiet with sleep. "The priestesses have a spell. Alean herself gave it to them for the sword sworn. Couldn't have a pregnant woman getting killed in a sword fight." She said the last with a wry note in her tired voice.

He stilled. "And if you want to have children?"

She yawned again. "They remove the spell when our term as sword sworn is up."

He relaxed, amazed at the relief he felt. Amazed at how much he wanted to have children with Rowena.

"Mom had to take an herbal drink," she mumbled. "Spell wouldn't work on her with Ba'nari. Probably all right though since she was only a sword sworn for a year..." Her voice trailed off into a quiet murmur he could no longer understand.

Within moments, her breathing evened and she slipped back into sleep. He smiled and let his tired body join her.

She surprised him by waking him next, her mouth moving over his cock in a slow, steady rhythm. He groaned and looked down the length of his body. She caught his gaze, held it as she continued to move her sexy lips up and down his erection. He was too big for her to take fully into her mouth so she squeezed and stroked the base of his penis with one hand while she sucked him.

He had no control over his body, no thought beyond the heat of her wet lips, the feel of her hands, the glint of lust in her dark eyes. He came with a shout that echoed among the trees, spurting into her mouth. She continued sucking until she'd milked him completely, then lifted her head, licked her lips and grinned.

The sight was almost enough to get him hard again.

When she crawled up the bed and snuggled next to him, he wrapped her in his arms. "You're right," he murmured, kissing her brow. "That's a very nice way to wake up."

She chuckled, kissed his shoulder then nestled her head on his chest. After only a few minutes, he felt her breathing deepen as sleep took her again. He slipped under with her, knowing he'd wake her again soon. And again before the sun rose.

CB&CRO

Kael blinked against the dawn light, yawned hugely and rubbed his chest. He'd barely slept all night, just a few short naps. Yet he felt better than he had in years. He rolled to kiss his *raynia* awake, only to find the bed empty. He sat up and glanced around. She stood near her pack, still naked, though he noted her sword and dagger were within easy reach. She stared at her trousers, her lips pursed as if she was deep in thought. He almost hated to say anything. He enjoyed watching her when she was unaware of his gaze. The unconscious emotions and thoughts flickering over her face fascinated him.

Finally, his curiosity got the better of him. "Good morning. Is something wrong?"

She glanced up and grinned. The smile was so bright, so unrestrained it took his breath.

"I'm just wishing I had a stream nearby to wash in." She shrugged, and faint color tinted her cheeks.

"I think I can help with that." He shouldn't. It was a waste of power. Power he knew he'd need later. But he couldn't resist her. He closed his eyes, focused, muttered the spell. At her gasp, he opened his eyes. A few feet from Rowena sat a small red stone tub with a fired enamel interior so dark it was nearly black. Steam rose from the water inside. Rowena's eyes were huge as she stepped up to the tub and gingerly dipped her finger into the water. She groaned, her eyes rolling up.

"That's amazing. Should I even ask how you did this?" She smiled, dropped her trousers and stepped into the tub.

The sheer bliss on her face as she sank into the water up to her neck had his cock hardening. And a part of him was intensely pleased he was able to provide her the small luxury. He'd never been sure if the increase in his powers, induced by his early trance, had been a good thing or a bad thing. Because of those added powers and the prestige of having forged a true mage sword, his position among the Heron had been elevated.

His father had used his son's newfound status on more than one occasion to accomplish his own political aims. Both his parents were encouraging him to enter into the political arena, take a place as a high councilor. But Kael didn't want anything to do with politics. He was a smith, a sword mage at their most elemental. And if his powers hadn't grown so much, he wouldn't have to worry about being anything more than a smith.

But as he watched his *raynia* sighing happily as she scooped warm water up over her head, he decided the increase in his power was definitely worthwhile. He might have been denied her for twelve years because of it. But now, he could give her things he wouldn't have been strong enough to give her before. And that was worth all the other hassles, and the long, long wait.

Rowena grinned and crooked an eyebrow. "Are you just going to lie there watching, or do you want to join me?"

He was out of the bed and climbing into the tub before she could finish laughing. He slid down behind her, cradling her between his thighs. It was a tight fit, but he loved having her ass pressed up against his cock and wouldn't have traded to a bigger tub for all the wealth in the Deep.

As he settled behind her, he noticed the tattoo on her shoulder blade. He'd seen it the night before, but this was the first time he could study it in the light. He fingered the intricately designed, multi-colored picture—a sword, the point aimed toward the sky, the blade and hilt wrapped in a vine heavy with purple and blue flowers.

She glanced over her shoulder at the tattoo he traced. "A symbol of my status as sword sworn," she said.

"I wouldn't have thought the sword sworn would wear such an obvious sign."

"Why not? We give fair warning to anyone we fight. We don't try to hide who and what we are. It wouldn't be fair to those we face if they didn't know what they were getting into."

His eyebrow arched. "Most wouldn't have such compassion for their enemies."

She shrugged, making the sword jump skyward. "Most aren't Aleanian sword sworn." She grinned. "Besides, it's in a place that's easy enough to cover if we have to hide the tattoo for any reason."

He chuckled and pulled her back against his chest.

"I just thought of something," she said, leaning into him.

His arms circled her and he cupped her breasts, toying

with her hardened nipples. "What?"

For a moment she didn't say anything, just hummed a sound of pleasure under her breath. Then, "The only towel I have is a hand-sized scrap of material. I don't usually get to take full baths on the road, unless I stay at an inn."

"You think I can manage a tub but not towels?" he asked against her ear.

She shivered and chuckled. "I think you could do just about anything. But," her tone turned serious, "it costs you power to do this kind of thing, doesn't it? I can feel it."

His eyebrows rose. "You can? You're not a mage."

"I'm an empath and we're *raynyn* so I can feel a lot of what you're feeling. Calling the bed last night, the tub this morning, you hesitated over doing it, just a bit. And then I could feel... I don't know. But all magic costs, doesn't it? So how much does this cost you?"

"Enough I can't do it every day, not enough that you need to worry." He kissed her shoulder, then worked his way up her neck to her earlobe. "I'll be able to handle Dorjan's wizard when the time comes."

"I didn't doubt that. I just don't want you to...well, to drain yourself just for me."

He laughed and pulled her ass tight against his erection. "Actually, I'm feeling quite anxious to drain myself *into* you." She made a sound between a laugh and a groan and rubbed against him. He held his breath, let it out very slowly. "Too much more of that, baby," he murmured, "and I'll be draining myself into the water."

She laughed outright then, dropped her head back to his shoulder and offered her mouth for a kiss. He accepted the offer eagerly.

"You know," she said against his mouth as her hand ran down his thigh, "we should probably take care of this for you, before we get on the road." She reached behind her, under the water and wrapped her fingers around his straining erection.

"Not worried about someone seeing us?" he asked, though it was hard to think coherently with her hand, warm and insistent, stroking his cock.

Her eyes widened. "I hadn't thought of that. I forgot the road was so close." She looked over her shoulder then shrugged. "If anybody passes and sees a full bed and a bathing tub in the middle of the trees, they probably won't believe it's real, so I imagine they'll ignore us, too."

He laughed then lifted her up in a movement so fast it made her squeal. He stretched his legs beneath her and settled her on his lap. "I think you may be a bit of an exhibitionist, *raynia*. Get onto your knees." He held her around the waist to help her balance as she crouched so her knees bracketed his thighs.

"Am not," she said, throwing him a very sexy pout over her shoulder. "I was only thinking of you."

"Well then, thank you for your consideration. Lean forward." She did, bracing her hands on his knees. The sight of her curvy little ass angling toward him made his pulse race. He reached between her spread thighs, dipping his finger into the wet heat of her, spreading her lips. He guided her back until the tip of his cock just entered her, then with both hands on her hips, he pulled her down hard, ramming home. She groaned and arched her back, her hands gripping his thighs.

He didn't need to encourage her to move. She lifted up, slammed back down, setting a hard, steady rhythm. Water sloshed back and forth with her movements, raising a gentle wave. As her pace increased, water splashed over the sides of the tub, but neither of them paid attention. He gripped her hips, his fingers digging into flesh. She was so tight at this angle it took all his self-control to keep from coming too soon. After the night they'd shared, he wouldn't have thought he'd have to worry about that this morning, but with her sexy ass slamming into him, her tight pussy gripping him, it was all he could do not to erupt.

When she reached between her legs and cupped his balls he thought his head might explode. "Rowena," he groaned, straining to hold back.

She answered his unspoken plea by squeezing his testicles, rolling them around as she fucked him harder, faster. Her breathing came in pants, her moans increased. When she came, her muscles clamped hard around him, pushing his own orgasm beyond his control. He collapsed back against the tub, his eyes closed as he tried to calm his heartbeat. He managed just enough energy to rub her hip and bottom with one hand, but the hand shook slightly.

"Do you think we defeated the purpose of the bath?" she asked, her voice breathy.

He grinned without opening his eyes. "Not my purpose."

Her chuckle vibrated through where their bodies were still connected. With a groan, she rose up on her knees, releasing him, and started to climb out of the tub. He grabbed her hips and held her for a moment while he said the spell that would bring two towels to the edge of the tub. She grinned over her shoulder at him as she plucked up a towel and stood to dry off. He watched through eyes narrowed to slits, enjoying the sight of her naked body glistening in the dawn light.

When he could stand, he dried off, dropping a light kiss on her lips before climbing out of the tub. The grass beneath the tub was soggy but thick enough to keep away the mud. She shrugged apologetically as she laid the towel on the dirt near her pack and stepped on it to get dressed.

"What will you do with all this now? Won't it take more power to send it back?"

"It'll return to its original location later this morning. Nature of the spell I used."

She pursed her lips, but didn't comment.

When they were dressed and her gear repacked, they started off again, leaving the bed and bathtub sitting like some strange elfin bedroom in the middle of the trees.

Chapter Five

Rowena sat at the back of the pub, carefully hazed from the men filling the commons. Anyone who looked her way would barely notice her. They wouldn't realize she was a woman, they wouldn't see the sword on her back, but they *would* feel the need to avoid her corner of the room.

This was the fifth pub, in the third town, over the last week. And she'd finally found what she wanted.

Dorjan was here. And he had the oracle with him.

The bulk of his army camped a league from the village, readying to move again, so the rumors said, as soon as Dorjan had finished some business here with the local governor. Dorjan was on a campaign, moving south to the lands currently held by a powerful warlord named Umbrico. Umbrico was one of the few eastern warlords bordering Dorjan's lands still strong enough to hold Dorjan at bay. Rumor had it the "witch" Dorjan traveled with was his secret weapon against Umbrico.

And if Dorjan had managed to break the oracle, then she would be a spectacular weapon against his enemies.

The poor oracle. Rowena hated to think what the woman was going through. During her week's reconnaissance in these lands, she'd learned enough to know the warlord had no pity and no mercy. The oracle was Valen. She would have tried to hold out against him. And he wouldn't have held back in breaking her.

Rowena left the pub, keeping herself carefully hazed as she stepped back into the bright light of the village street. It was still early in the afternoon but already the townspeople looked worn out by their day. She turned toward the top of town, the rich area where the local soldiers barracked and the governor lived.

She wasn't sure whether Dorjan's presence in this particular village was welcome news or not. True, she'd been tracking him. Had known she would meet him somewhere soon. The question was, did he know she was here? He knew she was coming for the oracle. Had the oracle told him where Rowena would be?

Too hard to tell. Even if the oracle could predict Rowena's movements, oracles revealed their prophecies in ways often hard to interpret until after events had unfolded, even when what the oracle said seemed to be perfectly straightforward. Rowena's own parents had fallen victim to false assumptions about a prophecy, so she knew they were easy to misinterpret.

And outside of that first group of mercenaries, Dorjan hadn't sent anything else to stop her or slow her down. Did that mean he didn't know where she was? Or was he simply waiting for her to come to him?

Her only option was to continue with her mission, taking as many precautions as possible. She knew the location of the oracle now, and the warlord. She just had to get the oracle back.

Easier said than done, she thought with a hint of wry humor.

The job of the sword sworn was never easy. And because they were so well trained, and so few in number, the sword sworn almost always worked alone. It wouldn't be the first time one of her sisters faced overwhelming odds, some with less help than she had. Still, getting the oracle away from Dorjan wouldn't be simple.

She did a quick reconnoiter of the area where the warlord was said to be staying. The governor's house, a large white stone dwelling next to the governor's official offices, was an imposing place, more like a prison than a home. Tall walls circled three sides of the building and turned in to blend seamlessly with the front façade of the house. The tops of the walls were lined with metal spikes. The front door looked out onto the road, and was built of thick oak, reinforced with steel brackets. Arrow slit windows broke the solid white front of the house and surrounded the door. City soldiers patrolled the street. Men wearing Dorjan's crest guarded the door.

The governor's office, a similarly imposing block of a building, rose up to the left of the house. Outside the office, on the side farthest from the house, two corpses still hung from a gallows, their bodies rotting in the heavy air. Rowena thanked Alean the wind was blowing the stench in the opposite direction.

She didn't dare remain in the area longer. None of the villagers came this way, only the soldiers. She left with one last glance at the governor's house and went to find Kael.

She spotted him hovering near a market stall, absently studying a rack of cutlery. The knives were dull and poorly made compared to anything the Heron would have. She watched his slight frown a moment and wondered if he just disliked the state of the cutlery or something else bothered him. He looked up before she was near enough to speak, his gaze locking on to her as she approached.

He looked her over, checking for nonexistent injuries, and

she shook her head. His protective instincts were both endearing and a little annoying. She was the sword sworn after all.

"Our man is here," she murmured when she could speak to Kael without being overheard by the passing crowds.

"And the oracle?"

"With him. They're barricaded in the governor's house. I took a quick look. It's a fortress and patrolled by both city soldiers and some of Dorjan's own troops. The rest of his army is camped about a league away. They're supposed to be moving on south from here once Dorjan finishes his business with the governor."

"Did you see Dorjan?"

"No. But the guards on the governor's door wore his crest."

Kael fell silent and Rowena let her gaze run over the crowded street as he digested her news.

Hinsol was a dirty, depressing place, not much different from the other towns they'd been in since entering Dorjan's territory. It wasn't completely desiccated, not like the deadlands held by the southern wizards. In fact, from the look of the fields and bands of woodland they'd passed on their way here, this had probably once been a prosperous area.

Dorjan was draining the land, though, to feed his soldiers and fund his wars. He was greedier than his predecessor, not content to keep the tentative truce the eastern lords had developed. He wanted to expand his territory. And slowly killed his own lands to do it.

Now, the villages were trampled, dust dry except where sewage had gathered wetly on the roads, the fields barren, the few forests thinned and ravaged. There was little game left, and the domesticated livestock looked lean and ragged. As Rowena and Kael moved down the narrow street, they passed a man herding a team of oxen so thin their heavy bones stuck out sharply against their tough hides. The people looked just as desolate, their eyes hard and dead, their expressions bland.

And they had no way to fight back against the injustice, the abuse of their lands. The warlord's armies were too strong, the soldiers policing each village too quick to punish dissent. These milling, grim people lived under a heavy yoke and could no longer see beyond their next, painful step.

It tore at Rowena, clogging her empathic senses. She blocked most of the despondency, but some still leaked in. Her Aleanian soul wanted to help, to aid, to rescue these people who could no longer help themselves. But she was one woman. Even a sword sworn couldn't fix an entire land. She could only hope that by taking the oracle back from Dorjan, his future efforts would fail and the leader who replaced him would be more forgiving and respectful of his territory.

She startled when Kael closed his hand around hers—her left hand, leaving her sword arm free. She turned to see him staring at her, his gaze full of compassion. It still took her breath away, how he knew without any words, how he seemed to understand her instinctively.

She forced a smile. "Let's find an inn. We have some planning to do, and I'd rather do it in the comfort of a room where we're less likely to draw attention."

They tried two inns before they found one that would give them a room. And in that one, Rowena had to use a little mental push on the proprietor. It wasn't that the inns were full. The innkeepers held most of their rooms in reserve in case the soldiers wanted one. The inns lost money, waiting on these whims. But they'd lose their entire business if one of the soldiers couldn't be accommodated. Rowena used her mental nudge in an empty establishment, leaving the innkeeper with plenty of rooms if he needed them. She didn't want to cause these people any extra misery.

"What else can you do?" Kael asked, his voice low and curious as they headed up the creaking back stairs to their second floor room. "Besides haze your presence and influence people's thinking."

She nearly smiled at the admiration in his voice. "I can do lots of interesting things," she said with a wink.

She hadn't had to use her full range of psychic skills yet. And Kael had only experienced one of her talents firsthand so far. In the first town they'd entered, he'd wanted to go with her on her forays into the pubs for information. She refused, insisting he stood out too much and it would be easier for her to go unnoticed. He looked her over with a frank and heated gaze that made her blood pound harder. "I doubt that very much, baby. You're too damn sexy to go unnoticed."

She grinned and gave him a little taste of what she could do. She only hazed his mind a moment, blurred his thinking just long enough that he lost sight of her. He stepped back, glanced around, his brow snapping down over his eyes. He knew she couldn't move the way he did, using magic. He'd be able to feel it if she used magic. The confusion on his face made her chuckle. When she released him and he realized she was still standing in the same place, his eyes widened, then narrowed.

She laughed. "It's harder to do on a mage," she assured him. "But I can make people see and feel what I want them to. No one in the pub will even notice me."

He hadn't argued with her going alone on her fact-finding excursions since. One day soon she was going to have to let him know the full extent of her psychic skills, talents she'd inherited from her father. She might not be full Gryphatar, but she could use her mind almost as well.

When they were safely ensconced in the tiny but remarkably clean inn room, Rowena collapsed on the bed with a sigh. She closed her eyes and drew in her emotions, trying to cleanse herself of the bitterness of the villagers. She couldn't afford to feel pity. If she had to face Dorjan in order to rescue the oracle, she might have to kill him. But doing so would leave this already battered land in chaos. The various groups within the warlord's army, as well as the neighboring warlords and the bands of mercenaries working for Dorjan, would battle until the strongest managed to wrest full control. And even then, the new leader might be no better than Dorjan himself.

But she couldn't afford to think about that, about whether killing the warlord would be good or bad for the people he ruled. Her mission was to rescue one woman, a very important woman to the Valen. And as sword sworn, Rowena would do whatever it took to complete that mission.

She felt the bed dip under Kael's weight but didn't open her eyes.

"This is hard on you," he murmured, his finger tracing over the creases on her brow. "The way these people are living."

"One of the side effects of Gryphatar empathy. I'll get over it." She pulled in a breath. "We need to plan."

"Later. First you need to relax."

Her eyebrows quirked up but she kept her eyes closed. "I do?"

"You do. You won't be any good to the oracle if your mind is muddled by pity and exhaustion."

His warm palm covered her cheek, slid down her neck, over her shoulder, cupped her breast. She sucked in a breath, amazed she could still feel such fire so fast. Especially since they'd barely kept their hands off each other for the last three weeks. They hadn't allowed the sex to slow down the journey, but when they took a break or stopped for the night, they found time for making love. *At some point, the intensity has to ease,* she thought, arching against his massaging hand. If they went on like this, they were going to exhaust each other.

She reached up to where she knew his head bent over her, intent on pulling him down for a kiss. But he captured her wrists and eased her arms up over her head. "You're feeling responsible for the lives of these people?" he murmured, kissing her jaw.

"No. But what I do might affect what happens to them next."

"And you feel responsible for that. You feel as if you should fix things for them, control the outcome."

She frowned, tilted her chin up as his kisses moved to the hollow of her throat. "Maybe. I know I can't. But..."

"But you want to."

She sighed. "Yes."

"You can't control everything. Sometimes, you just have to let go and leave the world to its own devices."

"That's hard for me. For any Aleanian. It's part of our basic philosophy to protect those not able to protect themselves. It's what we do. And it's hard to let go that responsibility."

She blinked open her eyes. Kael stared down at her, his expression intent. "I know," he said, his deep voice quiet. "But, baby, you can't protect everyone. Sooner or later, they're going to have to take care of themselves."

She curved her lips in a wry half-smile. "Tell that to the high priestess."

He dropped his lips to hers, his kiss gentle. She sighed against his mouth and arched up for more. When she tried to move her arms, his grip on her wrists tightened. "Kael?"

He smiled, his eyes sparkling with mischief. The look made her instantly suspicious. "Kael…" This time her tone stretched with warning.

His grin grew. "You need to let go," he said. "You need to get used to the fact that not everything is in your control."

"Around you? What control have I had?"

He chuckled. "A lot more than you think. You've had me wrapped around your finger since you were fourteen. But that's not the point. The point is that you need to relax, and you need to give over responsibility to someone else."

"Meaning?"

His eyebrow quirked. She felt that strange tingling sensation she got whenever he used his magic, and an instant later, she felt the cool brush of silk against her hands. She arched her head back to see a beautiful orange and gold scarf lying across her hands and upper arms where they were still held against the bed.

She frowned, completely confused now. "What's that for?"

In answer, he twirled the scarf into a thick rope of silk. She watched in wonder, keeping her now free hands above her head.

"This," he said, "is a device to help you relinquish control."

"Oh?" A suspicion started to dawn. "And if I'd rather not relinquish control?"

"Do you trust me?" He asked the question very seriously, looking directly into her eyes.

She startled, blinked. Paused a moment to consider. Did she trust him enough to give him the control he asked for? They were soul twins. He would never willingly hurt her, not physically. But he had hurt her emotionally. Hurt her enough that she'd been willing to reject the other part of her soul in order to avoid further pain. He never had explained why he'd disappeared for twelve years. If it came up, he changed the subject.

Did she trust him?

She stared into the sincerity of his expression, the patience as he waited for her answer. What could she tell him? She *didn't* fully trust him with her heart yet. But she was about to go into battle with him at her back. And she trusted him to be there when she needed him. She did trust his honor, his strength. She'd already trusted him implicitly with her body.

Did she dare give in to curiosity? Could she abandon control?

"I trust you in this," she said finally, letting out a long breath as she made her choice.

Something flashed in his eyes but was quickly hidden. She couldn't begin to interpret the emotion she'd seen. What she felt from him was a mixture of lust, concern, a need to please, a wicked thrill at having her under his control. And something else twined into it all. But she couldn't separate the strange feeling or put a name to it. The intensity of his lust overpowered everything else. Before she could think about the elusive emotion too closely, she felt the silk scarf wrap around her wrists, binding her hands together.

Her stomach fluttered with a mix of nerves and excitement. It had never occurred to her that she might like giving over complete control to someone else, letting someone else have all the responsibility. But then again, she'd always assumed she'd die a virgin so what did she know?

Kael secured the free end of the scarf to the edge of the iron headboard behind her, stretching her just enough to keep her secure but not so much that her arms hurt. He kissed her gently on the lips, then moved down the bed, removed her boots and tossed them aside. She wiggled her hips to help him slide her trousers off, and felt strangely exposed lying there with her lower body naked but her upper body still dressed. She squirmed under Kael's stare, impatient to have him finish undressing her.

He stood at the foot of the bed, his gaze raking over her. Her heart hammered. She wanted his touch so badly she could barely stand it. And because her wrists were tied, there was nothing she could do to speed up the process. After a moment, he gripped her ankles and spread her wide. He knelt on the bed between her legs so she couldn't close them, the leather of his pants rubbing her inner thighs.

She tried bending her knees, intent on wrapping her legs around him and pulling him closer but he eased her legs straight again with gentle pressure.

"Shall I tie your ankles too?" he asked, his voice deep and husky.

His excitement at the idea rolled through her, but her own heart jumped in panic. Somehow, she still felt like she had an element of control with only her arms tied. He must have sensed her hesitance, her trembling of fear because his eyes narrowed. A moment later, she felt the delicate touch of silk on her ankles.

"Kael, I'm not so sure about this." Was that actual panic in her voice? She didn't panic. She was a sword sworn.

He grinned, an expression that managed to be both reassuring and wicked. "I won't hurt you."

"I know."

"And I can have you free in an instant if needs be."

She swallowed, nodded.

"Trust me," he murmured, and moved off the bed to bind her ankles.

Almost against her will she found herself tugging at the binding holding her arms.

"Don't pull hard," he cautioned. "Silk is more forgiving than metal, but I don't want you to hurt yourself."

She forced herself to relax, but it wasn't easy. With her legs spread wide and secured to the short posts at the bottom of the bed, she felt more vulnerable than she'd ever felt in her life. Her muscles flexed, tensing and relaxing as she tried to adjust to her confinement. Her stomach clenched. And to her surprise, she felt herself getting wetter with each passing moment. Fear and excitement boiled through her blood in a heady mixture, similar to the sensation she got during a fight. Except she was never, ever this vulnerable during a fight.

Kael's eyes darkened as he stared. His chest rose and fell with each ragged breath. She could feel the greedy, possessive hunger rolling through him, and her heart pounded hard in answer.

"There's something about having you only half undressed," he murmured. He knelt between her bound legs and laid his palm against her mound. "Especially when it's this part of you that's naked."

He dipped a finger between her lips and caressed in long strokes that made her tremble.

"Not that I don't love your beautiful breasts," he added, his full attention on the juncture between her thighs. He dipped his finger just inside her channel, tempting, teasing, not entering far before he pulled out again.

She tried to arch against his hand, and he dropped his touch entirely. She groaned in frustration and dropped her head back against the pillows.

He chuckled. "Stop trying to control what I do to you. My game. My rules. All you get to do is enjoy. But you'll stay frustrated if you don't give in and let me lead."

"But..." She squirmed on the sheets, twisting her wrists. "Kael, you're going to kill me this way."

"No, I won't. Now lay still."

With no small effort, she complied, forcing herself to stop moving. He smiled and her stomach contracted with pure lust. He reached for the buttons on her tunic, easing them out slowly, only opening the tunic when all the buttons were undone. She arched up when he told her to, and he slowly unwound the linen binding her breasts. When the cool air hit her bare skin, she shivered and her nipples puckered. Kael groaned, cupped her, squeezing her nipples gently. She closed her eyes and savored the feel of his hands. She arched into his touch, unable to control herself, but to her infinite relief, he didn't pull away.

"You do have beautiful breasts," he murmured. He leaned forward and pulled one taut peak into his mouth.

Her arms flexed, an instinctive urge to thread her fingers into his hair and hold him close. The silk on her wrists pulled tighter. He took his time, suckling and kissing each breast, toying with her hardened nipples until she thought she might scream. She felt each tug of his lips as a line of fire directly to her pussy, pulling her tighter. An orgasm was building just from the feel of his mouth on her breasts. Her stomach clenched and her thighs flexed. She started to pant.

She wanted to pull her legs together to hold the sensation back, but the silk held her, keeping her open and vulnerable. Her hips bucked up, bringing her into contact with Kael's hard stomach. The feel of his muscles skimming against her overly sensitive skin made her cry out. He reached down and grabbed her hip in one hand, holding her against the mattress so she was no longer touching him.

Her body shook, trembling out of her control. She had no defenses, no relief. She teetered on the edge, so close a single touch would send her over. And still he drove her further, using only his mouth on her breasts. When he stopped, she almost cried. She was wound so tight she thought she might snap at any moment. She watched him, looking down at her, his gaze so hot she could feel it on her skin. Her body screamed with frustration and need, and there was nothing she could do. Nothing but wait for Kael.

He reached out and trailed a hand over her stomach. Her muscles bunched and shivered. "I had intended to draw this out longer," he said, his voice rough and quiet.

She moaned as his hand slipped over her hipbone, across her lower stomach. He moved off the bed and removed his trousers. She vibrated with anticipation and just a touch of fear as he crawled back on the bed—terrified he'd leave her hanging on this edge with no relief.

He braced himself above her, his cock poised to enter her. She wanted desperately to rub against him, urge him in, but she stayed perfectly still so he wouldn't move away. He rubbed his lips against hers, kissed her deeply and plunged into her. He pounded once, twice and she came, crying out against his mouth. Her arms and legs strained against the bindings as pleasure rolled over her. She jerked once against the silk ties and then relaxed, giving over completely to the feel of him inside her, the play of his tongue against hers, the hard rhythm he set.

There was nothing she could do, no way she could move. In the end, she had no choice but to allow him to give her pleasure and take his own. She let go all responsibility, all control and let him do what he wanted with her.

And what he did was heaven.

When he finally released her arms and legs, she was drained, sated and almost too tired to move. Only the overwhelming urge to hug him pushed her to force her slack body into motion. She draped her arms around his neck and held him. He nuzzled her throat, cuddling her close. And it came to her in that quiet moment—whether she trusted him with her heart or not, he had it.

Chapter Six

Rowena edged along the outer wall of the governor's house, keeping to the shadows and carefully hazing both herself and Kael from the two guards ahead. Earlier in the evening, Kael had discovered a small door through the wall circling at the back of the house. Two soldiers guarded it, but the area was shadowed from the main street at the front, giving Rowena and Kael more privacy to overpower the guards and gain entry to the inner yard. They'd been watching the house since full dark, timing the movements of the soldiers, watching for Dorjan. The warlord himself never showed. But Rowena hadn't really expected to see him.

They waited for an opening, a moment well past the middle of the night when the soldiers on the back gate looked bored and complacent. Then Rowena and Kael eased toward them.

Kael didn't dare use magic yet. He'd risk revealing himself to Dorjan's wizard if he did. Even though none of the rumors mentioned the wizard being in town, Rowena had no doubt the man would be here somewhere. Dorjan knew a sword sworn was coming for the oracle. He wouldn't be careless enough to bring her anywhere without the protection of his sorcerer.

So Rowena used her own talents to keep the soldiers from seeing her and Kael. It was harder than disguising only herself, but she managed, getting them within touching distance of the guards. Then she stepped up close to one and whispered in his ear. The man's eyes widened. He held perfectly still for several heartbeats. Then he dropped his sword and charged off between the few buildings that rose up behind the house, leaving his comrade to shout after him. The second guard suddenly realized he wasn't alone. He spun to face Kael, and Rowena knocked him unconscious with the pommel of her sword. She reinforced his unconscious state with a mental shove.

Kael raised an eyebrow. "I'm feeling a bit useless here."

She chuckled quietly as she jimmied open the door's lock. "Sword sworn are used to working alone. But you're a handy distraction."

He patted her ass affectionately and followed her through the door.

The courtyard beyond was barren and muddy. Rowena scowled. They must soak it on purpose as it hadn't rained in weeks, maybe months. She thought it an awful waste of water given the parched-looking state of the fields surrounding the town, but she couldn't argue with the logic of such a simple safeguard. It was hard to sneak around unnoticed if you left muddy footprints behind you. No wonder the lock on the door had been so easy to pry open. Unwelcome guests would never get through that back gate and into the house without leaving plenty of evidence of their presence.

Maybe they could take their boots off? Probably broken glass or some other nasty trick at the entrances to prevent that. She sighed. Well, they'd just have to take the chance and hope they weren't spotted before they found the oracle. She prepared to move out into the mud when Kael stopped her with a hand on her arm.

"Allow me," he murmured near her ear.

In a blink, the mud turned to dried, caked earth. Rowena

gaped. She'd felt the usual tingle of Kael's magic but so slight, she would have been convinced it was her imagination if not for the evidence of the dry ground. If the wizard felt that use of power at all, it was just possible he'd dismiss it as imagination too.

"Not so useless after all," Kael whispered, his breath brushing warmly against her neck.

"*Hmm.* I suppose you have your uses." She followed him this time, guarding their backs and trying hard not to smile. This was serious business—either one of them could be killed. But Kael had succeeded in relaxing her that afternoon and easing her sense of responsibility for those she couldn't help. She felt focused now, sharp. Able to face any challenge. And a little part of her enjoyed the danger of their situation. If she died tonight, she intended to savor the last minutes of her life. She was an Aleanian after all.

They made it to the house without attracting attention. She'd expected more soldiers to patrol inside the wall, but if they did, they were in another area. She tested the first door they came to leading into the house, found it locked and considered her options. Did she pick the lock or look for another way in?

She stretched out her psychic senses, hunting for the feel of a person beyond the door, a flicker of emotion, the familiar touch of a human mind. When she didn't feel anything, she made her choice. They might not get another chance to get inside without stumbling into a member of the household staff. She re-sheathed her sword, pulled out two thin slivers of metal from the pouch on her belt and knelt down in front of the lock. Kael stood over her, his sword in hand, watching the courtyard.

A few moments later, she grunted softly in triumph and stood. "There's no one in the room beyond," she whispered to

Kael, "but I'm not sure any farther than that. I need to find a single solider, or better a servant. Someone on their own. I only need a few minutes with them to get the location of the oracle, but I'd rather not get caught while I'm interrogating."

He nodded and eased open the door, going through first. Rowena closed the door behind her, carefully locking it again from the inside. Then she studied her surroundings, smiling slightly. As she'd suspected there were sharp metal barbs scattered across the inner floor—painful to bare feet but negotiable with boots. The room they'd slipped into was some sort of storage room, filled to the rafters with barrels and sacks. The barrels looked to hold mostly beer, and the sacks were filled with flour, sugar and various beans. Spices and dried meats hung from the rafters giving the room a pleasant aroma that made her stomach rumble. She grinned when Kael glanced at her and raised a brow. They'd eaten dinner at the inn, but the food hadn't been much better than her oatcake rations. This storeroom smelled like it would produce some very nice meals.

She eased open the only other door in the room and felt the touch of a sleeping mind as soon as she stepped into the large kitchen beyond. She put a hand to her lips to warn Kael, then eased toward the giant hearth at one end of the kitchen. In the ashes in front of the grate, warming his back by the still-glowing coals, lay the smallest boy Rowena had ever seen.

It hurt her heart to wake him, but if anyone knew where the prisoners were kept, it would be a kitchen mouse. She touched his mind, eased him awake and directly into her thrall. He wouldn't even remember being brought out of his sleep.

He grumbled a little, despite her empathic reassurance, and rubbed his eyes. She gave a gentle mental push to edge his thinking toward what she wanted to know. She wasn't as good at reading minds as her father or even her siblings. She could talk telepathically a little, and because of her empathy, she could usually interpret the information she picked up from other minds accurately. But it wasn't as easy for her as it was for her full Gryphatar family.

Fortunately, a sleepy little boy's mind was easier than most. She coaxed him toward the brief images of chains, the trembling of fear and fascination. And there it was, a clear image of the oracle locked in a dark room. She was sitting on a small bed with a thin mattress. One leg iron wrapped around her ankle and attached to a long, thick chain secured to the opposite wall. Her wrists were cuffed together in front of her, the manacles chained to the leg iron to make standing or walking awkward if not impossible.

Through the more prominent fear coloring the boy's thoughts, Rowena sensed his sympathy for the strange woman in the dark cell. He was terrified of displeasing the governor, yet he'd risked a beating to bring the oracle an extra chunk of bread for her supper. Rowena's heart tugged. She tried to remind herself she couldn't save the boy from his labors. But, oh, how she wanted to.

She stayed with him just long enough to learn how he snuck into the holding cell without having to pass many of the soldiers, then she eased him back to sleep. She hesitated by the hearth, reluctant to leave him behind.

Kael's hand dropped onto her shoulder. He leaned in and whispered in her ear, "He'll be okay, baby."

"The governor beats him, Kael." Her whisper sighed out full of resignation and pity.

"Don't worry. He'll be okay."

She felt a slight tingling, the flashing sense of Kael casting a spell. When the feeling subsided, she looked up at him. "What did you do?"

"Just a little protection spell. The governor won't be

inclined to beat him for some time. At least not until he's old enough to protect himself."

"You shouldn't have spent the power," she said, though her eyes misted, and she had to swallow hard around the lump in her throat. "But I'm glad you did."

She led Kael toward a door concealed behind a cupboard at one side of the kitchen. The door led to the hidden corridor she'd discovered in the boy's memories. At one time, the passage had been used by the servants to get around the house unseen, but it had fallen into disrepair over the years and was too dangerous to use now. The boy discovered it on accident and used it, despite the hazards, to avoid the harsh fists of the governor's men. Only a few people in the household still remembered the doorway even existed.

The corridor was pitch dark. They'd need light to get through, but she didn't want to risk Kael using a mage light spell. After a moment of searching, she found the lamp the boy had hidden just inside the corridor. She used a small coal from the kitchen fire to light the taper. The glass casing around the lamp was smudged and cracked but it still glowed enough to cut through the passageway's gloom.

With the images she'd gleaned from the boy's memories, she led the way through the narrow tunnel, down a flight of stairs, and deeper into the house until they came to the door that opened into the basement holding cells. She left the still burning lamp just inside the hidden passage and opened the door carefully, relieved to hear it didn't squeak. She looked out into a tiny room used for storing barrels of wine. There was barely enough space for Rowena to squeeze through. Kael nearly toppled the head-high stacks of barrels twice trying to ease his bulk through the narrow gap that led to the outer corridor. She could feel his need to curse and almost laughed.

At the uncovered doorway opening into the main part of the basement, Rowena stopped to study the surroundings. To call the place a prison was to flatter the damp, dank grouping of cells that lined the edges of the large square chamber. But to call it a dungeon would have been an exaggeration. It was as if someone had converted storage rooms into holding cells and hadn't bothered to either improve the atmosphere or make it worse.

The single guard on duty at the far end of the room snored softly in his chair—thanks to a mental push from Rowena. There was only one prisoner that she could feel. The oracle.

She pulled her sword from her scabbard and eased closer to the sleeping guard. Kael held back, watching the only two doors into the chamber—the main entrance and the secret tunnel entrance. She glanced back once and smiled a little at his alert and ready stance. It was nice having Kael to cover her.

She eased past the sleeping guard and glanced through the small slit window into the oracle's cell. A small woman with black hair lay curled up on a thin, lumpy looking mattress. The chains binding her arms and ankle were identical to the image in the boy's head, though the chain connecting her to the far wall wasn't as thick, and the chain linking her arm manacles to her ankle was longer than the boy imagined. The oracle still wouldn't be able to stand straight, but she could at least stand.

From Rowena's vantage, the oracle looked asleep. She tested the door latch, found it locked as expected, and eased back to the sleeping guard. The keys were half hanging out of a pocket, but they were attached to a chain secured somewhere inside the guard's clothes. Short of stripping him, she couldn't find a way to release the chain and free the keys.

She frowned, considering. If she had the same power as her father, she could simply make the guard get up and open the door for her. But she wasn't that strong. She could bend his mind so he didn't know she was standing in front of him but bending his physical movements to her will was a lot harder.

She pulled a sharp Heron dagger from her hip sheath and carefully pried one of the chain links apart. Not subtle, but it got her the keys without having to disturb the guard's sleep.

She unlocked the door to the cell then turned to check on Kael. He glanced back in the same moment and winked. She blew him a kiss and entered the cell. Two steps into the room, the oracle suddenly sat straight up in bed, her black eyes wide, her mouth forming a small "o" of distress. Rowena raised a hand to calm the woman, but the oracle shook her head.

"Get out. Don't—"

In the same instant, Rowena heard Kael shout her name. She turned to jump back out of the cell and felt like she hit a wall. Blackness enveloped her, sucking her under. She had a moment to realize she'd triggered a spell of some kind, an instant to reach out mentally to Kael, and then she knew nothing more.

Chapter Seven

Rowena came slowly awake, her head aching, her arms unaccountably sore. She tried to stretch out her senses to judge if there was anyone nearby before she opened her eyes. But her mind felt fuzzy, like it was stuffed with wool. She couldn't sense anything.

A tingle of panic started in her stomach. She controlled the urge to open her eyes quickly, instead taking assessment of her physical state. Her arms were pulled up tight above her head. When she shifted one hand in the tiniest of movements, she felt the cold metal of the manacle holding her up. Her shoulders burned from being confined to the awkward angle and her wrists were numb from holding her unconscious weight. Hot stone at her back burned even through her tunic, and sweat trickled down between her shoulder blades. She shifted a foot and found her legs manacled as well.

Not good, she thought, more annoyed than scared. She imagined she'd be scared soon enough, especially since her mental senses seemed to be blocked. But for the moment, her discomfort overrode her fear. She blinked her eyes open to face her surroundings.

Her head screamed as light speared into her eyes. She clenched her eyelids shut again, wincing. She breathed deep and slow through her teeth until the pain eased, then she opened her eyes more slowly. After a moment, her blurry vision cleared, and she looked around.

Her holding cell was more obviously built for purpose than the cell the oracle had been in—rough walls of thick gray stone, a single high window covered by bars that kept her in but did nothing to keep the weather out, a short wooden door to her left made of hard, impenetrable oak, to her right a straw mattress sprawled on the ground. Her chains secured her to the wall opposite the window. At the base of that wall, a rat scurried for covering shade.

She was alone in the little room.

Straightening to take the weight off her wrists, she groaned as muscles protested. Her legs felt rubbery and she had to lock her knees to keep them from giving out. Feeling came back into her wrists with a stomach-turning combination of tingles and pain. Mid-day light poured into the hot, sticky cell. She'd been unconscious for at least half a day.

As the pain in her head dimmed, she tried stretching out her psychic senses again. And again she came up against a barrier—like a wall of cotton. She could feel the rat, off to her right under the mattress now, but nothing beyond the walls of her cell.

Cursing under her breath, she forced herself to work out what had happened. A spell trap must have been set into the door of the oracle's cell. The spell had incapacitated her, giving her no time to get out or resist. She wasn't a mage so she couldn't have felt the trap. And obviously the protections the priestesses had given her hadn't been enough to protect against the effects of the spell. She wondered if Kael had felt it and that's why he'd called out to her.

Kael.

Now fear trickled in past her annoyance. Was he okay?

What had happened after she'd triggered the spell? Where was he? She had a split second to consider trying to reach him telepathically before the undersized door to her cell swung open.

"So. Awake at last."

A man nearly as wide as the door ducked into the cell. When he straightened, he stood as tall as Rowena. He was thickly muscled under the jerkin and leather trousers he wore. His dark hair hugged his scalp. His features were large but proportioned well. Three thin scars ran down his left cheek, white against the dark tan of his skin, and she could just see the edge of an intricate tattoo above the collar of his jerkin. He had a sword strapped to his hip, worn with the casual comfort of someone used to having the weapon there, and a second short dagger just visible above the top of his left boot.

Dorjan.

His pale gray eyes sparkled with a gleam of triumph that made her want to snarl. She watched the warlord closely as he stalked toward her, his gaze running over her body. Her hands fisted involuntarily before she could control the reaction. He smiled at the sign of her anger.

"I can hardly believe it," he said, his voice low and silky. "An actual Gryphatar. Well," he said with a shrug, "I know you're not full Gryphatar, obviously. You wouldn't be sword sworn if you were a shape-shifter. But you have family in Gryphaldin. An aerie. And I imagine they'll want you back."

Rowena's heart lurched and her eyes widened despite her attempt to keep the surprise from her expression. He knew she was part Gryphatar. And that's why he'd captured her? Not because she'd come to free his captive?

"Where's the Valen's oracle?" She risked the question, trying to gauge his intent. Frustration gnawed at her. For the first time in her life, she couldn't use her mental skills to read another human. Even her empathy was dampened. So she had to watch him closely for any physical sign of his emotions, something she wasn't as good at as a non-empath might be. She bit the inside of her cheek to keep from cursing in irritation.

"A couple of doors down," Dorjan answered, "doing what she's supposed to be doing. Awaiting my pleasure."

He smirked. His gaze dropped to Rowena's breasts and lingered. She gave in to her snarl this time, unable to control her rising anger.

He chuckled. "And you, my tasty morsel, will be serving my pleasure for many nights to come. Until your family agrees to my terms."

Rowena's fury moved deeper then, turning cold. He underestimated her if he thought she'd let him rape her while he blackmailed her family. Her expression closed up, her rage moving beneath a cold mask. She tested her mental skills again, found them still blocked and knew his wizard had put a spell on the room to suppress her natural talents. But outside this room...

She held herself perfectly still and didn't so much as flinch when Dorjan closed the space between them. He cupped her breast, squeezed hard. She didn't snarl, didn't curse, didn't struggle, didn't even alter her breathing. She stared at him, straight in the eyes, and showed no reaction to his touch. His smirk dropped.

He paced away, his muscles flexing and bunching as he moved. "That man with you, the wizard?" He swung around to face her, his eyes narrowing. "He abandoned you, you know. You should hire better help next time."

She knew, without having to feel his emotions, he was

trying to goad her into a reaction. She didn't give him one. She simply stared. Inside, she seethed. What did he know about Kael? Was Kael still alive? He had to be. They were bonded fully now. She'd know, even through the wizard's spell, if Kael were dead. So where was he?

Then a burst of inspiration hit her. Despite the spell, she *knew* she'd be aware of Kael's death. Did that mean he could still sense her? Was their bond strong enough to allow her to touch his mind, despite the spell? The wizard might not have known they were *raynyn*. From Dorjan's reaction, he didn't seem to know. And if he didn't, his wizard wouldn't. Rowena sent up a silent thank you to the oracle for keeping that one secret.

But to reach Kael and give him time to get to her, she would have to distract Dorjan. Her eyebrows popped up. And she smiled.

The warlord's gaze narrowed, his frown deepening.

She laughed out loud at the suspicion on his face and mentally called out to Kael. "You're probably right," she said to Dorjan. "It's hard to get a trustworthy wizard these days." She leaned against the wall as if she weren't chained but merely relaxing there. "Your wizard is good though. I didn't anticipate that spell in the oracle's cell." *Kael? Are you there? If you can hear me, react. I won't be able to hear you if you try to talk to me, but I can feel you. Give me a reaction of some kind.*

She nearly gasped aloud as a flood of emotions—fear, anger, longing, need, and relief—washed through her. The sheer joy of knowing Kael was okay overwhelmed her. And from the strength of his emotions, he wasn't far away.

"I pay good money to have the best wizard on hand," Dorjan said, smiling again. "Waging war can be expensive, though. I need more resources."

"Is that what you think you'll get by holding me? Money?" She chuckled. "Not likely. The aerie disowned me when I joined the Aleanians. Too mercenary for their blood." *Kael? I'm not sure where I am. I'm not in the governor's house anymore, though. Can you track me through this bond?* She felt such an absolute sense of determination from him it was as if he'd shouted "yes" in her mind. She smiled and hoped Dorjan thought the smile was for him.

The warlord tipped his head to one side, studying her. "I've never heard anyone refer to the Aleanian sword sworn as mercenary. Though, to be fair that is what you are, isn't it? A band of very well paid mercenaries. How much did the Valen pay you to retrieve their oracle?"

"A lot," she lied. The Aleanians and the Valen had an agreement of sorts. For something truly serious that threatened the clan, an Aleanian sword sworn would be sent out to help without charge. In return, the clan quietly protected one of the Malyk borders, a buffer between the Aleanians' homeland and the far northern empire. The link between the Aleanians and the Valen was kept quiet, though, because it could be considered an "act of war" alliance by the eastern warlords.

"Shame you won't be able to collect the fee," Dorjan said, "but I still need my oracle. She's brought me great success in the wars."

"I imagine. But how do you know how to interpret her prophecies? Aren't prophets notoriously difficult to decipher?"

"If she tries any fancy word games, she's punished. She doesn't play those games with me anymore."

A sudden welling of concern from Kael let Rowena know he felt her distress. It took all her self-control not to let Dorjan see her boiling fury. Bad enough he'd kidnapped and used an oracle. To hear he beat her or worse to suit his greed made

Rowena furious. Everything in her screamed to protect, to rescue the helpless woman from this brutal tyrant.

The only thing keeping her under control was the knowledge that Kael was closer. She could feel his emotions more clearly now, sense his presence. And the closer he got, she realized with a start, the easier it was for her to feel Dorjan's emotions. The spell keeping her psychic talents in check seemed to be weakening.

"What did your wizard do to the room?" she asked suddenly, pleased when she saw Dorjan start at the change of subject. It was a subtle reaction, just a twitch of his lips, but a reaction nonetheless. And better yet, she could feel his irritation and suspicion. She hadn't reacted the way he'd wanted her to at the mention of the oracle's punishment. He didn't like that she was acting contrary to his expectations. She checked a smug smile, and the tension in her stomach relaxed.

"When the oracle told me you were part Gryphatar," he said, "I knew we'd need protection from psychic challenges. And I was right to assume you'd have some of the famous Gryphatar skills, wasn't I?"

She tried a shrug but it wasn't very effective with her arms wrenched up over her head. "I'm an empath," she said because there was no reason to hide that part of her skill. "Whatever he's done is blocking that. It's kind of nice actually. Quite."

"Is that your only talent?"

His eyes narrowed. She felt his suspicion again. And his disappointment.

"Nothing else but being able to sense emotion?"

"'Fraid so. Not enough Gryphatar blood I guess. Not that I mind. Damned inconvenient to be stuck in Gryphaldin your entire life."

"Still..." He sidled closer, watching her carefully.

To her disgust, his lust surged again as he stepped near enough to touch her. The anger she felt flowing from Kael took her breath away. She had to swallow hard to keep from flinching at her *raynei's* fury. She didn't want Dorjan to think she was flinching from him. Any reaction would give him too much power.

"Still," Dorjan said again as his hands closed on her waist. "You can never be too careful in my line of work."

His gaze darkened and his attention turned to her lips. She forced herself not to dampen her suddenly dry lips or snarl in response to his nearness. She cringed inwardly, though. Dorjan was distracted all right, but not in the way she'd hoped.

"Where's your wizard now?" she asked, trying to get him back to the original distraction. "Protecting the oracle? I'm surprised you'd take the chance being alone with an Aleanian sword sworn." She spaced her words, making sure each came out calmly. Her skin crawled where Dorjan's hands flexed against her waist. Her stomach turned when one of his hands slid up to cup her breast again.

"I think you're helpless enough at the moment," he murmured. He licked his lips and let his gaze wander down to her breasts. "Between the wizard's spell and the chains..." He met her gaze. "I'd say you're at my mercy." He smiled and moved against her so she felt the bulge of his erection pressing into her stomach.

She couldn't stop her heart from pounding harder now. Couldn't completely hide her building disgust and anger. He wanted a reaction from her, she could feel it. He wanted her fear, wanted her to struggle. She resisted an intense need to fight, uselessly, only because she could sense Kael closer, very close now.

She hated feeling helpless this way with Dorjan. The feel of his hands on her, his body pressed against hers, made her physically sick. But worse, so much worse, was the obscene parody this made of her time yesterday afternoon with Kael. She tried hard not to link the two in her mind, to ignore any similarities between being tied and helpless for Kael and being chained and under Dorjan's control. The sheer rage pumping out of Kael now, flowing into her, helped keep her grounded and her disgust under her own control.

And it reminded her strongly that what she and Kael shared was something special, a loving act of mutual consent. What Dorjan wanted was rape.

She stretched out with her mind again. The warlord's emotions were stronger now. She could sense him easier. The barrier of the spell was coming down. She tried one small mental push, a subtly implanted suggestion. *You want to move your right hand away from my breast.* The hand painfully squeezing her breast lowered to her waist.

Dorjan looked up then, his eyes widening as he met her gaze. And she knew her sense of triumph must have shown. *Back away,* she commanded, pushing harder this time, ignoring subtlety. *Now!*

Anger fed her talent. Dorjan jerked backward. She couldn't control him physically with her mind, but she could force him to think what she wanted him to think. And she made him see horror in the face he stared at. She forced a nightmare into his mind. A nightmare with eagle wings and lion claws.

Dorjan scrambled away from her until his back pressed against the opposite wall near the window, his eyes wide with terror. He shook his head in denial, trying to force her out of his mind. And because he had a strong will, his efforts might have worked under normal circumstances. Her psychic talents had always been more effective in subtlety and illusion. She could

211

haze a mind better even than most Gryphatar. But she couldn't continue to force terror on someone who recognized the emotion as coming from outside himself.

Normally.

In that moment, though, she knew Dorjan couldn't shake her free, and she poured the illusion into him without mercy.

She didn't have time to analyze the increase in her power, the surge of certainty that she could drive Dorjan insane if she wanted to, because suddenly the door of her cell exploded outward. Door, frame, even part of the wall disintegrated in a flash of dust. And through the dust stepped Kael.

Rowena released Dorjan then, her senses overwhelmed by the sight of her *raynei*. An aura of energy surrounded him, crackling with his rage. His eyes glowed with it, his hair moved in a non-existent breeze caused by the swirling of magic around him.

"You dare touch my *raynia*?" His voice boomed in the small room, deeper, stronger than a human voice should be, thundering with power.

Dorjan's warrior instincts took over where most men would have collapsed into a puddle of jelly at the sight of the angry Heron. The warlord drew his sword, held it at the ready, never taking his gaze off Kael.

Rowena watched in helpless fascination as the two men faced off, circling, swords held in double-fisted grips. Dorjan was a few inches shorter than Kael, his reach not so long, but he was nearly Kael's equal in muscular girth. When their swords met, Rowena felt the reverberating clash through the stones at her feet. The fight was more impressive than any she'd seen, their skills nearly matched. Kael was better, and he was stronger. But Dorjan's movements were fed by the desperation of a man looking at his own death.

When Dorjan slipped under Kael's guard long enough to cut a slice along his arm, Rowena gasped and jerked at the chains holding her wrists. She swallowed the impulse to scream Kael's name. He didn't need the distraction, but that moment of terror had nearly overridden all her training. She forced her arms to relax to prevent the manacles on her wrists from cutting any deeper.

And then suddenly, the air changed. Crackled. Wavered with power like heat. Dorjan slammed backward against a wall, his body pinned, arms outstretched. For an instant, Rowena thought it was one of Kael's spells, but then she looked at him and saw his eyes rolling back in his head.

No! Not now! Not another seizure. Dorjan would kill him. And she was chained to the damned wall! She jerked at her bonds, hard this time and felt blood trickle down her wrists. "Kael!" She barely heard her voice above the pumping of her heart, the blood rushing through her veins.

Time slowed, the air thickened, every tiny detail in the room became clear and distinct. The sound of the rat, the strained breathing of Dorjan, the dirt filling the spaces between the gray stones of the wall. Her gaze shifted to Kael. He stood with his sword held in a double-fisted grip in front of him, the point angled toward the ceiling. His eyes were closed now, his expression taut, the muscles of his arms bulging. She drew in a breath to shout his name again.

And stopped.

A whisper wove through her mind, indistinct and overpowering. Not a voice. A feeling. But not Kael and not Dorjan. Something else. Something...familiar. The feeling wrapped itself around her mind, wove through her thoughts, tangled with her senses. There was a knowing, a belonging that tugged at her heart, brought tears to her eyes. *You're mine*, the feeling said. *And I am yours.*

"Yes," Rowena murmured. And the cuffs holding her wrists and ankles exploded.

She stepped away from the wall, her arms aching as they dropped to her sides. Muscle spasms and cramps nearly doubled her over. She winced, rolled her shoulders to speed up her returning blood circulation. Then she looked up and her gaze snagged on Kael's sword. It seemed to be...singing. Almost a purr. She held out a hand and the sword flew to her, slapping gently into her palm. When she closed her fingers around the grip, it felt as if the sword had been made just for her. It felt like coming home.

Sighing out a breath in wonder, Rowena studied the glowing purple blade, the faint but distinct symbols etched into the steel, the sharp edges that winked in the light pouring in through the cell's single window. She glanced up to see Kael watching her. He looked normal again, if pale, no sign of the seizure she'd been so terrified of a moment before. His green eyes sparked, his lips lifted in a slight smile that was at once hesitant and strangely triumphant.

"I don't understand," she said.

"The sword is yours. I always thought she was supposed to be. Her name is Ca'laez."

"A mage sword? But how is that possible? My mother has one."

He nodded, his smile quirked. "I worried about that too when I heard about Ba'nari. It's never happened in our recorded history that two mage swords claimed members of the same family. But it's happened now. The claiming can't be faked."

"Why didn't you tell me?"

"I couldn't. Not until Ca'laez claimed her owner."

Rowena nodded, but didn't really understand. She supposed there would be time later for all her questions. At the moment, she had a warlord to deal with and an oracle to rescue.

She turned to Dorjan.

He still hung against the wall, his arms spread wide, but the sword tightly gripped in his hand. His teeth were clenched, his jaw tight as he fought against the magical hold keeping him in place. *Are you doing that, Ca'laez?* she thought. And suddenly Dorjan was released.

Rowena gasped. It seemed she and her sword had a lot to learn about each other. *Did you dissolve the wizard's spell too?* she wondered.

"I don't know what's going on," Dorjan growled, distracting Rowena from her new weapon, "but you're both going to die now. I don't care how much you would have been worth."

Kael raised a hand, but Rowena stopped him with a nod. "I was the one he thought he could use," she said, without taking her gaze off Dorjan. "I'm the one he has to face."

The warlord laughed. "I don't care if you are a sword sworn, bitch. I've been a warrior all my life. I've run over armies. You don't stand a chance."

She grinned. "Well then," she said, barely repressing a chuckle. "Shall we?"

Despite her sore muscles, the wounds around her wrists and ankles, Rowena had never felt stronger, more coordinated, more sure of her skill. The sword flowed with her body, no mere steel tool, but a living thing that knew her thoughts almost as soon as she did, adjusting to her style effortlessly. The sword didn't actually do any of her fighting. It was simply the perfect weapon for her to wield. Adrenaline and joy surged through her blood. This was what a battle was supposed to be like, she thought as she rained blow after blow down on Dorjan's frantic defense. This was the art of it. The beauty.

In the midst of her awe and excitement, she forgot why she fought Dorjan. She didn't even feel rage or anger toward him anymore. He was an afterthought, a sparring partner while she learned to wield her new blade. She saw it in his eyes, the moment when he realized she would win no matter what he did. She was better, she was faster, she didn't need to use her psychic skills. She wasn't even trying hard.

He roared in rage and animal fear. Charging her, trying to drive her into a corner. She laughed and circled away. Shame the cell was so small. She needed more room to get to know Ca'laez better.

She was so caught up in the fierce joy of using her very own mage sword, she didn't anticipate Dorjan's desperation. Between one blink and the next, he shifted and swung his blade to line just under Kael's chin. She sucked in a gasp and took a step closer, but Dorjan shook his head.

"Don't. He's your *raynei*? Well, if you want him to live, you back off. I have no intention of dying in this stinking cell at the hands of a mere woman."

She would have pointed out that this "mere woman" had outstripped him in skill to such an extent that he'd resorted to taking a hostage, but she was too concerned for Kael to bother. Kael was weaponless now that the sword had come to her. And she could tell by the narrowing of his eyes, his slight grimace, that he hadn't protected himself magically from Dorjan's attack. It wouldn't take much for Dorjan to slit Kael's throat. And she couldn't close the space between them quick enough to prevent it. Fear trickled into her blood stream, spiking her adrenaline.

Can you do something? she asked Kael, mind to mind. She felt a distinct shrug. The sensation didn't make her feel better.

Fine. When the signal comes, move back out into the hall. She felt his question and said, *You'll understand when it happens.*

Then she turned the full force of her attention on Dorjan.

His eyes widened. He took a startled step forward, his sword moving away from Kael. Her *raynei* didn't hesitate. He faded backward into the corridor. Dorjan swung around in a wide circle, searching for two people he could no longer see. She allowed him to see her again when she knew Kael was well out of the way.

"What did you do? Where is he?" Dorjan advanced on her, but his eyes were bulging with shock.

"Despite everything you've done, I might have let you live," she told him, raising her sword, "if you hadn't threatened the life of my *raynei*. For that, no mercy."

All her Aleanian-trained compassion for life sank under the weight of her white-hot rage. And Dorjan didn't stand a chance.

When she stepped from the cell, her body shook as adrenaline left her system. Kael was waiting, his arms crossed over his chest as he leaned against the wall not far down the corridor. He lifted away from the wall and uncrossed his arms when he saw her. Without a word, she walked to him and fell into his embrace.

Chapter Eight

They left Dorjan's lands as quickly and quietly as they could with the battered oracle. The upheaval they left behind gave them enough time to get the woman away before anyone thought to come after them. Because of his fight with Dorjan's wizard and his passing of the mage sword, Kael's powers were too drained to transport them all magically, so they stole a couple of horses to aid their escape. To both Kael and Rowena's surprise, just being on horseback seemed to help the oracle.

They returned her to her grateful people two weeks later. She'd undergone such trauma at Dorjan's hands, though, her clan leader felt it might be years before she was fully healed enough to function as oracle again. But she was theirs and they intended to take care of her.

On the journey home, Kael waited with no little patience for Rowena to say something about their future together, something about the mage sword. He hadn't pressed her on the matter as they smuggled the oracle out of Dorjan's lands and back to the Valen. But now they were alone. And it was eating away at him, wanting to talk about what it meant that she owned the mage sword now.

He needed her to ask first, though, to broach the subject. It was left up to the owner of a mage sword to either ask for help from the Heron or not, to start the conversation regarding her new sword. Part of the Heron taboo—if someone didn't ask, there was no reason to tell because the less people knew of Heron business, the better. He was on the verge of breaking that taboo, though, if Rowena didn't start asking the right questions soon.

"Your powers are recovered?" she asked as they walked along the rutted road between wide stretches of grassland. They'd left the horses behind with the Valen. Rowena preferred to travel on foot.

"They are." That wasn't the question he wanted her to ask, but at least she was talking about something that might *lead* to the questions he needed to answer. He tried to make his tone light as he said, "A Heron doesn't usually have to pass on a mage sword to its first owner right after a deadly fight with a powerful wizard." As it was, the battle with the wizard had so weakened him he hadn't bothered fighting Dorjan with magic. Passing the mage sword to Rowena had drained what little he had left.

Despite his attempt to make light of the danger he'd been in, Rowena shivered in the early autumn air. "I'm glad you killed him," she murmured.

The oracle had, after a few days, told Rowena some of what the wizard and Dorjan had put her through. Kael could feel how much those stories hurt Rowena's compassionate heart, and he was only sorry he couldn't kill the wizard again for her.

"I didn't know it would drain your powers to pass on a mage sword," she said.

His pulse started to pump harder. Closer. But he resisted the urge to rush out a lot of information. This had to be handled carefully. "Only the first time. And it only affects the Heron who forged the sword."

She nodded, fell quiet again. He cursed silently. His

patience wasn't this good. He couldn't wait for her to ask. Screw taboo. He needed her to know.

"I always assumed the sword was meant for you when I forged it," he said, watching the side of her face closely. "Since meeting you triggered my trance."

Her head snapped up. "You mean, that seizure you had had something to do with Ca'laez?"

He felt some of the tension leave his shoulders. "It was the start of the initial trance a Heron enters when he forges a mage sword. My trance was earlier than normal."

"How long did it take to make the sword?"

There! A churning of satisfaction started in his chest. "Six years to forge, nearly three years to fully recover from the process."

Her eyes rounded. "Nine years!"

He watched as comprehension filled her expression.

"That's why I didn't hear from you? That's why you never came back to me?"

He nodded.

"But what about the last three years? Why did you avoid me for another three years?"

The pain in her voice tore at his heart. Gods, she still thought he'd been avoiding her. "My family counseled me to wait. My mage powers increased after forging the sword, and I needed to train them. The sword had to be claimed before I could talk about any of this. And..."

"And?"

"And my family was afraid if we fully bonded before your term as sword sworn was up, you could be killed and I would follow. They wanted me to wait until you were initiated as a full priestess first."

She turned back toward the road, her brow creased.

"I couldn't stay away though," he rushed to tell her. The confusion he felt from her was an ache in his gut. "I kept sneaking into town to see you. I thought by keeping my distance, we wouldn't bond. But I'd still be able to...to be near you."

She nodded but didn't turn to face him. "What made you decide to come for me now, then? I'm still months away from taking my vows. What changed?"

This was the part he wasn't sure he wanted to tell her. But they needed honesty between them now that he could give that to her. "After a while, it wasn't enough that I watched you in crowds, or training in the temple. I needed to be alone with you. So I...I snuck into your room."

"When?" she interrupted, cocking her head to one side.

"A few days before you left for the oracle."

She rounded on him then, forcing him to stop and face her. "That's why I was having those dreams about you? Did you do that to me? I couldn't sleep for a week!"

"Those only started when I snuck in?" He paused a moment, as her words sunk in, then said, "Your dreams were about me?"

She rolled her eyes. "Of course. Who else would they be about? I already told you, you ruined me the first time we met."

He couldn't help it. He smiled. And because he needed to, rather desperately, he pulled her into his arms. They hadn't been alone since rescuing the oracle. This was the first time they'd had a chance to talk. And the first time they'd been able to hold each other. Gods, he'd missed having her in his arms. As much as he missed being inside her.

To his infinite relief, she sank against him, resting her

hands on his chest.

"I'm sorry I didn't come to you sooner," he said. "I should have."

She shook her head. "No. Your family was right. I could have died at any point in my term as sword sworn. I wouldn't have wanted you to die too. But... Why didn't you tell me all this sooner?"

"Until Ca'laez claimed her owner, I couldn't discuss Heron business with you. And if you hadn't been Ca'laez's owner, like I thought you were supposed to be, I could never have discussed any of this with you. It would have damaged the honor of my family."

"Ah." She nodded, understanding dawning across her face. "Secrets and honor I understand something about." She leaned in close and kissed him briefly.

Too briefly for his state of mind. His cock was hard, pressed against her soft stomach, and trying to think beyond getting her naked was becoming difficult.

"So then...why did Ca'laez take so long to claim me?" she asked, her gaze on his mouth.

"Damned if I know," he snarled. "You'll have to ask her because she's refusing to tell me. Just says we needed time. Whatever the hells that means."

Her eyes narrowed. "She talks to you?"

He nodded. "All Heron can talk to the mage swords. You may be able to with time. But not all owners can talk directly with their swords. Depends on the bond."

"It would be nice to be able to talk to her," Rowena murmured. "Was she the one to break the spell on my cell that was blocking my powers?"

"That was partly Ca'laez, partly the wizard's death. The

spells weren't designed to outlive him. I doubt he thought he'd be killed by a single mage. He was pretty powerful. But Ca'laez forced the spells to degrade faster than they would have naturally after the wizard was killed."

"That was nice of her," she said. Then she leaned forward and kissed him again, lingering longer this time.

His pulse jumped and his arms flexed around her. There was more he needed to tell her, but that could wait for a little while. The grass was long. And the road deserted. He started to walk backward, taking them into the grass. She followed without resistance.

"I've missed this," she said against his mouth. "I'm glad to know you can sneak into my room at the Temple. That will make things easier."

"What do you mean?" He was too busy working the buttons loose on her tunic to notice the catch in her voice.

"Since I can't move to Heron's Deep and you can't leave, at least we'll be able to see each other often."

She pressed closer and he forgot to breathe for a moment, almost missing the point of her comment.

As he realized what she'd said, though, he eased her back so he could look in her eyes. "Actually, I've been thinking a lot about our living arrangements." She stiffened in his arms and it didn't take her empathic powers for him to realize she was afraid he'd ask her to live in the Deep. "Now that I've passed on my mage sword," he said, "and forged the only one I'll ever forge, I'm no longer bound to live in the Deep."

"You're not?"

He shook his head. "In fact, I've already bought a little house in the city."

"You did?"

He smiled at her surprise. "I did. You can look out the front door at the Temple."

"How did you find something so close?"

"Well, it took me three months of negotiation. But I couldn't pass the place up after I'd seen it. I knew you wouldn't be able to live far from the Temple."

Her gaze narrowed and a sly glint touched her expression. "Who owned it?"

He grinned. "Your high priestess is some negotiator. I probably paid twice what the cottage is worth."

She chuckled, then laughed loudly and wrapped her arms around his neck. "You bought us a house. Already." She looked into his eyes. "And you don't have to live in the Deep. You can stay with me? You'll be there every night and during the day when I can sneak away?"

It was his turn to laugh. "I'll be there whenever you want me, baby. As often as you want me. Will you live with me there?"

"Of course! Kael. I love you." She froze the instant the words left her mouth.

He stopped breathing. Her eyes were huge. She looked more vulnerable than he'd ever seen her, even when she was chained to a wall at Dorjan's mercy. "Do you?" he asked, wonder in his voice. She nodded.

They were soul twins. They were only whole when they were together. But hearing this strong, intelligent, sexy woman say she loved him made his world seem right. "Good," he murmured, placing a gentle kiss on her lips, "because I love you too, *raynia.*"

She smiled. And pushed him back into the grass. Kael laughed on his way down, happier than he'd ever been in his life.

About the Author

To learn more about Isabo Kelly, please visit www.isabokelly.com. Send an email to Isabo at isabo@isabokelly.com or join her Yahoo! group newsletter to join in the fun with other readers as well as Isabo! http://groups.yahoo.com/group/isabokellynewsletter.

Thief of Hearts

J.C. Wilder

Dedication

To Crissy and Jessica, two ladies of style, wit and infinite patience—love you!

Chapter One

Year 2024

Death was too good for Dennis McRae.

Harper landed on the stone balcony with a soft scrape of shoe leather and a gentle exhale. Her gloved fingers grasped the carabineer clip and she released her climbing harness from the nylon rope. She'd used the contraption to leap from one balcony to the next in the hopes of avoiding a painful landing on the gravel garden path two stories below. She glanced over the rail and her gut clenched. She hated heights, which, considering her profession, was pretty amusing.

She removed the harness and carefully tucked it behind a planter where it wouldn't be found until she was long gone.

The biggest problem with Dennis was that he was her stepbrother so killing him, while a pleasant thought, was out of the question. Not only would it really piss her father off, not that she considered his anger a serious consequence, but her stepmother loved her son. There were times Harper doubted the woman's sanity. Her son was evil on two feet and her father was the meanest son of a bitch she'd ever had the misfortune of meeting.

What had that poor woman done to deserve such men in her life?

Crouching before the double doors, she was a slim shadow among the shadows. The night air was cool against her flushed face. Tonight was the perfect night for a second-story job. Clouds obscured the fat moon and the weather was temperate. She grinned when she remembered her last job had been in the mountains of Colorado during a blizzard. It had taken her the better part of an hour to gain entry to the house and another twenty minutes to warm up enough so that her fingers could work the safe. By comparison, tonight's assignment would be an easy job.

She eyed the expensive electronic door lock and her lip curled. This mechanism, while pricey, wasn't enough to keep a determined thief out of a cowshed let alone a multi-million-dollar house such as this. She opened her miniscule evening purse and removed a slim leather wallet.

Lock-pick tools were a well-dressed girl's best friend.

Extracting a wire pick, tension wrench and a credit card-sized frequency scrambler, she set to work on the lock. It was lucky for her that Ross "Blackie" Ryan, the homeowner, was hosting a party for his fourth wedding anniversary to the sour-faced Mrs. Ryan, the source of his current wealth. The lavish event coupled with an engraved invitation had enabled Harper to gain entry to the house and the grounds. Only the family wing and Blackie's private offices were off limits to the partygoers. She smiled. Of course this was the one place she intended to infiltrate.

Her research, which had included a fair number of sizeable bribes, had revealed that the extensive alarm system protecting both the house and grounds had been disabled for the duration of the party. This meant Blackie's office safe and its contents were vulnerable to her clever fingers.

The frequency scrambler disabled the electronic signal on the lock turning the tiny light on the card from red to green. With the aid of her lock pick and wrench, the well-oiled tumblers glided together then released with an almost female sigh of surrender. Harper enjoyed the surge of triumph when the door opened a few millimeters. Cracking a safe or opening a locked door was more satisfying than just about anything she'd ever experienced in her professional life. Both skills were hard-earned and she was quite proud of her prowess. In the burglary business, she'd been known as Houdini as there wasn't a lock yet invented that could keep her out.

She returned the tools to their case then tucked it into her purse. Rising, she slipped into the office before closing the door behind her. She took a moment to draw the heavy drapes so the illumination from her laser light wouldn't be seen from the outside. She produced the slim light from her purse and turned it on.

The office was definitely a man's domain with rich, dark wood and walls painted burgundy. Floor-to-ceiling shelves covered the far wall though the leather-bound books looked as if they'd never been opened. Her lip curled. Buying books as a decoration was pretentious in her opinion. Books were the doorways to magical worlds and they should be read and savored, not used as an accessory to a tastefully decorated room. She was struck with the sudden urge to liberate them.

A broad fireplace occupied the far end of the room and a neat stack of real logs was arranged in a brass bin. Her brow arched. Maybe Blackie was richer than she'd realized, as trees were in short supply thanks to rampant home building in the early years of the century. At one end of the room, arranged before the fireplace, was a comfortable grouping of leather chairs and a low-slung couch.

Her nose wrinkled. Definitely old-fashioned.

At the opposite end of the office was a broad desk. No doubt the imposing piece of furniture and Blackie's overbearing presence had cowed many a subordinate as they sat in one of the two wing chairs situated before it. Was it in this very room that Dennis had learned his balls were in a noose?

Probably. Blackie would enjoy destroying a man's life all the while sitting in the lap of luxury surrounded by his security team, Cuban cigars and his imported, hand-carved desk. She walked toward it, sweeping the light around to survey the area.

Now, if I were a gutless, spineless blackmailer, where would I keep the evidence?

Sliding the slim light behind one ear, she began a methodic search of the desk drawers. Mentally damning both Dennis and Blackie, whom she called "The Prick" when in private, she focused on her task.

In her opinion both men would get whatever they deserved without anyone having to lift a finger. Her stepbrother, the up-and-coming politician, for screwing around on his wife and Blackie for being the crooked, unscrupulous bastard he was. Harper had tried to warn Dennis when he'd made friends with the mobster more than a year ago but the lure of needed campaign funds had been too hard to resist.

Her lips firmed. Dennis also had a bit of a gambling problem he was desperate to hide. The biggest mistake her stepbrother had made was to allow Blackie to unearth this little fact. It hadn't helped that The Prick had his finger in the gambling pie as well as neo-synthetic drugs, prostitution and blackmail.

She shut the center drawer then moved to the next one.

Her stepmother didn't know about her offspring's potentially career-limiting shortcomings. If Blackie did as he'd threatened, not only would Marianna be shunned from the society life she adored, she'd be thoroughly humiliated. The woman might be shallow but she had a good heart, when she remembered she had one at all.

She reached for the final drawer.

Harper was pretty sure that Dennis didn't have a clue as to her former occupation any more than anyone else in the family, all he knew was that she *knew people*. She was a woman who could get things done, especially when the task in question involved the wrong side of the law. Her family overlooked that little tidbit as her connections could be handy in times of need. Dennis certainly had no clue that when he'd come to her with his perfidy, she'd be the one sneaking around Blackie's office cleaning up the mess.

She eased the drawer shut.

Nada.

Harper had come out of her self-imposed retirement to perform this one last job and steal back the evidence the mobster had against Dennis. After this, her stepbrother and the rest of her family were on their own.

She rose from her crouched position, her gaze focused on a painting on the wall behind the desk. Most people didn't realize how obvious it was to place a safe behind a painting. Not only was it portrayed in every movie on the planet, it simply wasn't a viable option if one wished to keep its location a secret. It took space to hide a wall safe and the average thickness of a wall simply wouldn't accommodate most safes. Alterations would have to be made and any accomplished thief would obtain the blueprints to a house before ever setting foot on the property.

Needless to say she'd had the blueprints within six hours of making the decision to break into the house as she was a very proficient thief.

Harper moved her fingers along the bottom of the ornate frame until she located a small metal piece. She pushed against it and the painting swung toward her.

Bingo.

Her chest grew tight with excitement when the safe was revealed. It was top of the line but it was an older model, probably came with the house. She smirked. It might have been one of the best in the late twentieth century but it didn't stand a chance of keeping its secrets from her.

There were very few things as dangerous as a resourceful, determined woman.

Harper withdrew a small bundle from her cleavage. Her trusty listening device, much like a stethoscope, felt like an old friend in her hand. Unwrapping the wires, she slid the tiny earpiece in her ear then placed the other end against the safe directly over where the tumblers were located. Flexing her fingers, she leaned forward and began working the lock.

With her whole being focused on her work, the only sounds that registered were her breathing and the soft clicks in her ear as she turned the dial. To her, cracking a safe was as familiar as putting on makeup or easing into a much-loved pair of blue jeans. She grimaced when she turned the dial too far and had to start over again. She was rusty and she knew it. Back in her prime she could've opened a safe such as this in just under two minutes. She glanced at her watch.

Four minutes so far.

She licked her lips, her gaze focused on the dial.

Click, click, click, tick...

Her heart stopped when the final tumbler clicked into place. Holding her breath, she opened the door with a soft snick. Inside were a neat stack of envelopes, several leather-bound ledgers and an impressive tower of velvet jewelry boxes.

She bit her lip as her gaze danced over the collection of items. Knowing Blackie he probably had several million in jewels stashed in this one safe.

It really was too bad she was retired.

Chase couldn't believe his eyes or his luck when he'd spied the figure on the second-story balcony. It had to be Harper as he'd recognize her mouthwatering ass anywhere. He dropped his slim cigar to the floor then ground it out with his heel. No other second-story pro would have the balls to break into a house while the owners, one hundred and fifty party guests and a legion of security guards were in residence. His gaze skimmed the shadowy figure. And to top it all off she was wearing a sexy evening dress guaranteed to slay a man with one glance at those neck-to-floor legs of hers.

How well he remembered those legs.

Chase held his breath when she opened the French doors and slipped into the office. It would appear that the beautiful thief was going to do all the hard work for him this evening.

With the grace of a ballet dancer, he climbed onto the balcony rail of the guest suite and made the leap to the office balcony. His gloved hands connected with the railing and he pulled himself up with ease.

He was pleased to see Harper still had the same, deft touch with locks that she'd been known for. Houdini had been a legend in second-story work though he'd heard she'd retired more than a year ago. He dropped to a crouch before the doors to peer inside through a narrow slit in the drapes. It would seem the stories of her retirement had been greatly exaggerated.

His former lover stood over the desk with a laser light tucked behind her ear as she searched the drawers. Her movements were economical, swift yet efficient. She moved through each drawer, her search thorough, yet she took great care to not disturb the contents of the desk.

What was she looking for?

Her task completed, she rose and her gloved hands were empty. She stood for a moment, her gaze fixed on a painting behind the desk. She slid her fingers along the bottom of the frame, it swung to the side to reveal a safe.

Now, that's what I'm talking about.

She was hard at work on the safe when Chase reached for the door handle. Rising, he held his breath as he slipped into the room, counting on the fact she'd be too immersed in opening the safe to notice his arrival.

It wasn't hard to detect the differences between the Harper he'd known and the woman standing before him. In the past she could've opened this safe in a matter of moments and that was with her eyes closed. Now, she labored over the task like a master painter would over his latest work.

In their line of business, being slow increased the chances of getting caught and she'd definitely been caught this time.

He slipped out from behind the curtains, his gaze still focused on the beautiful thief. Her posture was tense though she seemed to be completely unaware of his presence. In the past he'd never have managed to sneak up on her. It seemed Harper had been in retirement just long enough to lose her edge.

Lucky him.

If it were possible, she'd grown more beautiful in the past five years. Her black hair was contained in a complicated twist on the back of her head leaving the length of her slim neck exposed. He'd always loved that part of her anatomy. There was something undeniably erotic about the bare curve of a woman's neck.

She wore gloves and a long-sleeved black dress that clung to her tight, athletic frame. The skirt was short, ending several inches above her knees, but it was her legs that had his mouth watering. Long, shapely and clad in sheer black stockings, Harper had the most amazing legs and he well remembered the feel of them wrapped around his waist as he'd taken her beneath him. Bemoaning her mere five feet, five inches, she'd always worn stiletto heels and he was quite pleased to see she'd retained that particular habit. His woman hadn't changed completely—

His woman.

His chest went curiously tight. Five years ago she'd thought she'd caught him in a compromising position. Without giving him a chance to explain, she'd packed her bag and walked out of his life. He rubbed his hand over his chest. If she hadn't come home early that day, if Susan hadn't come by in the midst of an emotional meltdown, if he hadn't held her as she'd cried and been more on guard when she'd grabbed his face for a passionate kiss, would he and Harper still be together?

The safe opened and she made a soft sound of satisfaction. He glanced down at his watch. Seven minutes. Definitely not as good as the old Harper had been, not by a long shot. He crossed his arms over his chest and adopted a careless stance.

"It's about time, Harper. My grandmother could've opened that safe faster than you and she's been dead for ten years."

Chapter Two

Chase.

Harper froze when the familiar voice spoke behind her. Even though it had been years since they'd been in the same room, she'd never forget his deep voice. It had haunted her dreams since the day she'd walked away from him and their relationship.

Mentally she cursed herself for getting caught on the job. It stung to know that for the first time she'd been seen, let alone getting nailed by *him*. She'd really lost her touch.

Her heart stuttered and she turned, her gaze sliding over his familiar face. He hadn't changed much in the past five years. If it was possible he'd grown more handsome. Then again with his Black Irish good looks and charisma, Chase could charm any woman into his bed within minutes of their meeting. It had certainly worked that way on her.

"Do you mind? You're blinding me." His voice carried a slight tang of Ireland, the land of his birth.

"Mind?" She presented him with her back when she began searching the contents of the safe. "I don't mind one bit."

He chuckled and the sound sent shivers of awareness down her spine. Her nipples tightened and she scowled at a stack of envelopes she held. He'd always had that nerve-tingling effect on her. A few more minutes in his company and she'd be ready to shed her panties and mate with him like an animal.

"What are you doing here?" She flicked through the envelopes, scanning the neatly printed names on the front.

"I could ask you the same."

"Yeah, well, I asked first." She made a mental note of the prominent names listed on each envelope. Two senators, a Hollywood actor, three local politicians and a few leading businessmen were among them. She stopped to open the envelope with the actor's name. Pulling out several glossy photos, her eyes widened when she saw the famous face buried in another man's crotch as he gave an award-winning performance of another sort.

My my, Blackie has quite the little side business going on.

She stuffed the photos into the envelope and continued flipping through the pile until she spied Dennis's name.

"It would appear we're here on the same mission."

Chase's sexy burr sounded close to her shoulder. She shivered and the lace of her bra chafed her sensitive nipples. Damn him for being so sexy and her for being so weak where he was concerned. Her body betrayed her every time and in the end he'd used that weakness to deceive her.

"What have you found?" His breath caressed the nape of her neck.

"Nothing that concerns you." Turning away, Harper shoved the envelopes, save the one with her stepbrother's name, back into the safe. Opening it, she removed a stack of glossy photos. After looking at a few, she knew that these would definitely incriminate her Senate-bound stepbrother. If they were released to the press, his career would be over and his mother would never dare show her face in public again. She looked into the envelope and spied the negatives in the bottom. Now what kind of blackmailer was stupid enough to keep the negatives and the photos in the same place?

Sloppy, sloppy.

Satisfied she had what she'd come for, she folded the envelope and tucked it into her bodice.

"How are we on the same mission?" She checked the safe to ensure that she'd disturbed nothing else. He would know soon enough that she'd stolen the envelope as Blackie wasn't a stupid man. Funnily enough, he was one of the only people who knew of her criminal past.

"It appears we're here to accomplish the same end, impeding Blackie's latest sideline," Chase said.

"Indeed?" Harper shut the safe door, giving the dial a quick twist to secure it.

"Hey, now." Annoyance was thick in his voice. His brogue was always thicker when he was aroused or aggravated. "You could've left that open for me."

"Naw." With a sharp smile she propped her hip on the desk. "You said your granny could open that safe faster than I." She nodded toward the safe. "I just wanted to see how a *pro* would do it."

His eyes glinted. "I'll just bet you do, darling."

Her breath caught when he reached for her, his fingers brushing the hardened tip of her breast. Heat sparked across her skin and raced down her abdomen to center at the apex of her thighs. She fought the urge to press her legs together to relieve the pleasant ache.

"If I may?"

Harper wasn't sure if she was relieved or disappointed when she realized he only wanted the tiny microphone that was still in her ear. With a mocking smile, he tugged on the slim wire until it came free.

"You can't bring your own toys?" She handed him the light.

His brow arched. "Why bother when yours are warmed up?"

"I'm timing you." She looked at her watch.

"You do that."

She'd always enjoyed watching him on the job. Chase approached everything with a single-minded determination to get the job done right the first time, even in bed. On the job, he was a no-nonsense thief and it was his ability to concentrate in the worst of situations that aided him in achieving his financial success.

He had a way of focusing his attention on a woman in such a manner that fooled her into thinking she was the end-all-be-all of his existence. Seeing that he was a philandering liar, this was a handy talent for him to possess.

Her eyes narrowed. He'd claimed she was the one he loved yet he'd screwed around on her. As long as she lived she'd never forget the feeling of unreality when she'd walked into their apartment and caught him in a lip lock and his hands firmly planted on their neighbor's DD's.

Her heart and trust had been shattered and the memory lingered, sharp edges and all.

She swallowed hard and pushed away the ever-present ache that made itself known when she thought of that night. None of that mattered now as the past was long buried. Ancient history had never interested her, especially when it was her own.

Harper's gaze moved over his back. He looked good though.

Bastard.

Was it too much to hope that he'd pined for her, gotten fat and lost his hair? She was annoyed that his dark hair was loose and the thick waves made her fingers itch to touch them. He wore a black turtleneck, black jeans and a black leather belt around his still-slim waist.

Her gaze caught on his firm backside. She'd always loved his ass. It was high, tight—he ran for miles every morning—and the perfect size to sink her nails into as he'd thrust into her. Chase had the stamina of three men and was able to maintain an erection for hours. In bed, he was every woman's dream.

Too bad he was a complete, amoral dick outside of it.

The safe door opened with a metallic sigh and she glanced at her watch. Two minutes.

Figured.

"You always were good at safe cracking," she muttered.

"And you are quite talented with lock picks, much more so than I." He gave her a wide smile and she couldn't help but return it. "That's why we made such a good team—you were strong in my weakest areas and I was strong in yours." He handed her the microphone.

"And you had so many weaknesses," she drawled.

"You were my biggest weakness and you know it."

Her smile froze. "Your biggest weakness was screwing around with other women and that had nothing to do with me."

"No, my biggest weakness was a King Kong-sized ego coupled with immaturity and you're right, it had nothing to do with you." He pulled out the same envelopes Harper had held just minutes before.

She blinked. "Honesty? What a concept."

He shrugged. "It's been a long time, Harper. I'm not the boy you once knew."

"And for that the world is grateful, I'm sure. I'm only glad I discovered your philandering before I made the mistake of marrying you."

His movements slowed and his head came up. His dark gaze met hers. "So you would've married me at some point?"

"Possibly." Uncomfortable, she shrugged. "Who knows what would've happened if you'd have kept your dick in your pants?"

In reality she'd been dying to marry him though she'd had doubts about his fidelity long before it had been confirmed. It had seemed that every time she'd turned around a different woman was throwing herself at him. His handsome face and accent drew them in and with no effort on his part. While he didn't encourage them, he also didn't do anything to discourage them. She'd loved him with all the passion her twenty-four-year-old heart had possessed, and he'd crushed it with his carelessness.

He chuckled and resumed flipping through the envelopes. "You always were blunt." He selected two, folded them in half then slid them into his back pocket.

"And you always were a shameless charmer." She shoved away from the desk and headed toward the balcony door. "And I need to leave before we're caught in here."

"Ah, not quite so fast." He replaced the envelopes and shut the door before swinging the painting back into place. "How were you planning to get out of here?"

"Are you talking about this room or the house in general?" She looked down at her party dress. "Through the front door. I, unlike others," her gaze moved over his mouthwatering physique, "was invited to this event and I have every right to be here."

"But not in this room."

"Yeah, well, when one invites people to their house they can only expect that someone will be nosy." She headed for the balcony door. "Have a good time making your getaway."

"Harper—"

A noise sounded from the hallway and her heart almost stopped. There was a jingle of keys then a muffled curse.

"I'm telling you, I heard someone in here," a voice hissed from the other side of the door.

Harper spun and scrambled for the door and Chase cut her off.

"We'll never make it," he hissed. His iron hand caught her wrist and hauled her toward the couch. "Lay down."

"W-what?" She gaped at him.

"Now, Harper."

"But—"

One minute she was standing and the next she was on her back. His big body covered hers, crushing her into the supple leather of the couch. He grabbed her light and turned it off, shoving it into her bra. His scent, familiar and arousing, invaded her senses even as he forced her legs apart. He draped one over the back of the couch.

"Just go with it, Harper. Our lives may depend upon it."

Stunned, she heard the doorknob rattle even as Chase ripped her panties with a single yank. The fragile silk gave way beneath his brutal assault, leaving her bare, exposed. He tore off his gloves then reached between her thighs, parting her damp flesh with nimble fingers. He scooted down her body to perch between her thighs.

His mouth covered her and she moaned, her back arched when his tongue zeroed in on her clit. One finger entered her vagina only to be followed by a second, stretching her, filling her with heat, friction. This man, only this man, had known how to turn her on with a single-mindedness that had never failed to steal her breath.

His tongue stroked her aroused flesh and Harper closed her eyes. Hunger, a hunger she hadn't realized even existed, clawed at her mind and ravaged her body. Against her will, her back arched higher to press against his talented mouth, her hips moving in response to his finger thrusts. Desperate to hold him in place until she received the release she craved, she clenched at his silky hair until her hands fisted. His tongue aggressively stroked her aroused flesh, each touch sent tension to spiral throughout her body.

Harper knew she was lost when, even as the door opened and someone hit the light switch, she came apart with a powerful scream.

"Get off of me," Harper hissed.

Even with her spicy taste hot on his tongue and the echoes of her cries still burning his ears, he was all too aware of the men standing in the doorway. He'd hoped they'd open the door, see them, then have the decency to back off. It would seem these baboons didn't take a hint or understand discretion.

His cock gnawed at his zipper and he wanted to tell them to fuck off. The urge to spread his woman out on the couch and take her for a hard ride was almost overpowering.

Someone cleared his throat.

"Gentlemen." Chase's voice was mild. "If you would give us a moment, please."

"Certainly, sir. We'll be waiting in the hall." The voice carried both a hint of amusement and warning. Chase had no doubt their voyeurs would be waiting for them when they exited the office. That gave an added wrinkle to an already complicated exit plan for both of them.

The moment the door shut, Harper went wild beneath him. He was forced to lunge to the side or risk being impaled with a lethal-looking high heel. With all the grace a partially debauched woman could muster, she rolled off the couch. Yanking her dress down over her hips, she stalked away. Her face was flushed and her movements were agitated when she turned on him. If looks could kill he'd have a dagger stuck in his heart and would be bleeding to death in moments.

"Don't you *ever* touch me again." Her whisper was furious. She gripped the back of one of the wing chairs for support and her aquamarine gaze met his. "You lost that right a long time ago."

"Be reasonable, Harper." He walked toward her. "We were about to get caught by Blackie's goons with our hands in the cookie jar. A little humiliation is a small price to pay to keep our heads attached to our shoulders."

"Whose humiliation? Your crotch wasn't just displayed to perfect strangers."

"There's no way they could see around me. My body blocked their view; all they could see was your spectacular legs."

She didn't believe him; he saw it on her face. Her eyes narrowed. "Fine, but don't ever try anything like that again," she snarled.

His heart twisted. The need to touch her again was strong. There were two things in life he couldn't resist, the lure of a difficult job and the beautiful Harper, the only woman to steal his heart.

"I'm pretty sure I couldn't set up this scenario again if I tried," he said.

She ran her hands over her hips, smoothing the tight fabric into place. Her hair was slightly mussed but if anything those loose silky strands made her look even more alluring and much more approachable.

"Very funny." She tore off her gloves and stuffed them into her tiny purse. "Let's get out of here." She headed for the terrace doors.

"We can't leave that way, we have an audience outside." He moved to intercept her. "And judging from what they just witnessed, they expect to see a very *together* couple exit this room."

Her lips tightened and he felt a pang in his gut that he hadn't had the chance to taste them.

"Damn." She bit her lower lip and he fought the urge to throw her down on the carpet and kiss her. "I guess we'll just have to brazen it out and leave via the door."

Adrenaline burst through his system. Exiting the Ryan household before the theft could be detected would be a challenge, one that Chase would relish. Blackie was a cowardly bastard and he deserved a little dose of his own medicine.

He smiled. "Are you up for the game, Harper? One more for the road as it were?"

She looked up at him and a smile tugged at her mouth. Amusement lingered in the crystal depths of her eyes and he was catapulted back in time when she'd looked up at him like this every day. Damn, he'd missed her.

"Oh, yeah. Let's see if you can keep up, old man. In case you've forgotten, I am a brilliant actress."

He chuckled. "Harper, there isn't a thing I could forget about you."

Her eyes turned to ice and her smile faded. "Even as you were fucking another woman? How gallant." She moved toward the door. "Let's get this over with as I find your company distasteful and I long to be rid of you."

He felt a momentary rush of panic at the thought of losing her again after finding her only minutes before. They still had *it*, the undeniable rush of heat and awareness that had only occurred with her. Ever since she'd walked out the door he'd been struggling to find that same feeling and though he'd bedded dozens of women, not one of them made him feel as complete as she did. There was no way he could take the chance she'd give him the slip and disappear into the night.

He headed her off, reaching the door just seconds before she did. Her fingers brushed his wrist when he took the doorknob. She frowned up at him. Before she could react, he pulled her close and kissed her on the temple. The scent of her perfume was spicy and arousing. Resisting the urge to kiss her properly, he reached into the bodice of her dress and removed the envelope she'd taken from the safe. Her eyes widened and he waggled it in her face.

"Just a little insurance policy," he said.

Her brow furrowed as anger swept her face. "You bastard, that's mine. Give that back." She lunged for the envelope and he held it over her head, his arm full of enraged woman.

He chuckled, enjoying the feel her body against his. "Technically it isn't your property and we both know it." He tucked it into his pocket with the other two envelopes he'd taken. "I can't take a chance on your sneaking off and leaving me here to face the consequences alone."

The look of hurt on her face was unmistakable. The wounded look in those amazing eyes felt like a blow to his gut.

"You think I'd do that?" Her voice was fragile.

He wasn't falling for it.

"In a heartbeat."

She scowled and leapt for him, her heels connected hard with the top of his foot. With one arm, he grabbed her around the waist and swung her to the side then wrenched the door open with his free hand. Her long legs tangled with his and Chase allowed himself to stumble. Twisting, he landed on the floor with an armload of hot, angry woman.

Damn, she was beautiful.

The security men towered over them. With their surly expressions, identical dark suits, crew cuts and matching radio earpieces, they looked like twins.

Harper's fingers dug into his shoulders and her body was pressed as tightly to him as if she were glued in place. His hands slid to her hips and he flashed her a lazy smile.

"I guess we just made a spectacle out of ourselves again, darling," he drawled.

Her smile was more of a grimace as her teeth were gritted. "We really shouldn't allow this to become a habit, dearest."

His smile widened when she tried to loosen his grip by wiggling only to realize that it was his erection that was digging into her belly, not the contents of his pockets. Her eyes grew large and a soft flush raced over her cheeks.

Yes, I'm very happy to see you.

Harper scrambled to her feet and he followed suit. Easing his arm around her waist, he anchored her into his side. She froze for a moment then leaned into him, her body soft and supple against his. It felt...right.

"Please forgive us, gentlemen. I'm sure you'll understand that Ms. Wilde and I will be returning—"

"Mr. Ryan would like to speak with you before you return to the party." Drone One spoke, his gaze flicked over Harper in a dismissive fashion.

"He's waiting just down the hall." The second one spoke and his gaze, which was fastened to Harper's breasts, wasn't nearly as impersonal as his partner's. Chase wanted to smash his fist into his face.

"Do you hear that, darling?" Harper's voice was light and playful. "Blackie wishes to see us. How lovely. We can extend our best wishes to him and his wife on their anniversary."

"If you will follow us," the first one said.

"Lead the way, gentlemen." She flashed them a dazzling smile though both men seemed to be immune to her cheer.

They fell into step behind the guards, his arm still secure around her waist. He couldn't help but smile when he noticed her inquisitive fingers prod him in the side when she felt his pocket for the envelope. Smoothly, he caught her hand and raised it to his lips even as her nails dug into his fingers.

Minx.

Chapter Three

Years as a thief had perfected Harper's acting skills. She could blend in with the cream of society or feel at home in the seediest bars in town. Even without the aid of a mirror, she knew her smile would appear genuine, her expression bright and welcoming to any observer. She was a woman at ease in her skin. Little did anyone realize that while she might appear calm, her emotions were in an uproar.

She was both angry and disappointed she'd been caught breaking into the safe. During her years in the profession, she'd never been caught, not once. There'd been a rare occasion in which it had been a close call. Once a homeowner had made an unscheduled return and she'd been forced to secret herself in a tiny bathroom cabinet for over an hour while the lady of the house repaired her makeup, but never had she been caught in the act.

Then there was the sudden reappearance of Chase.

Walking beside the man she'd once loved was a surreal experience. They followed the security guards along the main hall. After all this time, why did he have to turn up now? She'd been devastated when she left him and it had taken her a long time to even contemplate seeing another man. Chase probably had no idea how badly he'd hurt her with his infidelity. For a long time, she'd turned the incident onto herself, blaming herself for not being sexy enough, too flat-chested or just plain boring.

Just how messed up was that? He'd screwed around on her and she'd ended up blaming herself, for a few months at least. Luckily for her, she'd managed to wake up and place the blame squarely where it belonged.

On him.

As if he knew she was thinking about him, he placed his hand over hers and gave it a gentle squeeze. In response, she dug her nails into his flesh until his muscles tensed.

Even though she'd managed to convince herself that she hated him for what he'd done, it was obvious that her emotions were far more tangled than she'd ever imagined.

She desired him, there was no question about that, but sex was a bad basis for a relationship. How did she really feel about him? Chase had made her laugh more than any man she'd ever met. She'd always felt physically safe with him and even though she'd had doubts about his fidelity, she'd never doubted he'd keep her confidences safe. Too bad she couldn't have trusted him with her heart.

They walked through a set of double doors into a brightly lit sitting room. Blackie and another man were the only ones present. Both stood near a small bar on the far side of the room, their heads together in a private conversation. Both men turned and she forced her smile wider.

"Blackie," she laughed and released Chase, "how lovely to see you again."

His tense expression smoothed and he smiled. "Harper, you look more beautiful each time I see you."

She forced herself to not shudder when he took her hands and gave her a chaste kiss on the cheek.

"Flatterer." She flashed him a brilliant smile. "How is your wife doing? I haven't seen her yet."

He made a soft tutting noise. "Well, if you'd stay out of the private rooms and join the party maybe you would have a better chance of running into her."

While his tone was teasing, she didn't miss the thread of steel that ran through his words. Warning her off, was he? *We'll just see about that...*

"Now, Blackie." Harper gave him a pat on the arm then moved past him toward the bar. "You and your wife have been together for some time now so you know what it is like to be in love." She giggled; something she wouldn't dream of ever doing under normal circumstances. "We just can't keep our hands off each other, can we, darling?" She reached for a bottle of brandy and a glass.

"That's right, dearest."

"Blackie, have you met my partner...Dick?"

In the mirror over the bar, she watched Chase's jaw tighten. Their gazes met in the glass and she couldn't help but smile. Score one for her.

"No, we haven't met." Blackie moved forward and took Chase's hand in a firm masculine shake. "Ross Ryan."

"Richard Lake," Chase replied, his smile smooth, practiced. "You have a lovely home here."

"Thank you, Dick." He looked at Harper then back to Chase. "Now tell me how you met our lovely Harper."

The inquisition begins...

"We've known each other for years, business associates actually." He gave her a loaded glance. "It was only recently that we found each other again."

"Very recently." Harper took a slug of the brandy, enjoying the heat, which rushed down her throat. She moved toward Chase and slid her arm around his waist. "It was nothing short of...magical."

Blackie chuckled. "Ahh, magical. That explains how you two managed to open my locked office door."

Chase's brow furrowed. "Locked?" He looked down at her. "The door wasn't locked, was it, peach?"

"Well, darling," she purred, "I couldn't tell you as my hands were full at the time." Her voice dripped sexual innuendo. "You opened the door, my love."

His smile promised retribution and he chucked her on the chin with his finger. "That I did, babe."

She flashed an innocent look at Blackie. "I'm sure the door was unlocked otherwise how could we have gotten in?" She gave a careless shrug. "We're hardly in the habit of breaking into locked rooms and having wild sex on couches."

"And yet that's what you appeared to do—"

"I'm sorry if we caused an uproar. I didn't even realize that was your office." Chase's arm tightened around her waist. "I'm afraid I didn't take time to look around the room as I was busy with other enticements."

Harper forced a laugh then leaned her cheek against his chest as if he truly were the love of her life. "Isn't he just a living doll?"

A rumble of laughter started in Chase's chest, which he covered with a cough.

"Well..." Blackie looked at his security person. "It seems my team has been lax in their assignments this evening." He gestured toward Harper and Chase. "Shall we go downstairs and rejoin the party? Dinner will be served in just a few moments."

Harper wasn't fooled by his cool smile. Blackie knew they were lying but there wasn't a damned thing he could do about it, now at least. He turned toward his security men as if to dismiss them.

She and Chase were safe, momentarily, but who knew when the mobster would think to open the safe? Once that happened, there'd be no way to lie their way out of the situation. Their only recourse was to rejoin the party and make their escape as soon as they could.

"Oh lovely, I'm starved." Harper put her glass on a table and linked her arm through Chase's. "And I'm to be escorted to dinner by two handsome men; what could be better than that?" She held out her arm toward Blackie.

He looked down at her, his expression momentarily irritated before he smoothed it over with a slight smile and a nod.

"Of course, Harper. It would be my pleasure."

I'll just bet...

They were being watched.

Chase's gaze moved around the dining room, picking out the security guards with ease. Even dressed in tuxedos, their military haircuts and the radios they wore in their ears caused them to stick out in a crowd.

Amateurs.

With so many eyes upon them, getting out of here would be tricky. So far Blackie hadn't left his sight so Chase was pretty sure the theft was undetected. Ever the considerate host, Blackie had moved through the room with his wife by his side.

They shook hands, smiled and made small talk with their guests until the dinner bell had rung and the party had shifted to the buffet table. The dining room was packed and the noise was tremendous. A legion of black-clad servers moved between the tables refilling wine glasses and clearing away used dishes.

For now they were safe, but the situation was tenuous at best. Their lives were on the line, the clock was ticking and here he was eating grilled tuna steaks and drinking champagne with his woman by his side.

It just didn't get much better than this.

"What are you thinking about?" Harper asked.

He speared a bite of fish. "How does it feel to have your personal and professional lives collide?"

She shrugged, her face averted. "I'm retired, this is my life, my real life now."

"If you're retired then what were you doing upstairs? Revisiting your previous life?"

"Just taking care of a friend."

"But you miss the rush of a job well done."

She shrugged, her attention focused on her plate. "Not really—"

"Don't lie to me. You forget that I know you, the real Harper Wilde. Who in this room knows who you really are? Or what you are?"

"What I was." Her tone was brittle. "Only two people in this room know who I was, you and Blackie."

"Blackie? How did that happen?"

"Hell if I know. I suspect he stumbled over Ramon Garcia, the man who makes the custom alarm deactivators in Brazil, and he spilled his guts. Blackie suspects but he's never broken me and he's never had any hard proof." She smiled. "And I don't see that situation changing any time soon." Her smile faded. "Sometimes it's hard to live with so many secrets."

He placed his hand over hers. "We all have our secrets, Harper."

"Some more than others." She nodded in the direction of the exit nearest to them. "We have four guards here in the dining room and one stationed at the main doors. The best way out of the house is through the music room on the north side. It has an open terrace and we should be able to slip out then make our way through the gardens and into the parking area."

"Sounds like a plan. We can make our escape after dinner. According to the wait staff, they will be presenting the cake in the ballroom following dinner. That should be enough to keep everyone busy for a few minutes."

"And when do I get my envelope back?" she asked.

"When we get out of here. I told you that I cannot take a chance on you abandoning me."

She poked at her fish. "As if you would ever be helpless."

He leaned over and whispered in her ear, soft strands of her hair tickling his mouth. "I liked it much better when you were helpless."

"When was I ever helpless with you—"

"Remember that night I had you tied to my bed? I was inside you and you were screaming my name over and over again." He brushed his fingertip along the outside of her little finger and he felt her tremble. "When I had my mouth on you and your taste was on my tongue—"

"Chase—"

"Dick."

He scooted his chair as close to hers as possible and draped an arm around her shoulders. With his free hand, he reached for her knee. Her flesh was firm, warm beneath the silk of her stockings. "I want to touch you. I'm going to slide my fingers against your clit—"

"Not here." Arousal had caused her voice to drop.

"Yes, here. Now."

The clinking of a knife against crystal brought his attention to the front of the room near the dais.

"Ladies and gentlemen." A tall man stood at the podium near the head table. "My name is Jerry Fontaine and I will be your host for this portion of the evening."

His voice faded for Chase when he skimmed his fingers up the inside of her thigh. She'd always had the best legs and he couldn't wait to get her into bed where he could properly appreciate them. He wanted to lick every inch of her body and worship her as only he could do.

She was aroused, her breathing had deepened though she held herself ramrod straight. They'd been lucky to secure a small table at the back of the room and while they were sharing with two other people, the couple had finished their dinner then ducked outside for a smoke, leaving Chase and Harper in relative privacy.

He leaned toward her, his mouth brushed her ear. "Open for me, babe. Let me inside."

She made a noise in the back of her throat and her thighs relaxed. He nudged them apart and parted her slick folds. His fingers found her clit with ease and he was pleased with how wet she was. Stroking the hard bead, Chase enjoyed the desperate strangled sound she made. Her hand landed over his and she sought to stop him.

As if.

She was close to coming. Harper had always had a thing for public sex and she possessed a hair-trigger that never failed to amaze him.

"Chase—" Her voice was a mere whisper.

"Come for me, Harper. Let me feel your release."

She turned her face into his shoulder and he tipped his head to shield her flushed cheeks. Her breath was hot against his throat and he was more turned on than he'd ever been in the past. She made a silky noise and he caught her mouth with his own. Her fingers clawed at his and he swallowed her whimpers of release, his tongue savoring the heat and taste that was uniquely hers. He gentled the kiss along with the movements of his fingers.

Her eyes were luminous and her lips were reddened from their kiss. Heat seared his flesh, his cock hard beneath the zipper of his jeans. As he removed his hand from between her thighs, the crowd burst into applause.

Chapter Four

Harper walked beside Chase. Her grip on his arm was strong because she feared if she released him her wobbly knees would betray her. Her cheeks colored when she thought of what had just occurred in the dining room surrounded by a hundred strangers.

It was...arousing.

Shocking.

Chase had always had that effect on her. He turned her on and made her more aware of her body than anyone else. She'd dated and had sex with numerous men since leaving Chase but never had she found anything that came close to what they'd had together.

You're still in love with him...

The thought almost jolted her off her feet and she stumbled on her slim heels. Chase's grip tightened.

"Are you okay?" he asked.

She nodded, not sure she'd ever be okay again. How could she still be in love with a man who'd betrayed her in the most intimate way a man could betray a woman?

You never gave him a chance to explain...

She looked up at his handsome face and her stomach clenched. She wouldn't survive another broken heart from this man. Not that he'd indicated a future relationship was what he wanted from her. So far he'd only shown an interest in sex and finding a route out of the house.

"Now where?" he asked.

His voice jolted her back to reality. They walked along the main hall back toward the ballroom. Judging from the roar, most of the attendees were already partaking of the bar as they awaited the cake presentation.

"The music room is the second door on the left. It's the only room where the exit is shrouded by shrubs on the outside." She nodded toward the left. "Start making your way over there."

"Act as if you're hot to jump my bones, babe."

"That won't be hard since you just had your fingers in my crotch," she muttered.

He laughed and hugged her closer to his side. She enjoyed the warmth and strength of his big body. Oh, how she'd missed it, the simple things like walking side by side. Just breathing the same air was a sensual experience with this man. She wrapped her arms around his waist and leaned into him as if she'd had a little too much to drink.

"Come over here, baby." He spoke loud enough that those closest could hear him. He gently steered her toward the music room doors. "I think I need a kiss."

Harper gave a throaty chuckle. "You need more than that, big boy."

Out of the corner of her eye, she saw the two guards who had been trailing them since they'd returned to the party. Chase braced her against the broad door then leaned down to nuzzle her throat.

"How are we doing?" he whispered.

"Fine, they're by the dining room doors."

His mouth caressed her throat and she tried to ignore the sensations he'd ignited in her blood. Sheesh! She'd already had two mind-blowing orgasms and it hadn't dulled her need for him one bit. Was she sex-starved?

Yes!

His teeth nipped her earlobe and she shuddered. "I'm going to open the door. I can guarantee they will come over here and stand by the doors so we'll have to make it good. If they think we're going at it then it will buy us more time."

Harper snorted. "I'll handle my end of the bargain, you just see if you can keep up with me, big man." She leapt into his arms and twined her legs around his waist. Her bare crotch caressed his jeans-clad erection and her eyes threatened to roll back in her head at the delicious sensation.

"I see I have a tough job ahead of me." His eyes gleamed with amusement.

"You have no idea..."

The door swung open and Chase stumbled through it. Their lips met and Harper sank deep into the sensual darkness created by his mouth, his tongue. He turned and braced her back against the wide oak door to slam it shut. Pressing her mound against the ridge of his arousal, she felt his shudder. Dear God but she wanted this man with a fever that made her dizzy. With every fiber of her being she hungered for him and that hunger demanded to be appeased.

His fingers tangled in her hair and within seconds he'd freed it from the confines of her French twist. He angled her head back to accept the purposeful sweep of his tongue against hers and she moaned into his mouth. His big hand cupped her buttock and gave it a firm squeeze.

She whimpered against the onslaught of need and rubbed against him in a vain effort to pacify the growing heat between her thighs. Her body wept for his and she ached for him to fill the emptiness inside her, to feel his cock against her flesh as he slowly fucked her into release.

Her nimble fingers grabbed his turtleneck and wrenched it upward to reveal his muscular chest. She kneaded and stroked the thick pads of muscle that comprised his impressive six-pack. Her fingers sought out his flat nipples and she gave them a tweak to elicit a groan from him. She sucked on his tongue, swallowing his cry.

She didn't want to break the kiss but she burned to feel more of him. She pulled away then relaxed her legs, sliding down his body until she stood on the floor. His big arms were braced on the door and his breath was hot against her temple as he struggled to regain control.

"I need to feel you inside me." She reached for him, her fingers on his belt.

"Wait." His hands covered hers. "Do you really want this? Here?"

"Yes."

His handsome face was a blur in the dim room. She needed to be close to this man. For this one moment in time, he was hers and hers alone and she knew she had to grab this opportunity or risk losing it forever. Their lives were in danger but for some reason she wasn't terribly worried, she knew it would work out somehow. On the other hand, regret was a terrible thing to live with and she had no intentions of doing so ever again.

"Come here." Chase took her hand and led her to a chaise lounge near the terrace doors, their escape route.

He kissed her as if he would never let go and together they sank onto the lounge. Her head swirled as he possessed her mouth, taking her to heights she'd only found with him. Their tongues tangled as their hands stroked and explored each other. Hers ventured across his broad chest while his slid under her skirt.

"Mmmm." She purred when he stroked her inner thighs. She grabbed the hem of her dress and pulled it to her waist. "Touch me, Chase. I need you inside me."

"With pleasure." He ripped open his jeans before he seized her knees. Pulling her thighs apart, he insinuated his slim hips between them.

She arched her back and a loud moan escaped her when his cock brushed against the core of her desire. She felt weak, feverish all over. Reaching for him, she moved her hands over his thick erection. Stroking the broad head, she loved the way his eyes narrowed and his breathing deepened. The sense of power was heady. He gave an involuntary thrust against her hand.

"Stop, Harper. I want to be inside you when I lose my mind," he hissed.

At that erotic image, she went breathless, unable to speak. With his cock in her hand, she guided him to her pussy before she released him. He pressed forth, the blunt tip of his erection against her dampened folds and she moaned.

Moving his hand between her thighs, he caressed her flesh with long slow strokes until she was crying, her hips moving in a sensual dance. He slipped a finger in, sinking deep into her vagina. Harper shuddered at his touch, instinctively drawing her knees up to take more of what he offered.

A sigh escaped her when his thumb brushed her clit. She wound her arms around his neck and drew him close as the world tilted wildly beneath his knowledgeable hands. His slow strokes grew more rhythmic and her hips rocked in response, her inner muscles subtly clasping his finger as she answered his mating call.

Impatient now, Chase removed his fingers and replaced them with the broad head of his cock. Harper moaned, straining against him as he entered her, stretching her, filling her. He barely gave her time to appreciate the feel of him inside her before he began to thrust. He coaxed soft moans from her as he moved and her hips joined his in the ancient dance.

Fire rippled through her body to gather between her legs. She closed her eyes, concentrating on the sensations that rocketed through her blood, bone and every fiber of her body. Strong hands held her steady as he hammered into her, each thrust taking her higher than the last. Her nails dug into his shoulders as he forced her body into accepting his domination.

She screamed with the force of her release, her thighs high and tight around his waist. He continued to move, slow rippling movements that caused her release to roll over her in long, slow waves. She never wanted this feeling to end.

She'd barely caught her breath when he began thrusting again. Within seconds, another cry was wrenched from her lips as a harsh groan exploded from him. With his head thrown back and his face contorted, he came deep within her.

When Chase gave a particularly earthy groan, Harper had to slap her hand over her mouth to stifle her laughter. She stood in the open doorway while he was nearer the inside door performing his vocal gymnastics. Through the narrow crack under the door there were several dark shadows breaking the light. The security guards were standing in front of the door, listening to the sounds of their supposed lovemaking.

Chase's voice reached a sharp crescendo that sent her scampering across the room toward him to add a scream or two of her own. The sounds of their faux lovemaking were pretty authentic in her opinion. Their voices mingled when they reached their staged orgasms. With a few final sighs, they joined hands and tiptoed toward the open door.

Harper shot a look over her shoulder. The shadows visible though the crack were still in place. Mission accomplished. They slipped outside.

"This way," Chase hissed. "My car is in the north parking lot with the rest of the hired help."

"Gotcha."

The clouds had parted and the moon was full as they made their way along the side of the house. The ballroom was on the other side of the house and the gardens were located in the rear. No doubt there would be a few guests outside sneaking a smoke but that was no problem. Having a few guests witness their escape wasn't what Harper was worried about, it was the armed security that concerned her the most.

"Showtime," he murmured.

With her heart in her throat, Harper slipped her hand into the crook of his arm and they stepped onto the gravel path. A few other couples were walking through the gardens and techno-dance music poured through the open windows

"So close and yet so far." Harper's gaze was fixed on the slope that separated the parking area from the gardens.

"Don't worry, we're almost there."

She flashed him a brilliant smile. "I'm not worried."

"Liar."

"I keep forgetting, we're being truthful this evening. I didn't know your kind was familiar with that trait."

He shook his head. "Are you ever going to let it go?"

"In case you've forgotten, you broke my heart so you'll have to excuse me if I seem a little bitter."

"I'm surprised you didn't break your knees jumping to conclusions," he shot back.

"Jumping to conclusions? What do you mean?"

"You never gave me a chance to explain—"

"What was there to explain? I walked in and found you half-naked—"

"I'd just gotten out of the shower—"

"And your face just happened to fall into Sharon's massive bosom? I'm so glad you had a soft place to land."

"Harper, I know you won't believe me but I loved you so much—"

She gave a choked laugh. "That is not the way to prove you love someone."

"I spent years looking for you but it was as if you'd vanished off the face of the earth. I knew your name but nothing about where you were from or where your family lived. I had no idea where to look and anyone I asked either knew nothing or was very tight-lipped about you."

Her friends still in the business would've reacted that way. Most were closed-mouthed about their personal lives as it enabled them to live a somewhat normal family life. It was all a part of the job.

But could she ever trust Chase again?

His arm tightened and he shot a glance over his shoulder. "We need to keep moving, love. The lights are on in the office we just burglarized."

Harper's heart quickened and she lengthened her gait to match his. Just as they passed a fountain, one of several in the gardens, she heard a whistling noise then the head of the statue exploded into pieces.

She screamed and ducked.

"Run!" Chase took off in a sprint, her hand now secured in his. "They're shooting at us."

"No kidding."

They ran down the path and Harper regretted her sexy, stylish shoes. She wished she were wearing tennis shoes but she didn't have a pair made for evening wear.

They zigged and zagged among the fountains and garish statues in an attempt to make themselves a harder target to hit. Dirt and gravel were being kicked up on the path by shots that missed their mark and several pieces struck Harper's bare legs.

They ran up the slope next to the parking lot, the only part of the journey completely bare of cover, and Chase ducked behind her when her shoes tripped her up. She hit the grass face first and swore loudly.

Scrambling to her knees, Harper grabbed handfuls of his shirt when Chase scooped her up with ease. She heard a faint whistling sound then felt Chase jerk. His curse was as lusty and heartfelt as hers had been.

"What's wrong? Are you hit?" She tried to get a good look at him and he shoved her forward, almost knocking her over. "Keep moving, babe, they're still firing. It's the black Zephyr on the end."

With her heart in her throat, she ran toward the sleek car. He unlocked it with the remote and she dove into the passenger seat while he took the driver's side. The engine sprang to life with a throaty purr then he threw it into gear, backing out so fast the tires kicked up gravel onto the gleaming paint.

They moved forward and she screamed when the back window exploded inward. Men in suits swarmed over the slope and spilled into the gravel lot. Several held guns pointed at them and judging from the muzzle flashes, they were definitely firing.

"Get down, you fool." Chase grabbed her head and shoved her into the footwell out of harm's way.

Metallic pings exploded against the sides of the car and he gunned the engine. She clung to his muscular thigh as they sailed over bumps and it felt as if they were off road. The car fishtailed just before the squeal of rubber against asphalt sounded. She released her breath.

"Are we safe yet?" she hissed.

"Barely."

Harper sat up and pushed the hair from her eyes. The powerful engine purred as they flew down the road toward town, only minutes from the dubious safety of normal society.

"You realize they will follow us," he said.

"I'd be surprised if they didn't." She twisted around in her seat to look out the non-existent back window. The road was empty. "But we're safe for now."

"And that's all we can hope for."

Relaxing into the seat, she had to giggle. "That was the worst getaway in the history of second-story work."

"Definitely not our best."

"Not even close, it was awful." She rubbed a shaky hand over her forehead. In the faint lights of the console, Chase's face looked as hard as a rock, his jaw was set and his eyes were narrowed. "Are you okay?"

"I'm going to head for Avon Lake and then we can switch. I'll need you to drive into town."

Harper frowned and looked behind them again. "Okay, why?"

"I've been shot."

Chapter Five

Chase slept like a stone, silent and unmoving. Harper sat by his side, both exhausted and numb. Her eyes burned from the multitude of tears she'd shed while he'd slept. She barely remembered their nightmarish drive into town. After forcing him to pull over at the first opportunity, she took over the wheel, knowing if she'd taken him to a hospital there would have been a lot of unwanted questions from the police. Lucky for her, the years of second-story work granted her nerves of steel. Pushing all personal feelings aside, she'd taken the back way into town and contacted a specialist for Chase's injuries.

Dr. Owen Short was no longer a doctor thanks to a massive malpractice lawsuit but that didn't stop him from practicing. Most people still called him Dr. O and now he made his living tending to the illnesses and accidents of a select few who would require his services without the interference of law enforcement.

Chase could have died tonight. They both could've, and for what? Slowly her gaze shifted from his pale face to the blood-stained envelopes on the bedside table. To keep three amoral people from being publicly humiliated by Blackie? What was a little humiliation in comparison to a human life?

Nothing.

Her tired gaze moved back to his sleeping face.

Never in her life had she been quite so terrified as when she realized Chase was hurt.

She loved him.

Even before he'd bled all over her dress or he'd put himself in harm's way and had taken a bullet for her, she'd realized she was still in love with him. In retrospect, hearing his voice behind her in Blackie's office should've been a given. Now she knew it had only been a matter of time before they'd stumbled across one another again. It was as inevitable as the sunrise.

Her eyes stung.

Sometimes knowledge could be a terrible thing.

Exhausted, she turned to the side in an attempt to relieve her numb buttocks. It didn't help. Blindly, she stared out the window. The rising sun was just beginning to pinken the sky and it was past time for her to leave. Chase was safe here with Dr. O and she needed to get back to her life—

"I fell in love with you the first time I laid eyes on you."

Harper blinked. Her mind was so numb that it didn't register it was Chase's voice she heard. Slowly she turned toward him and their gazes met. He looked tired and his face was so incredibly dear to her that she never wanted him to get away, at least not without hearing the truth. She licked her lips as a soft warmth bloomed in her chest.

Damn, how she loved him.

"You don't say." Her voice was wobbly.

"Do you remember when we met? We were in Prague at the reception for the President of the United States. I was there to scope out the building and you were there to liberate the Comtesse de Longue's family jewels."

Harper smiled even as a single tear ran down her cheek. "I made almost a half-million dollars in one fell swoop that night.

Served the harpy right as she should have never swiped them from her twin sister."

"You wore a red dress with a slit on the side that showed off your spectacular legs."

"And you wore a tuxedo that stopped every woman's heart in the ballroom." She sniffed.

"I was never unfaithful to you, Harper. Susan came over in tears because her boyfriend had broken up with her. She was in pain, distraught and she'd grabbed my face for a kiss and you just happened to walk in at exactly the wrong moment."

"The story of my life."

Chase watched her closely. Dark circles marred her eyes and her mouth was drawn with exhaustion. Never had she looked so beautiful to him. Would she give him a second chance?

Harper sighed and rubbed her cheek. "Maybe I was being irrational," she said. "But when I saw you in that woman's arms, I just went crazy."

"You were waiting on me to cheat on you," he said.

"Yes, I think I was."

"I'm not surprised. The men in your life haven't been exactly trustworthy individuals." He took her hand. "But I am. When I give my love, it is for always and forever, Harper."

Her shoulders slumped. "I really blew it, didn't I?"

"No, you didn't."

"So where do we go from here, Chase? Do you think we start over again?"

He released the breath he didn't even realize he'd been holding. "I think we'd be stupid not to."

Her gaze met his and in the depths he saw relief and love there—love for him. He was one lucky man.

"I love you, Chase." Her voice was hushed.

"I love you, too, Harper." He caught her arm and hauled her into the bed with him. She curled into his side as if she'd been born to assume that very spot. "We need some one-on-one time together. How do you feel about going to Europe? Italy, maybe?"

"Tuscany."

"That sounds like a plan. I hope you don't mind a slight detour to Paris."

"Why Paris?"

"Well, I have this job lined up and I could use a good locksmith..."

About the Author

To learn more about J.C. Wilder, please visit www.jcwilder.com. Send an email to J.C. at wild-2112@jcwilder.com or join her Yahoo! group to join in the fun with other readers as well as J.C. http://groups.yahoo.com/group/thewilderside.

Look for these titles

Now Available

Sacrifice
Deep Waters
Stone Heart

hot stuff

Discover Samhain!
THE HOTTEST NEW PUBLISHER ON THE PLANET

Romance, fantasy, mystery, thriller, mainstream and more—Samhain has more selection, hotter authors, and everything's available in both ebook and print.

Pick your favorite, sit back, and enjoy the ride!
Hot stuff indeed.

WWW.SAMHAINPUBLISHING.COM